Duncan tu... ... ...re you truly here, or am I dreaming?''

''I'm here,'' Samantha said softly.

He frowned. ''Why did you come? Didn't I tell you not to?''

''I guess I don't take orders very well.''

He studied her for a few seconds. ''This isn't the Samantha Wilder I know.''

''Well, this is the one you haven't met yet.''

''Why did you come, Sam?''

Fear leapt out from behind the Brave-Sam persona she'd invented on the way here. ''I knew,'' she began in a quivering voice, ''that if I let you ride off without me, I'd never see you again.''

He took a step toward her, then stopped. ''You have to go home, Sam. I don't know what I was thinking, letting you stay this long. I must be out of my mind.''

''I thought you were glad I was here.''

''I'd have been glad to see another pair of hands no matter who they belonged to.'' He rubbed a hand over his face. ''I didn't mean that the way it sounded.''

''I know you didn't. Now, get into bed.''

He stretched out on the bed and sighed, seeming to melt into the mattress.

Sam started to step away, but he caught a handful of her skirt. ''Stay. For just a minute?''

She sat down beside him and shoved an errant curl off his forehead. He caught her wrist and nipped at the tip of one finger, sending chills racing up her arm.

''You're like a balm to my soul, Sam Wilder.'' He cupped the back of her head in his hand and brought her lips to his. ''No one's worried about me . . . in a long time.''

Fatigue had stripped him of his reserve and bared his soul for only her to see. Strong, proud Inspector Duncan McLeod lay before her, a mere mortal man. She leaned down and kissed him again, savoring the softness of his lips, his warmth. Then she laid her cheek against his and threaded her fingers in his dark curls. ''I love you,'' she whispered. ''You deserve to be worried about.''

Dear Romance Reader,

In July of 1999, we launched the Ballad line with four new series, and each month we present both new and continuing stories set everywhere from medieval England to the American West—the kind of passionate, romantic stories you love best, written by the most gifted authors. At the back of each book, we tell you when you can find subsequent books in the series that have captured your heart.

Premiering this month is **Light a Single Candle,** the first in the dramatic new trilogy *The MacInness Legacy*. Written by sisters Julie and Sandy Moffett, the series is about three long-separated sisters who discover their heritage includes witchcraft. Talented newcomer Pat Pritchard is next, with the first in a pair of books about two men whose lives are changed by a game of poker. Meet the first of the delectable *Gamblers* in **Luck of the Draw.**

Reader favorite Kathryn Fox returns with another of her *Men of Honor* in **The Seduction** in which an intrepid young reporter looking for scandal in gold-rush territory finds passion instead. Finally, beloved author Jo Ann Ferguson introduces a heartwarming new series called *Haven*. In **Twice Blessed,** when an orphan train stops in this small Indiana town, a shopkeeper becomes an instant "mother"—but when she meets a widowed father new to town, she dreams of becoming a wife.

There's romance, passion, adventure to spare. Why not read them all? Enjoy!

Kate Duffy
Editorial Director

MEN OF HONOR

THE
SEDUCTION

KATHRYN FOX

ZEBRA BOOKS
KENSINGTON PUBLISHING CORP.
http://www.kensingtonbooks.com

PROLOGUE

The Isle of Skye, June 1884

A sea breeze swept up the rocky slope, caressing the bobbing wildflowers and tossing Duncan's hair. He snatched a blossom from its stem and added it to the bunch in his hand. Was there ever a June so glorious? he wondered, straightening to gaze across the bay to the lonely rocks jutting from the sea. Long ago, the monoliths had been part of the Isle of Skye, he imagined. Then some accident of nature had cut them off from the mainland, leaving them barren and alone, tantalizingly close to the green shoreline. Even on a splendid day like today, they brooded, the sea nibbling away at their feet.

He shook off the romantic musing and returned to his flower gathering. Elizabeth would like these. The pink ones were her favorites. He held the delicate blossom up to the morning sun and wished he knew its name. He'd never paid much attention to the wildflowers that rioted across his homeland in the summer.

Until Elizabeth.

He shifted the growing bouquet to his other hand and set off across the meadow to the cottage in the distance. He'd wake her up with the delicate fragrance of the bloom she loved. She didn't expect him back before dark and he could imagine her asleep, her hair glowing in the shaft of sun that fell across their bed in the mornings. She'd be warm and scented with milk from the baby's recent nursing.

Though exhausted, his body stirred with thoughts of his wife and the hour they'd spent together before he went to work last night. Dark hair tossed about her shoulders, she'd climbed atop him and controlled their lovemaking to satisfy her own desires. He'd nearly been too weak-kneed to walk the two miles to the village.

The door was slightly ajar and the house was silent. He slipped inside and closed the door behind him. He peeked into the children's rooms and found both lost in angelic sleep, Lizzy with her tiny fist beneath her cheek and baby Sarah asleep on her back.

He tiptoed down the hallway, careful to avoid the loose, creaking board. Soft voices came from the bedroom, the words indistinguishable. He moved closer and the sounds grew louder. Cold premonition washed over him as he paused with a hand on the door. Did he want to walk into this room, he asked himself, his blood chilling, slowing in his veins? Did he want to destroy all he had or turn away and try to forget what was now unmistakable?

He pushed the door open and saw first Elizabeth's slim back, her tiny waist, and flared hips naked and smooth. Her hair was loose and slid across her bare back as she moved back and forth. For a moment the room was lost in a brilliant flash of light created by Duncan's own mind, a grateful blinding. And then the picture returned and he noticed the pile of men's work clothes on the floor.

For an interminable second his heart stopped beating and he wondered if he were dead, if he'd been somehow spirited away, salvaged from the pain that was sure to come.

"Elizabeth?" he said.

She sprang away, yanked the covers up around her breasts, then turned to face him. Rob McDonald rose from the bed, naked and bold, evidence of his lust still visible and ready.

"Elizabeth?" Duncan said again. "What's the meaning of this?"

She glanced at Rob then back at Duncan. "It is what you see, Duncan."

There was no regret in her eyes, no surprise or shock. Only the confidence of a sated woman.

"Rob?" Things seemed to be swirling in slow motion. Perhaps he was dreaming. Perhaps he'd fallen asleep shoveling fish.

"I've taken Rob as my lover."

What mortal woman says such words to the man she's lain with for three years, the man she's allowed to touch her both with hand and mouth in places no other has.

"Your lover? Does what we have here mean nothing to you?"

"My children mean everything to me. And I'll be taking them with me when I go."

Duncan dropped the bouquet and the petals of the wilted flowers scattered across the polished floor.

Like shattered dreams.

"But last night . . ."

She smiled softly, her hair mussed and tousled. "Last night was good-bye."

"You climbed on me, woman, and nearly pumped me dry. Are you saying you felt nothing for me then? Nothing for our home?" The buzz of disbelief vanished and anger cut sharp angles into him.

"A home can be had for the price of rent, but a man that satisfies me has been harder to find."

When had his gentle wife become this wanton, smirking at him while clutching their worn sheets to her breasts? Wonderful breasts with pink crests that made her jerk and beg when he teased them with his tongue.

Had he been so blind as not to see? How many mornings had she kissed him good-bye at the front door, then opened the back door for Rob?

"We've been at it for some time, Duncan," Rob said, bending to pick up his pants, seeming proud of his nakedness. "She just didn't know how to tell you."

"Get out of my house," Duncan said between clenched teeth, dreading to wake his girls and have Lizzy see her mother like this.

Rob smiled. "She's coming with me. It'll be your house alone now."

"I was going to tell you tonight," Elizabeth said, scooping up her nightgown and tossing it over her head. "I've packed the girls' things."

"You expect me to let you take away my daughters, without a fight?"

"You can let me or be dragged to jail. I've spoken to Constable McGee about the way you beat me. He's said if I wanted to press charges, he'd lock you up."

The remaining of Duncan's control unraveled. "Beat you? I've never laid a hand on you and I never would."

"Whether 'tis true or not doesn't matter now," she said with a lazy smile. "Constable McGee'll be summoned if you don't let me leave in peace."

She'd planned this well. How many nights had they lain together naked, caressing, teasing, speaking of the day's events while she planned this betrayal?

"You can go and good riddance, Elizabeth, but I want the girls to stay with me."

Elizabeth laughed. "You with a baby? How would you feed her?"

"She's mine, dammit," he stormed. "She and Lizzy and you."

"You can't own what you don't have and you don't have us, Duncan."

"Why? Can you at least tell me why? Is he better in bed than me? And what should that really matter?"

"Oh, it matters," she said with a tittering laugh. "But money matters more. He has it and you don't."

Duncan swung his full attention to Rob then. He was the son of a baron, a bully and a dandy, both hated and courted by the villagers. He'd left a string of women pregnant or brokenhearted or both, according to gossip. But nothing had ever been proven. No one dared cross the McDonalds.

With an excruciating lack of modesty, Elizabeth leisurely dressed and finally stepped around the bed to where Duncan seemed to be rooted to the floor. Surely, he was asleep in the fishery, leaning on a slimy shovel, dreaming this nightmare.

"I can't say I didn't love you once," Elizabeth said softly, her breath teasing his ear. "You gave me two lovely daughters. The McDonalds will see they're given everything they desire.''

A canvas bag fell onto the tops of his feet. "It'll be less confusing for Lizzy if she doesn't see you before we leave. It'll be easier for her to come to accept Rob as her father that way. I've packed a few of your things. Stay at the fishery until I've moved out.''

"I'll not let you take my children away from me," Duncan said, stepping backwards, anger blinding him.

"You have no choice. In a few days, we're moving to Rob's house and the guards at the gate will make sure you don't come inside.''

Elizabeth stepped forward. Her eyes, once filled with love, were now cold and calculating. She rose on tiptoe and brushed her lips across his cheek. "Good-bye, Duncan.''

CHAPTER ONE

San Francisco, California, 1898

The horsehair sofa itched.

Her corset was too tight.

Sam Wilder fidgeted and Aunt Sophia's heirloom china cup rattled ominously against its companion saucer.

Lips pursed, ankles crossed, demure smile in place, Aunt Sophia shot Sam a glance of pure, icy disapproval that could have turned the cup of steaming tea into a small brown iceberg.

"Samantha, dear, do be careful of the china. As I'm sure you remember, this set of dishes came over from England in the late 1700s with my dear Uncle Ezekiel." Aunt Sophia leaned toward the other ladies seated in her parlor. "He was the true aristocrat of the family," she added with a self-confident nod.

Sam drew a deep breath, or what had to pass for one with the corset sawing across her midsection, and tried to shut out the thousandth recitation of Aunt Sophia's lineage. Instead, she focused on her aunt's thin lips and planned another escape.

This time she'd run away to Africa. She'd stow away aboard some southbound steamer and work her way to the Dark Continent. Once there, she'd write about great hunters, see lions and elephants, and—

"Samantha, dear?"

Sam blinked and her aunt's face came into focus.

"I've called you twice, dear. Were you daydreaming about some of your foolish notions again?"

The words were sugar sweet, delivered in the syrupy, cloying tone Aunt Sophia had mastered almost immediately after Sam came to live with her. The same tone that reprimanded her for not keeping her room neat, not hanging her dresses in the wardrobe according to usage and color, and not facing life as a woman with the proper dread.

A woman's life is to be devoted to service, Aunt Sophia would preach.

Or . . . *a woman's worth is measured by the degree of her meekness.* Another favorite.

And best of all . . . *a woman's role in the more intimate points of marriage is to simply endure with her dignity intact.* Endure? What exactly did that mean? And what *were* those mysterious intimate points her aunt had spoken of so frequently in the last few weeks? Ever since she'd been marked for the marriage market.

"Samantha, I've asked you a question. Please do me the honor of paying attention when I speak to you."

The tone rankled, but Sam swallowed down the biting

response that sprang to her tongue. "I'm sorry," she answered obediently. "What did you say?"

Another icy stare, backed up with the silent promise of another lecture.

"Mrs. Thornton asked if you were looking forward to your coming-out party. I assured her you were."

Sam turned to smile at the chubby little woman with the sweet smile. Sam liked Emma Thornton despite the fact that she chose Aunt Sophia as one of her friends. She was one of the few of her aunt's entourage she could stomach. "Yes, I am. Very much." *I'm dreading every second of it.*

"Who have you chosen as your escort, dear? Certainly not Oscar Timmets?"

Sam lifted her lips in what she hoped passed as a smile. In reality, she was gritting her teeth. "In fact, yes, Oscar has agreed to escort me."

A collective gasp went up around the room, bouncing off the heavy drapes and the dark, baroque furniture, kept draped until Aunt Sophia chose to impress someone with her wealth. Sam glanced at her aunt. She looked uncomfortable. That, in itself, was worth the scolding Sam knew was imminent. No young man in all of San Francisco would have agreed to escort Sam Wilder anywhere. She basked in the safety of her rejection by the marriageable male population. That left only dear, sweet Oscar.

Her best friend.

Her reluctant partner in mischief.

With him, Sam could be herself. He already knew how horrid she could be at times, knew the darkness that had haunted her since her parents' death ten years ago. And he loved her anyway. A wisp of guilt intruded. Oscar was smitten with her, in love with her as a woman while she loved him dearly as a brother and a friend. She pushed the thought aside. Understanding the complex relationship between them took more thought than she was willing to contribute at the moment. After all, she was being faced down by four hungry lionesses.

"My dear, do you think that's a wise idea? Dear Oscar is a fine young man in some regards, but he is hardly a fitting escort for the niece of someone of the social prominence of your aunt," Matilda Osgood chimed in, her multiple chins wagging.

Sam lifted her own chin as the narrow-mindedness got the better of her civility. "Oscar is my friend and a far better man than Robert Potkins."

Matilda's eyes bulged as she huffed with indignation. Robert Potkins had been a prime catch as escort for Matilda's less-than-congenial daughter Hannah, who was also being placed on the marriage market.

"Would you like another petit four?" Aunt Sophia urged, grasping the silver platter and holding it out to the assembled matrons.

The conversation swung from her to Hannah and her latest fashion success, fueled by her mother's money. Sam endured the chatter, knowing the day would get darker once the inspection committee left.

"How could you have embarrassed me like that?" Aunt Sophia's voice bordered on a cat-like growl.

Sam curled her legs underneath her on the window-seat cushion and braced for another verbal onslaught. "She was saying bad things about Oscar. And besides, Hannah Osgood has the personality of a snake."

"It's not your place to voice that opinion." Aunt Sophia jammed her hands on her hips and paced away, her back rigid. "Your chances of making a good marriage depend on your cooperating within the society of this town, Samantha." She sighed, her back turned. "How can I make you understand that?"

"I don't want to get married. Not to any of these pampered dandies, anyway. I want to travel and write about the new places and things I see for Uncle Harry's paper."

Her aunt pivoted, her eyes snapping anger. "Since your sainted mother died, I have tried to conform you to the world we live in. I considered it my duty to my sister to take her only child and raise her properly. I only wish I'd had influence over you sooner so that I might have chased some of your father's foolish ideas out of your head earlier."

Anger, hot and immediate, filled Sam. Biting words crowded into her mouth, begging to be let out. She'd idolized her father and his wonderful stories. A ship's captain, a gentle rogue with dancing eyes and wavy hair, Ben Wilder had captured her mother's heart and soul. They were married in secret and proceeded, almost immediately, to conceive Sam. She still had memories of their happy life in the little seaside cottage her father had built. Until an impetuous sailing trip cut short both their lives. Sam closed her eyes and conjured from memory their faces, love for her and each other shining in their eyes.

She opened her eyes. "I'm glad you didn't, Auntie, or else life here would be unbearable."

Her aunt seemed to shift backwards slightly, as if physically struck by the words. She opened her mouth, but no sound came out. Another wave of guilt overcame Sam and she regretted the biting remark. Her aunt and uncle had taken her in when she had no one else.

They'd given her a roof over her head and food and warmth. They were not to blame that they were emotionless, barren creatures with no imagination or vision. They traveled adequately in the tiny circle of existence they'd created for themselves, never looking to what might lie beyond, never envisioning what life might have been. They were the product of their own childhoods, lived within rigid requirements and mores that dictated their every thought and action.

"Auntie, I'm sorry," Sam said, scrambling out of the windowseat.

"Is something wrong?" Uncle Harry opened the door and poked his balding head inside. "Matilda Osgood had up a fine head of steam when she nearly ran me down on the walkway."

"Your ungrateful niece may have finally secured her spinsterhood."

Uncle Harry glanced at Sam, fleeting compassion in his eyes. "What did you do this time, Sam?"

"They were saying unkind things about Oscar. I only defended him."

Uncle Harry looked to Sophia. "The coming-out party?"

Sophia nodded. "Of course. What else?" She pivoted on her heel and glided out of the room, scattering righteous indignation in her wake.

Uncle Harry looked at Sam and shook his head. "You do know how to irk her."

"I'm being sold like a . . . a . . . side of beef."

"This is how it's done, Sam. We're only concerned for your future."

"If you were really concerned for my future, you'd let me write for the paper."

Harry wagged his head from side to side. "You know that's a forbidden subject."

"Only forbidden by Aunt Sophia. You understand, don't you?"

He stepped into the room and eased the door closed with an uneasy glance over his shoulder. "I still remember what it's like to want to see over the next hill. But you're a young woman, Sam, and the safest future for you is as a wife and mother."

"That's not what Papa would have said."

Harry stared at her, a wistful look in his eyes. "No, I don't expect he would have said that at all. But Ben's not here." He sat down heavily in an upholstered chair. "There was a time in my life when I very much wanted to go to sea."

Sam raised her eyebrows. "Really?"

"As does every young man, I guess. But I had the good sense to see that business was my strength, not sailing, and I have made a good life for us all with that ability."

Sam dropped to her knees at his side and gripped his forearm. "I've never thought you and Auntie weren't good to me. And I am grateful for what you've done. But I'm old enough to make my own decisions now. I want to write. I want to travel and see what else there is besides pastries and charity balls and seamstress appointments."

Harry put a hand on her head and smiled softly. "You remember the effort it took to get Sophia to agree to let you write the obituaries? I suffered her wrath for a month."

"Haven't I done a good job?"

He caressed her hair. "You've done an excellent job.

Never have there been obituaries written with more . . . compassion.''

"Then let me write stories, features. You know I can write. I've proven that, haven't I?"

"The life of a reporter isn't one for a lady, no matter her abilities. It's smoke-filled rooms and no sleep. Long, dangerous trips into difficult situations. Even if you could endure the trials, you'd never be accepted. It's a tight brotherhood, one hesitant to accept newcomers, and especially a woman." He slid his hand down her cheek to cup her chin and tip it upwards. "I promised your father's memory to see you well raised and provided for. I intend to keep my word."

"Did you get it?" Sam closed the door to the hotel storeroom and shivered in the dampness.

Oscar pulled the newspaper out of his suit coat and held it out in the dim light of the single candle he'd brought. CANADIAN GOVERNMENT SENDS MOUNTED POLICE TO SECURE GOLD IN THE YUKON. The words marched across the front page, invoking vivid images of handsome men in red coats; of glittering gold nuggets just waiting to be plucked from the earth; of opportunities for unbridled greed. Just the stuff reporters lived for.

Sam snatched the publication out of his hand and flopped down on a stack of flour sacks, unmindful of her white ball gown.

"You'll get your dress dirty," Oscar said, yanking her to her feet by one arm and spreading his overcoat out for her to sit on.

"The Yukon. Think about it, Oscar. What an adventure! It's untamed and wild and surely full of characters worthy of a story."

"Every reporter in the United States is headed there, Sam."

"Where's the other article?"

Oscar slowly pulled a folded piece of paper from his pocket. "Won't your aunt miss us inside at the ball?"

Sam shook her head. "Not for a while. I told her I felt like I was going to throw up. Her first comment was, of course, to be careful of my gown." She snatched the paper out of his hand and unfolded it. MINER CLAIMS MOUNTED POLICE ARE STEALING THE GOLD CANADA TRUSTED THEM TO GUARD.

"The *Bay Star*'s a rag sheet, Sam. Everybody knows that. You can't believe anything they print." He waved a hand at the ragged paper. "I wish I'd never shown it to you."

"But this story is based on an eyewitness account. This man says here that there's hundreds of thousands of dollars in gold in the hands of the Mounties. All of them can't be honest. There's a story opportunity here."

"There probably isn't even a witness. The *Bay Star* probably made up the whole story. I tell you they can't be trusted to print the truth."

"But you work for them sometimes."

"I only take photographs and nothing else." He shrugged his shoulders and adjusted his glasses. "A man's got to work. Besides, they're not the only paper I work for."

Sam scanned the article, then lowered it to her lap. "Wouldn't it be a grand adventure if you and I could go there and uncover the scandal?"

Oscar guffawed. "You and me in the Yukon? We're

hothouse orchids, Sam, compared to the men and women who've made that trip. We wouldn't last a day.''

"You give us far too little credit. Remember that time we camped out all night alone on the beach? Nobody knew where we were and we had nothing except some matches and a blanket. We did all right then.''

"We were eight, Sam, and we were sleeping fifty feet from your house. You ate too many cookies and threw up on my pillow.''

"Still, the principle's the same. We were independent and adventurous. Don't you want to know what that feels like again?''

Oscar looked down at his shiny shoes. "I imagine lots of lives alternative to the one I lead. But I've come to accept this as my lot. I take pictures of weddings and funerals and families who want to be immortal. There's no glory or adventure in it, but it's an honest living.'' He glanced up shyly. "One I hope to someday share with a wife and children.''

"But what if we went? Think of the photographs you could take. We'd be famous. Our names would be on the front page of every paper in the nation. Especially if I'm the one to uncover the crime.''

"What would you tell your aunt and uncle?''

Sam creased her brow and chewed the side of her mouth. Inspiration struck. "I'd leave a note telling them you and I ran off to get married. I'd say we've been having a torrid affair right under their noses. Auntie would be so humiliated she'd take to her bed. Uncle would pace and sputter, but he'd stay by her side. No one would come after us. Then, after a few months, I'd send a telegram and tell them where we are.'' Sam again pushed away a whisper of guilt. "They wouldn't really worry about me if they knew I was with you.''

Oscar stared at her as if she'd just sprouted two heads. "You're out of your mind. Your uncle would have the Pinkertons on us before the sun set."

Sam stood and brushed off her dress. Muted strains of a waltz floated to them from the hotel ballroom. "I know this sounds absurd, but somehow I don't think he would. Something about the way he spoke of my father the other day . . . Once I was out of Aunt Sophia's grasp and my escape couldn't be traced to him, I don't think he'd try to bring me back. I think he'd let me have this adventure."

Oscar snatched the article out of her hands. "Forget it, Sam. Forget you ever read this." He folded the paper and slipped it inside his jacket. "You've got more immediate problems." He held out his arm to escort her back into the ball before they were both missed.

"What?" Sam rearranged the skirt of her gown and hooked her hand through Oscar's arm, bracing herself to smile until it hurt.

"I overheard Robert Potkins talking to your uncle. He said he'd like to take you for a carriage ride on Sunday."

CHAPTER TWO

Chilkoot Pass, the Yukon, 1898

A tiny, black thread of humanity wound up the steep wall of Chilkoot Pass, disappearing into a brilliant blue sky. Sam shifted from one freezing foot to the other, keeping her eyes on the horse's rump in front of her.

"Where are you bound, my lad?" a voice asked in clipped British tones. She looked up and saw the man in front of her staring over his shoulder at her.

Sam cleared her throat. "Dawson City." The words came out in a hoarse squawk instead of the masculine voice she'd hoped for.

"I say, a rough place. I'm bound for the gold fields myself."

He turned completely around and Sam let her gaze drift away from his face.

"Say, you're a young one. Are you here alone?"

"No. This here's me brother." She grabbed Oscar's sleeve and hauled him in front of her, shielding her from the man's assessment.

Sam felt Oscar tremble and could imagine his Adam's apple bobbing in his throat.

"I say, that's not much of a horse you have there."

Sam glanced at the brown mare pulling their sled of supplies. Indeed, she was not an excellent example of horseflesh, but she was the only horse left in Dyea. At least the only one they could afford.

"You lads know Commissioner Walsh has issued an order that says all stampeders have to have six months of supplies with them before they can go over the pass."

Sam nodded. "Yep."

He squinted at her, then eyed the sled full of supplies suspiciously. "And five hundred dollars cash?"

Sam paused, but Oscar nodded emphatically. "Yes sir, five hundred dollars in cash."

"Did the two of you run away?" The man shifted to the left to look at Sam again, a glint of suspicion forming in his eyes.

"We're orphans," Oscar spit out and Sam cringed at the cliché. She smothered a smile, looked down, and shoved her hands into her pockets in what she hoped was a dejected manner.

"Poor lads—"

The rest of the man's words were cut off by a deep, troubled groan that shook the ground.

The chatter of voices ceased.

"Avalanches," the man said with a glance at the summit looming ahead of them. "They started last night. The Chilkat natives refused to go one step further this morning and left all these men stranded with their supplies."

Sam glanced at Oscar and then at the heavy shelf of snow hovering above them. The weather had been unseasonably warm and whispered warnings of impending disaster had circulated among the natives hired to pack and carry supplies for the stampeders. The mountain was talking, they had grumbled, then disappeared into the morning sun.

"Mr. Langhorn up there assures me this is normal," the man said with a nod to the crowd in front of him. "He's been up this pass three times this winter with no incident. Silly, suspicious aboriginals."

Then, as if in response to his irreverence, the mountain groaned again and the thin line of people near the summit disappeared. The entire side of the mountain seemed to be sliding toward them. Sam stood mesmerized, watching the wall of snow and ice sliding toward her, burying people and equipment before it.

"C'mon Sam. Run!" Oscar grabbed her arm and dragged her backwards, his photographic equipment flopping around at his side. She felt her pack slip off and momentarily mourned the loss of her reporter's notes.

They plunged straight downhill, caught up in the crowd running with them. A man in front, weighted down with a huge pack, fell and rolled under their feet. There was no time to think, no time to stop and help. Sam jumped over him and continued on. Someone grabbed her coat and fell, almost dragging her down, too, except for Oscar's hand pulling her along.

The roar turned into a growl, stinging them with tossed bits of ice and snow. Sam looked up from watching her feet to see the terror on Oscar's face before the snow engulfed them.

Breathtaking cold wrapped its arms around Sam and

shoved her forward, yanking her feet from beneath her. She tumbled over and over until her head spun. Somewhere along the way she bumped against another body, also caught up in the avalanche's fury.

Suddenly, she stopped rolling and silence descended, roaring louder than the avalanche that entombed her. She struggled, unable to move her arms or legs or turn her head. Icy crystals scraped her eyes. Gray light surrounded her, a feeble promise of freedom above the weight of the snow.

"Be still." The whispered words worked their way into her terror and she recognized Oscar's voice. His body lay on top of hers, his breath hot on her ear.

All the newspaper stories she had read in her research on the gold fields in the Yukon came back in stark detail. Avalanches punctuated frozen winters. Stiff, frozen bodies were exhumed after months and weeks of burial and some were never found.

"I don't think we're under too deep," Oscar whispered again. I can see light through the snow. Let me see if I can dig out."

Sam waited, but Oscar never moved. Assuming he was wedged in as tightly as she, she attempted to move her hands. Nothing. Her feet. Nothing. Swallowing down rising panic, she tried to think beyond their present predicament, invoking a childhood habit of chasing away fears and doubts.

She let her thoughts drift back to two weeks ago, to the day she'd convinced Oscar to come with her. They'd alternately argued and discussed her plan over the weeks following her party. With every confrontation, Oscar had squelched her idealism with his logic. Finally, she'd stamped her feet and said if he wouldn't come with her, she'd go alone. He'd relented and here they were. Buried in an avalanche.

"Try to move your head," Oscar croaked.

Sam nodded a little, able to move only a fraction within the cocoon the heat from her skin had melted in her icy tomb.

Oscar sighed against her. "Thank God you're alive."

Sam supposed people always suffered from a guilty conscience just before they had to face those sins for the last time, but hers seemed particularly heavy at the moment. She knew Oscar had come because he wanted to, not because of any temper tantrum of hers. Because he wanted to be with her.

The cold began to recede, replaced by a lethargic warmth. Even through her thick coat she could feel Oscar's breathing even out, his body relax. Were they dying, drifting off into some eternal unknown together?

She'd tipped the scales of Oscar's indecision by convincing him he'd have photographic opportunities those other feature photographers only dreamed about. After all, she'd said to clinch her argument, for an American paper to uncover the scandal in the Yukon would be quite an accomplishment. Especially since Canada and the United States were quibbling over the position of the Yukon border and ownership of the gold fields. The American reading public would gobble up the gory details. Her name would be synonymous with truth and justice and Oscar's photographs would be famous.

After all, thousands of dollars in gold were flowing out of the Yukon. And the handful of Mounted Police sent to administer law and order couldn't all be angels. Somebody was lining their pockets. And in their trek here, there had been whispered rumors among the passengers leaving the Yukon, rumors of thievery and lies

among the Police. And she'd assuaged her guilt some-
what when her suspicions graduated to rumor.

Silvery dreams, shattered into thousands of discon-
nected pieces, replaced rational thought. Memories,
long since tucked away, resurfaced. Sam felt her body
relax, her breathing slow.

Scrape. Scrape. Muted sounds worked their way into
her scattered thoughts. How long had she been asleep?
Or was she dead? Faint voices, steady and even, roused
her. Go away, she thought, and let me sleep.

More scraping sounds, and something in her roused.
She searched a numb brain. What was that sound? Somebody was digging above her! She opened her mouth
and found that the snow in it had melted. When she
tried to cry out, the sound was muffled and faint. "Listen, Oscar. Somebody's coming."

She waited for Oscar's whispered breath against her
ear, but he made no response.

"Oscar." Sam concentrated on the weight above her.
It stirred with the faint rise and fall of breathing.

The voices beyond the ice grew louder and deeper,
then Sam felt Oscar's weight lifted off her. Light poured
in, turning the inside of her tomb into thousands of
diamonds.

"Here's another one, laddie." A rich Scottish brogue
filled her ears and she felt a hand slip under the belt
that cinched her oversize coat close to her body. Yanked
out of her peaceful nest, she welcomed the bright sun
with a small prayer. Strong arms slipped beneath her
shoulder and knees, clasping her close to a brilliant red
coat.

Sam squinted against the bright sun and tried to raise
an arm to shade her eyes, but her muscles refused to
cooperate. Crunching footsteps carried her, then laid

her down on a blanket spread on the snow. A face moved between her and the light and she stared into brilliant blue eyes beneath ominous, bushy black eyebrows.

"This one's a lass! Tommy, bring me another blanket." The brows knitted together and long lashes swept away the look of concern and replaced it with snaps of anger.

"You must have left your sense at home, lass." He tucked the blanket close around her, huge hands accomplishing the task in seconds. "What are ye doin' here? Where's yer husband?"

He swept off a broad Stetson hat, revealing black, curly hair that touched a red collar with dark blue epaulets. Gold emblems caught the sun, then released it in a shower of light when he turned to glance over his shoulder.

Sam opened her mouth to deny the existence of this assumed mate, but caution whispered in her ear. "I don't know where he is," she said with what she hoped to be panicked concern.

"There was a laddie buried with ye. We thought that might be him."

"Is he . . . ?" A cold hand gripped Sam's throat and held on. Poor, dear Oscar.

"No, he's a mite scratched and cold, but he'll live. He's luckier than most."

The blue eyes darkened to sapphire and glanced at something over her head. Sam rose on her elbows. Bodies were scattered all over. Some were covered with blankets, others still lay in their icy tombs, limbs protruding at odd angles. A few red-suited Mounties walked among the bodies, while other parties of men dug frantically at the disheveled snow. Up along the ridge of the pass, bare rock shone where snow had blanketed before.

Jarring cold seemed to crawl inside her and coil itself around her insides. She started to shiver, hearing her own teeth clatter. She lay down, gripping the blanket tightly to her chin, and the foolishness of her idea descended, now unabated by enthusiasm. She could have gotten them both killed. What was she thinking, coming all this way just for a story? Well, now she had her story.

She waited for the rise of adrenaline to come, as it always did when she was faced with adversity, but her body responded instead with a wave of nausea and more shivering.

"Are ye a whore?" The question jarred her out of her fright.

"What? Certainly not." She clasped the blanket closer to her chin. "What kind of man are you?"

He smiled, crinkling the corners of those blue eyes. "I'm Inspector Duncan McLeod of the North West Mounted Police. I was wondering if you were one of Shorty's replacements."

"Well, Inspector McLeod, do you ask all the women you see that question?"

His direct gaze was unsettling. He was sizing her up, assessing her. "Nay, only the pretty ones," he answered, his brogue rolling off his tongue like honey.

"Where is Oscar? I want to see that he's all right."

"Your husband? He's fine, wrapped up over there." Duncan pointed behind them to where a group of men had clustered around a single man holding a cup firmly between two hands. "I'll take you to him." He stood, towering over her, then reached down and gently guided her to her feet. Sam stumbled and her head swam. Standing, she could better see the devastation the wall of snow had wrought. Packs and supplies littered the snowfield, sobering evidence that bodies lay beneath.

"My God." A cold wind swept down from the pass and sprinkled Sam's face with icy crystals. But not even the icy water that bathed her face could erase the gnawing nausea that returned to grip her. As she moved toward Oscar, a group of rescuers lifted a body from the snow. The arms and legs were bent and entwined and the bloody face was almost unrecognizable. Sam looked at her feet, concentrating on putting one in front of the other, trying not to look at the body as it met the snow, limp like an abandoned rag doll. Somewhere, someone waited for word from that man, waited for a letter or telegram that said he was all right. Sam had read such pleas in newspaper articles back in San Francisco and an article about families left behind planted itself in her mind to haunt her.

The world began to darken and Sam stumbled. I am not going to faint like some ninny, she told herself, taking a deep breath and wishing away the encroaching shadows. *I am not going to give him proof of what I see in his eyes, that I have no business here.*

But the shadows moved in closer and Sam stumbled again. A firm hand caught her elbow and she tried to shake him off, but the sudden movement was all the shadows were waiting for and they swooped in to claim her.

Duncan ducked as the top of the tent opening scraped off his hat. Wind buffeted the canvas sides, making a sound he was learning to hate. He put the bundle in his arms on the one cot, and straightened. A winter's worth of anger rose in him as he looked down into the youthful face. She was barely more than a child. What was she doing here, in what was probably the wildest place on earth? And what husband in his right mind would bring her here?

Duncan set a kettle back on the one eye of the barrel stove and opened the door cut in the side. Seeing only orange embers, he tossed in a couple of sticks of wood and blew on the ashes until flames licked at the new offerings.

He took off the beaver gloves, knelt by the cot, and whisked away her scarf and hat. A tumble of deep, auburn curls fell out and framed a delicate face. His hand slipped into her hair as he raised her head to shove a pillow underneath; he paused for a second to let the strands slide silkily across his rough skin. Many years had passed since he'd admired the softness of a woman's hair against his skin.

"Ah, lass. There's places that need you more than here. I oughta horsewhip that skinny husband of yours."

Her eyes opened. "I don't have a husband."

Duncan sat back on his heels and frowned. "Then who's that lad out there taking pictures?"

Her eyes widened for an instant. "Oh, Oscar. Yes. We're only recently married and I guess . . . I guess I forgot." The lie rolled out as easily as if it had been God's truth. She was a natural born liar. A trait true to her sex, he thought bitterly.

"You forgot your husband?" Shoving to his feet, Duncan turned toward the singing kettle. "Must not be much of one," he said under his breath. *Or you're not much of a wife.*

"Where is dear Oscar?"

Hot coffee hissed as it hit the bottom of a tin cup.

"Last I saw of him, he was setting up that contraption of his outside."

"I have to go." She rose to her elbows, then paused. "How long were we under the snow?"

Duncan handed her the cup. "I don't think you'll be goin' anywhere so soon. Drink this first."

Her eyes challenged him, then she took the cup from his hand. "How long?" she asked again over the rim.

"You were under the better part of an hour."

She watched him as she took a sip. "How did you find us?"

"I saw your husband's foot sticking out of the snow."

Her expression never changed, but the cup in her hands quivered slightly. "May I see him, please?"

Duncan turned, but her voice stopped him. "Thank you, Inspector McLeod." Duncan ducked outside, sweeping up his hat on his way. The brilliance of the sun against newly turned snow was blinding, yet its beauty was blotched by the rescue efforts. More Mounted Police had come down from the summit to help; small parties were scattered across the snow, engaged in what were surely fruitless searches. More than two hours had already passed since the slide and those not already found were now asleep in cold graves.

Stupid, foolish greed. With a sigh that fogged on the cold air, Duncan moved toward Oscar, whose head was hidden beneath a large, black cloth, looking into a box camera.

"Your wife wants to see you," Duncan said.

"This is a great shot," the voice beneath the cloth said.

"I said, your wife wants you."

Oscar drew his head out and frowned. "My what?"

"The two of you should be a good pair. Both of you have bad memories."

"Oh. My wife. How is she?"

Duncan frowned as Oscar's eyes wandered back to the avalanche. "She seems fine. Frightened."

Oscar gave the scene before him another wistful glance. "I guess I should go in and see her. Will you excuse me?" He set off toward the tent with deliberate steps.

Duncan flipped back the cloth and peered into the camera. All of the morning's tragedy was framed in that tiny hole. The reality of it was jarring and Duncan straightened quickly.

What could two people so young and inexperienced be doing here? he wondered, watching Oscar enter the tent and drop the flap behind him. The intimacy inferred in that action teased a tiny hurt deep within Duncan. Young. In love. Fearless. Hadn't he once been that way himself?

Dragging his gaze away, Duncan moved to meet more men lugging survivors toward the only tent.

CHAPTER THREE

"I know I should have come sooner, but that shot. Sam, you won't believe the power in that one picture."

Oscar spun on his heel, then plopped onto the end of the cot. "Thank you for talking me into coming with you."

Sam laughed and set the cup down. "After what we've just been through, you're thanking me?"

Oscar drew himself up exaggeratedly. "Firsthand experience. That's what we journalists thrive on."

"*Thrive* is not the word I'd have used. *Depend,* maybe. Oh, Oscar, I thought you were dead." Sam felt tears tease the corners of her eyes. "And all I could think about was that I'd talked you into coming."

"What an experience." Oscar leaned closer, his eyes alight with enthusiasm. "I could almost feel the life ebbing out of me before that gent with the shovel dug me out. Near death. You know, I've read stories about such things and myths have existed down through the ages about seeing the beyond. This could make a wonderful story."

Sam smiled at his eagerness, but felt none of it herself. She felt tired and old. Like one who has seen and learned things they shouldn't have, she realized with bitter irony that she and Oscar had subtly exchanged positions. "Go on and take your pictures. I'm going to rest here just a little longer, then we'll go and see if we can find any of our things."

Oscar sprinted out of the tent and Sam let her head fall back against the pillow. It smelled musty, but laced with something else. A thick, earthy smell. Like smoke. Pipe smoke, that was it. She turned her head and inhaled, remembering her father's penchant for a briarwood pipe. Was this where Inspector McLeod laid his head? She glanced around the tiny dwelling, its sides flapping ominously in a buffeting wind. But it was devoid of personal items.

She closed her eyes and let her mind settle on Inspector McLeod. He seemed a congenial enough fellow. Perhaps he would be willing to give her some information on the Yukon and the gold fields. She couldn't let him know what she was about, though. He would, of course, be too clever to divulge any information relating to the thefts she was sure were taking place, but maybe she could lure him into making a slip. After all, he was a man alone for a long time. Surely he could appreciate a pretty ankle when he saw one. Men's tongues had been loosened with less.

Or so she'd been told.

She sat up, grateful that the room no longer swirled when her head left the pillow. Outside, muffled voices raised and she shivered, wondering if they'd found a body or another survivor. Bending over, she peeked beneath the cot. Nothing, save bare boards that did little to insulate from the cold creeping up from underneath.

The tent flap opened and Duncan ducked inside. "We're bringing in more survivors. You'll have to share your shelter."

Guilty at lying about when she was perfectly fine, she stood. "Can I help with the wounded?" Now why did she say that? Blood oozing from a paper cut made her head swim.

"Yes, lass. And thank you."

The tent flap opened wider and another constable stumbled in and deposited a man in the spot she'd occupied only seconds before. Blood congealed on a horrifically broken arm, bone protruding from his torn sleeve. Sam swallowed.

"Are you all right?" Duncan's hand closed around her arm.

"Uh-huh," she said with a nod.

His grip tightened and the skin beneath his fingers warmed. "He needs you, lass."

She nodded silently and sat down on the edge of the cot.

"We're making bandages out of sheets," Duncan said, shoving a strip of cloth into her hands. "Bind him up like he is. We'll do better once we get him down to Sheep Camp."

By sunset, four people were stuffed into the tiny tent. Sam found herself in the role of nurse instead of patient, binding injuries and administering sips of water warmed on the tiny barrel stove. With the encroaching night came the creeping horror of loss. Bodies were to be hauled down the hill to Sheep Camp where a large tent had been set up as a morgue. Inspector McLeod's tent housed the most seriously injured, those that could not be readily moved. All across the snow pack, lanterns bobbed while search parties with dying hope dug up more bodies.

Sam turned when Oscar entered, his face gray and drawn. "Inspector McLeod says he's got more men coming down from the summit to take these lads down."

With the loss of the light, Oscar had been forced to abandon his photography and assume the role of rescuer. Their adventure had turned into a nightmare.

Sam turned around and looked into the fixed eyes of the man whose hand she held. While Oscar spoke, he had slipped away, his life's blood oozing from a deep wound in his abdomen. Revulsion washed over her. She'd never looked death in the face, even though she'd written many obituaries. Death had seemed merely a passage from obscurity to brief prominence with a parade of relatives and accomplishments. The finality of it had never fully dawned on her.

She swiped a hand over the man's eyes, closing his unseeing eyes as Inspector McLeod had instructed, shivering against the feel of skin still warm even in death.

"Tell him we have one less casualty to move."

Inspector McLeod pushed the tent's flap aside and entered, filling up the already crowded tent.

"He's dead," she stated simply, and stood.

The Inspector's face sobered, sadness darkening his blue eyes. "Poor bastard." He glanced up. "I beg your pardon, Mrs. Timmets."

So, Oscar was embroidering their lie. Samantha nodded.

"Are the others ready to move?"

She nodded again. "Yes." Whole sentences were becoming harder and harder to form.

With arms like tree branches and seemingly bottom-less energy, Inspector McLeod scooped the first patient into his arms, mumbling something soothing when the man groaned weakly. He'd be lucky to survive the hard trip down the incline. One by one the injured were loaded onto a large sled hitched to a horse, and for the first time Sam remembered their mare.

"Did you find a horse where we were buried?"

Inspector McLeod glanced over his shoulder, then jerked his chin toward a rescue party hitching up another sled. "She kicked her way out of the snow. Never saw anything like it."

"How about the rest of our supplies?"

He shook his head tiredly. "Just your husband's con-traption and your pack. The harness apparently broke."

All their supplies were gone. Luckily, their five hun-dred dollars was safely sewn into her clothes.

"Climb in there with the wounded and I'll take you all down."

A lantern dangled from a pole strapped to the side of the sled and in his buffalo coat, Inspector McLeod looked more like a grizzly than a man as he moved to the horses' heads.

"Aren't you going to ride down?" she asked as she and Oscar scrambled in between the legs of the three wounded men.

He shook his head. "Too much weight on the poor horse. I'll walk."

Guilt pricked her again and she scrambled over the side of the sled. "I should walk, too, then."

The Inspector stopped and turned. "Somebody needs to ride with the men."

Sam looked back at Oscar, practically swaying on his feet. "He can ride."

Inspector McLeod raised an eyebrow.

"He hasn't been well at all this winter."

Oscar threw Sam a grateful glance, climbed in, and settled down with his back to the sled's side.

"Gitup there," Duncan said and the sled slid forward. Sam hurried to his side to walk in the slick, hollowed-out trench.

"Mrs. Timmets—"

"Please call me Samantha. After all, with what we've been through, some familiarity is warranted, don't you think?"

He chuckled, the sound a deep, comforting rumble.

"And what should I call you?"

"Inspector McLeod."

"Oh."

Here was the perfect opportunity to get some information and she couldn't even manage to charm his name out of him.

"But you can call me Duncan," he said with a smile. Well, at least she thought he was smiling. Even with the faint light of the lantern, the wide brim of his hat made it difficult to see his face.

"How long have you been in the Yukon?"

"About a year."

"Have you spent all your time here, on the summit?"

He nodded. "I'm being reassigned in the spring, to Fort Herchmer in Dawson City."

"Really? How exciting. I understand Dawson City is an exciting place."

"*Exciting* isn't the word I'd use. *Dangerous,* maybe."

"No, definitely exciting. I'm going there myself . . . I mean, my husband and I."

She felt his gaze rake over her as she stumbled and

his hand caught her arm to steady her. "What will you do there?"

So far she'd given him more information than he'd given her. Not a good start for an investigation.

"Oscar . . . my husband . . . is interested in setting up a photography shop there."

"Photography? I suppose there's a market for such in the States."

"How did you know I was from the United States?" His investigative talents had eclipsed hers again.

He turned his head and smiled. "American women are easy to spot."

"And how's that?" Sam asked, her hackles raised by his condescending tone.

"Bold. Brash. Curious."

"And Canadian women aren't?" Her irritation showed in her words and she wished she could bite back the comment.

"Some of them."

Well, she'd certainly done well in that exchange. She waited but he didn't comment further, keeping his eyes on the bobbing lanterns in front of them.

"Why did you join the North West Police?"

"Nosey, too."

"I beg your pardon?"

"American women. Nosey."

"I was just trying to make polite conversation, Inspector."

"I wanted to see the West. This seemed the perfect way to do that."

"How long have you been in the Police?"

"Fifteen years."

Funny, she wouldn't have guessed he was old enough

to have that much time in. He must be about . . . She turned to look at him. Maybe thirty or thirty-two.

"I was twenty-one when I enlisted."

Sam glanced away, bested again. Did he read minds? Or cast spells? Or some other magical thing designed to make her feel like a complete fool?

"You and your husband think there's a market for a photography shop in Dawson City, do you?"

"Oh, yes," she said, falling back into her role. "Back home the public is ravenous for pictures of the Yukon, the gold fields, Dawson City."

"Ravenous?"

"Hungry."

He smiled. "I know what it means."

"You're laughing at me." There, she'd resorted to whining. Where was the soon-to-be-world-renowned woman reporter who'd gotten out of bed in Sheep Camp this morning? Had she left her buried in the avalanche?

"No, lass. I'm not laughing at you. Just haven't heard such words in a long time. Were you a writer before your marriage?" He cocked his head toward Oscar, now fast asleep in the bobbing sled.

"Yes, I was. I wrote for a ladies' magazine. Recipes, sewing, and the like."

"Uh-huh," he replied. "Do you plan to do some writing while you're in Dawson City?"

"Well, I haven't decided yet. I feel that my energies would be best concentrated on being a good wife to my husband and supporting him in his work." That sounded nauseating even to her ears.

"I think young Oscar there is a lucky man. To have such a devoted wife," Duncan replied with finely honed, unmistakable sarcasm.

"When do you think the pass will be open again?"

"In a few days. You're eager to get to Dawson?"

"Yes, we are."

He turned full toward her, his eyes dark and serious in the faint light. "This land is not for the ill-prepared nor the foolhardy. Lives are made and lost in days. Remember that."

Then he fell silent and Sam trudged beside him in that silence until the dim lights of Sheep Camp came into view. Residents rushed out to give them a hand and Duncan was swallowed up by the throng of helpers. So, he was going to Dawson City, too. To join the Mounted Police detachment there—the men who handled all the gold, made all the legal decisions, dispensed frontier justice. Yes indeed, Duncan McLeod would be a contact worth keeping.

Sheep Camp was not the Eden Sam remembered from the day before. What had been quaint houses were now shacks lining a mud-churned street. White canvas tents squatted in between. Even brushed by the pastels of a winter's dawn, the town seemed shabby and trampled. The wounded were quickly swept away by helpers, the dead carried to the makeshift morgue.

"What do we do now?" Oscar asked, clambering over the edge of the sled, clutching his camera equipment.

"Find a place to sleep, and to buy more supplies."

They slogged through the ankle-deep mud, relieved only partially by the half-sunken boardwalk that bordered the odd collection of stores. A crooked sign advertised HOTEL on the front of a two-story building and Sam heaved a sigh of relief.

She stepped into the doorway and up to a counter constructed of cast-off packing cases.

"You want a room?" the clerk demanded, glancing between them.

"Yes—two, please."

"Ain't got two. Got one. One bed."

A bare floor would do, Sam thought, as long as it was dry. "We'll take it."

"That'll be a hundred dollars."

"A hundred dollars!?" She glanced at Oscar. One fifth of their remaining money and not nearly enough to allow them passage back across the pass.

"No, thank you," she replied and hurried back out into the street. "We'll just have to find someplace else," she said, glancing around the settlement. A horse tied to a ramshackle building pawed the churned and muddy ground.

"There," she said, pointing. "That's a barn. We can sleep in the hay."

"Hay makes my nose run and makes me sneeze," Oscar complained.

Sam set off toward the barn. "At this moment, I don't care if your nose runs off down the street on its own. I'm sleeping in this hay." She stopped in front of the skewed door and gave it a yank. It swung open easily. Pausing for her eyes to adjust, Sam heard moans and whispers coming from within—clearly, even to innocent ears, the telltale sounds of lovemaking.

"Sam, there's somebody in there," Oscar whispered.

"I don't care. I'm dead on my feet and all my clothes are wet through. If they can bear it, so can I."

She stepped inside and the sounds intensified. They were coming from near the back of the one-story building. To her left was a pile of new, fragrant hay.

"Shouldn't we say something?" Oscar whispered, close on her heels.

"I doubt they'd hear or pay attention." She swung her pack off her shoulders, breathed a sigh of relief, and fell backwards into the fragrant mound.

The moans settled into a steady rhythm.

"This isn't proper," Oscar said in a nervous voice as he settled into the hay a few feet away.

"I don't care what's proper," Sam replied, beginning to drift off to sleep. Intervals between the sounds lengthened, as did the intensity. Then, both voices moaned loud and long, and settled into soft coos.

Sam nodded and heard the participants rustle themselves out of their love nest and shuffle toward the door, their voices blending in hushed whispers. The door creaked open, ground shut, and all was again quiet.

Sam rolled onto her side, scattered thoughts receding to the depths of her mind as sleep overtook her. Despite her nonchalance to Oscar about the couple in the barn, her curiosity had played a part in her decision to stay. What did two people do that made them moan like that? And if the process was so painful, why did people seem to be so enamored of it? Or not, according to Aunt Sophia. What was this great mystery between men and women?

She rolled to her back, something deep within her disturbed by her line of thought. Going to Dawson City was the most exciting thing she'd ever done, she assured herself, a new beginning for dull Samantha Wilder. Perhaps she'd find out new things about herself in Dawson City. Perhaps she'd find love, she allowed herself to dream. And maybe she'd find out what all that moaning was about. Yes, definitely, she'd put that on her list of things to investigate.

They slept through the day, miraculously unnoticed. Twilight fell, soft and hazy, before Sam opened her eyes. A tune tinkled from some off-key piano and a high, quivering voice floated eloquently over the noise. Someone was singing an old, sorrowful ballad, "The Songs of Summer," that Sam remembered hearing her mother hum. Intrigued, she rolled out of the hay and slipped out the door, unnoticed by Oscar.

Following the music, she found herself outside the door of what was obviously a saloon. She peeped over the half door. Smoke settled in a soft curtain and patrons in rickety chairs stared at a makeshift stage and a beautiful, willowy woman in a flowing dress. Her hands held dramatically under her chin, she warbled the mournful notes of the song.

At the side of the stage stood a tall, dark man, one foot propped on a chair seat. Inspector Duncan McLeod gazed at the performer, one hand cupping his chin. Sam slipped inside unnoticed and skirted the back of the room, quickly stuffing her hair up inside her hat. Finally, she slid into an empty seat that gave her a good view of Duncan. With rapt attention, Duncan watched the woman, a soft smile curling his lips. His Stetson was balanced carefully on his bent knee and a dark lock of hair fell across his forehead.

Something within Sam moved—a clenching, no, more like a stomach cramp, she observed, committing the sensation to memory for later assessment. But her analytical thoughts stopped when the woman glided across the stage and offered Duncan a dainty hand.

With a smile, he accepted her outstretched fingers and kissed them. She then leaned down and kissed the dark curls on the top of his head.

The room exploded into applause and she pulled her hand away, even though he clung to her fingers briefly before releasing her. She floated back to the center of the stage, bowed, and then disappeared between two tattered velvet curtains. Duncan clamped his hat back on his head and ducked through other curtains dangling at the side of the stage.

An unexpected zing of jealousy stung Sam. So, Inspector McLeod had a lover. Why was she surprised? In fact, why did she give that possibility a second thought? Of course he had a lover. Or a wife. A man that handsome had a string of women after him, no doubt. And the canary on the stage was certainly a cut above most of the women she'd seen so far in the Yukon Territory.

She rose and slipped back out of the room unnoticed. When she reached the barn, she found Oscar still sound asleep. Fearing for his health, she pressed a hand to his forehead and found him perfectly cool.

"Oscar," she said, shaking his shoulder.

"Huh?" Rubbing his eyes, he sat up and stared at her blearily.

"We have to find some supplies. We've slept all day."

"How are you going to buy them at night? Surely the stores are closed."

"I'm not going to buy them. I'm going to steal them."

"Have you lost your mind?" he asked. "Sam, what has gotten into you?"

"We have five hundred dollars. We have to have that cash and two months' supplies to be allowed over the summit by the Mounties. What else do I need to explain?"

"You could start with why an intelligent woman would suddenly turn into some . . . *outlaw* once she's out of sight of her controlling uncle."

"I'm not turning into anything. I'm just making do. That's what adventurers do. They improvise."

Oscar stood and swiped at the bits of straw clinging to his gray, rumpled suit and dusted off his bowler hat. "You're going to improvise both of us into jail. Let's just go home, Sam. I'd say this trip wasn't meant to be. There'll be other stories."

Sam started for the door. "Not for me, there won't. As soon as I set foot back in San Francisco, Aunt Sophia is going to marry me off to the first available bachelor and I'll spend my life changing diapers and weeding . . . rutabagas."

"That's quite a story, Sam. Perhaps you could also add that you'll be doing that weeding barefooted. One day you'll be a fine writer. If it doesn't kill you first."

"You can stay here and make fun of me if you want," Sam said. "But I'm going to steal us some supplies."

CHAPTER FOUR

"It's locked."

"Of course it's locked," Oscar whispered. What did you expect?

"If I only had a hairpin."

"You've read too many dime novels, Sam. No one ever really picked a lock with—. Well, I'll be darned."

Sam clamped the pin between her teeth, waggled her eyebrows, and eased open the door. The scent of leather and tobacco rolled out to engulf them. "I put one in my pocket," she whispered, returning the hairpin to its hiding place.

The soft squeal of a mouse made them both jump, their breathing heavy on the silence. A cat trotted by without a glance, the unlucky rodent dangling from its mouth.

"We'll need pemmican," she said, pulling a can of the dried meat concoction from the shelf. "And some flour. We'll get a sack of that on the way out. You hid the sled behind the rain barrel. Right?"

"Yes, I hid it properly."

Item by item, Sam chose their supplies. She piled them all in the center of the floor and expertly laced the batch together. "Now, let's get the flour and get out of here." Dragging a fifty-pound bag, they backed out the door and closed it softly behind them. Out came the hairpin and Sam jimmied the door until it was locked.

"Where's the sled?" Sam whispered when a glance behind the rain barrel yielded nothing.

"I swear I put it there," Oscar whispered back.

"Are you lads looking for this?"

They whirled and faced a Mountie, legs spread, arms crossed over his chest.

"Inspector McLeod?" Sam asked, peering underneath the broad hat.

"Nope, Constable Finnegan."

Sam's heart sank. "We lost our supplies in the avalanche, you see. And we only have five hundred dollars in cash. We have to have the supplies *and* the cash to get over the summit. So, Constable, we were driven to the sin of theft."

She adopted her most contrite expression.

"And a fine excuse that is. But not the best I've heard. Do you have any others?" He spoke with a thick Irish brogue.

"Nope. That's my best one at the moment."

"Then it's off to jail with the likes of you." He grasped both their coat collars and hauled them along beside him.

Welcome warmth spilled out of the little log building and, for a brief moment, Sam was glad they'd been caught. She couldn't remember the last time she'd been warm.

"We've got no jail proper," Constable Finnegan said, "so I'll have to shackle you to these cots." He brought out two sets of heavy leg irons as Oscar looked at Sam with widened eyes.

Constable Finnegan gently guided Sam to sit on a cot, then knelt and placed the iron collar around her ankle. He did the same for Oscar, then stepped back and crossed his arms. "The two of you are a bedraggled lot, to be sure. What are you doing in the Yukon Territory?" Riotous red hair poked out over his ears and a droopy red moustache dominated his upper lip.

"Well, my husband, Oscar there, is an accomplished photographer and we plan to set up a shop in Dawson City."

"A photography shop?"

Sam nodded and smiled the sweetest smile she could muster.

"You're not headed for the gold fields?"

"Oh, no. Oscar's health is very delicate," she explained and Oscar obligingly coughed.

"Uh-huh," the constable said, shifting his weight to the other hip. "You think there's enough photographs that need taking to feed the two of you?"

"Why, of course. The whole country is hungry for pictures of the Gold Rush. And men will want photos to send back home to their loved ones."

"You know, Mrs.—"

"Timmets. Samantha Timmets."

"Mrs. Timmets, the reason stampeders are not allowed to cross the summit without two months' provisions and five hundred dollars cash is to keep people such as yourselves from dying for lack of good sense."

"Whatever do you mean?" she asked with feigned innocence.

"I mean that the two of you look like good customers for that morgue down the street."

Oscar's Adam's apple bobbed and he glanced over at her, terror written all over his face.

"You two are the ones Inspector McLeod dug out of the avalanche yesterday, aren't you?"

"Yes."

Inspector Finnegan stroked his wide moustache and squinted one eye. "Tell you what I'll do. Mind you now, this is a one-time opportunity. I'll just settle with old Mr. McFarland for the supplies. And you and your . . . husband can take your supplies and your cash and be on your way as soon as the pass is open."

"Oh, Constable Finnegan. That's very kind of you," Sam said.

"Now, things don't come without a price."

She stared back at him. "What's your price?"

"That you take a picture of McLeod and me."

She breathed out with relief. "We'd be glad to do just that, Constable. What about in the morning so we can catch the early light?"

Finnegan nodded and knelt to release the leg irons. "Now just in case you get any more ideas about thieving here in Sheep Camp . . ." He rattled the manacles that chafed against her ankle.

"No, Constable. Just as soon as the pass is open, we'll be on our way."

He released the irons and stood, coiling the chains in his hands. "Good. I'm holding you to your words, now."

"I promise, Constable Finnegan, that we won't get

into any more trouble," Sam said, holding up her right hand for good measure.

"You were lovely tonight, Emily." Duncan eased the door to the bedroom closed and slid one hip onto the edge of a table.

Emily turned from the cracked mirror and smiled softly. Duncan's throat constricted and he drew a troubled breath. She was an angel—soft, delicate, fragile.

"Thank you, Duncan."

"Have you given any more thought to my proposal?"

She turned back to the cracked glass and carefully removed hairpins from the shiny coil on her head. Waves of silky black hair tumbled down her back. Combing delicate fingers through the strands, she turned. "You know I can't."

Duncan slid off the table, moved to her side, and took her fingers in his. Desperation edged into his thoughts. If he couldn't convince her, she'd slip away unnoticed and disappear as she had so many times before. "I'm not a man to beg. You know that. But I will if that's what it takes. I'll beg on bended knee if it will change your mind."

She stared down at their joined hands, then squeezed his fingers. "You know I love you, but I can't marry you. Your heart is too big, Duncan McLeod. If you let the whole world in, it will trample you and then I'll have no Duncan to come back to."

She was like the crocuses that bloomed through the snow. Beautiful, rare, often unnoticed except to those who knew they existed.

"I'd make a poor wife. Life in Dawson City would grow dull and I'd be off. You know that."

Duncan glanced down at the rough board floor. She was slipping away and there was nothing he could do. "As the wife of an officer, you'd be under my protection."

She caressed his cheek. "Your heart would be a precious gift to any woman. I cannot take it under these conditions. Sacrificing yourself for me won't set things right, Duncan. You know that. Nothing will right the wrong done you. I'd only make your pain worse."

She released his hand and stepped back. "I have an engagement at the Wild Horse Saloon in Dawson City through the summer. Let's enjoy the time we will have there and not think about the future."

"You never think of the future, Emily," Duncan told her. "You live your life a day at a time, an hour at a time, with no thought for tomorrow. I'm offering you a way to put the past behind you, and me, and start new."

She moved away with that gliding gait of hers, as if she floated inches above the ground. As she peered into the mirror, her face became wistful, softening into the expression that set his knees to trembling in dread. "The past and I have become fast acquaintances, soulmates. It wasn't meant for us ever to be parted. One is only allowed one soulmate in life, Duncan. I beg you to find yours."

Howling wind whipped snow into dervishes, flinging the icy pellets to torment man and animal alike. Sam pulled up the collar of her coat and hunched her shoulders against the onslaught. Behind her, Oscar trudged through the churned snow, struggling with the fifty pounds of flour on his back. Hours ago they'd reached

the Scales, their location when the avalanche had taken
so many lives more than a week ago, and breathed a
sigh of relief as they crossed the relatively flat terrain.
Before, the blanket of snow had been smooth and glistening. Now it was rugged and treacherous and hiding
bodies yet undiscovered. Sam kept her eyes ahead, concentrating on the summit that reared above them.

"We're almost at the Golden Stairs," Oscar said, his
voice muffled by his upturned collar. Sam shaded her
eyes and gazed up at the line of people and animals
struggling to maneuver steps chopped from sheer ice.
But beyond that nightmare lay the summit and the
North West Mounted Police detachment . . . and Duncan McLeod.

Sam scolded herself and tucked her chin further into
her coat. She couldn't entertain such foolishness. A man
was the last thing she wanted or needed. Especially a
Mountie. Again, she ran her headline through her
mind. THOUSANDS OF DOLLARS IN GOLD DUST EMBEZ-
ZLED BY NORTH WEST MOUNTED POLICE. Those simple
words would solidify her career. Never again would she
have to beg Uncle Harry for a job at his paper. In fact,
she could probably name her assignment, if she was
careful. Where would she go? she mused. Tombstone,
Arizona? Colorful name. Lots of action. Dodge City?
Maybe the logging country in northern California? Lum-
ber barons dealt in millions of dollars every day. Perhaps
she could repeat her victory.

"Watch your step." A hand grasped her arm and she
looked up into Duncan's blue eyes.

"Mrs. Timmets," he said in a soft baritone. "How
nice to see you again. And you, Mr. Timmets."

Oscar chuffed his disapproval, but she paid him no

attention. She doubted Duncan meant the words, but she was glad he said it anyway. "And you, Inspector."

"I thought we agreed on Duncan and Sam," he said softly as he guided her hand to the rope balustrade strung along the trail up the mountain.

"Duncan." She gripped the rope and took the first icy step.

"I hope to see you on top. It'll be dark by the time you reach the summit," he cautioned.

She nodded and moved away, pushed from behind by the crowd that followed.

Sunset was spectacular from the top of the Chilkoot Pass, the disk of light dying in a palette of cold colors. The lonely detachment consisted of a single canvas-covered shack with rough board floors. Sam trudged in the line to enter the building, pay their customs, and follow the flow of people out.

She ducked to enter the building and was immediately assaulted with the odor of mold. Two cots sat on the other side of the customs counter with supplies piled around them. Moisture permeated everything. Papers, the wooden counter, even the boards under their feet bore a sheen of moisture.

Inspector Robert Belcher looked up from scribbling on a soggy piece of paper. Quickly, Sam gave him a description of their goods and handed him the money required. He took the payment, wrote out a receipt, and handed it to her with a smile and a caution to be careful.

Outside, weary travelers were settling down to camp for the night. Some had brought tents; others spread quilts on rough boards provided by the Police. Sam was glad she'd thought to steal a small canvas tent while on her foray through the store. When she found Oscar, he had a fire going in a small rock firepit and was heating a can of beans in a bright aluminum pan.

"Breathtaking, isn't it?" Sam said with a nod to the west and the last ribbons of a dying sunset.

"I'm so tired I can't appreciate anything at the moment but this can of beans," he grumbled.

Sam glanced toward the customs house and two snow-dusted Inspectors just stepping over the summit. They paused, glanced toward the small tent town, then continued on to the office.

Sam turned away. Tomorrow night they'd be at the Bennett detachment where, if they were lucky, they could catch a boat all the way to Dawson City. Then, she could begin her real work.

Evening deepened and Oscar crawled under his blanket and was asleep instantly. Sam sat and stared into the fire until the precious firewood dwindled to coals. Restless, she walked through the little temporary town, too edgy to sleep and too tired to think. Overhead, stars filled a clear sky, winking and flirting with the mere mortals down below.

"The night sky is one of the things I love about the Yukon." He appeared at her elbow and her senses came to alert.

"It's beautiful," she agreed.

"Look there." He pointed to the north and faint dancing ribbons of light. "Northern lights. Not much of a show tonight, though." Sam had seen the lights many times since they'd set out, but never before had they seemed so bright or so magnificent. She knew with a bitter and ominous twist of her heart it was because he stood at her side, his touch inches away.

"Some nights they fill the sky with light." He laughed

softly. "Then I swear I can hear singing. You know some of the natives say they're spirits of the dead, singing."

She turned toward him, even though she'd warned herself not to. Not to look into his dark blue eyes. Not to watch for the twitch of his mouth just before he smiled. Not to imagine what it would feel like to be held in his arms.

"Where is Mr. Timmets?"

Sam took a breath and wiped all those traitorous thoughts out of her mind for fear he'd see the truth in her eyes. "He's asleep."

"And you're out for a stroll alone?"

"I'm sure all these men are far too tired to entertain the idea of accosting a woman."

"There are other dangers. High winds. Cold. Step off an edge and plunge hundreds of feet. Other perils a consummate troublemaker like yourself can find to get into."

Anger, then amusement, rushed through her. She turned away for fear he'd see her smile. "What are you doing out here? Shouldn't you be asleep, too?"

"Same thing as you. Stargazing. I like to see the evening sky over the lake. There," he pointed past her nose and she pivoted to follow.

"A lake? Where?"

"See that smooth coating of snow down there?" He stepped close behind her until she could feel his breath ruffling the edge of her hair. The sweet aroma of pipe tobacco swirled around them both.

"That's Crater Lake. Look at the stars."

She had to admit he was right. Millions of sparkling bits hung low over the dark, rugged mountain range that thrust upwards on the other side of the lake.

He leaned closer, his breath brushing her hair away

from her face. "In spring, the grass is green and the lake is a shimmering mirror by day. But at night, it reflects the starlight. Clear beautiful points of light. Winking. Twinkling. The world is peaceful then, quiet. Sometimes you can hear a wolf calling to its mate."

"That sounds beautiful," Sam managed to say, wondering if her pounding heart sounded as loud to Duncan as it did to her.

"You should share this with your husband. Starry nights are made for young lovers." Was there a note of wistfulness in his voice?

He stepped away suddenly. "Good night, Mrs. Timmets."

"Good night, Inspector McLeod."

He walked away, leaving Sam to wonder if he was a sorcerer as well as a mind reader.

Lake Bennett, Canada, May 1898

"River's clear!" The cry echoed across the tent city on the banks of the Yukon River. Sam scrambled to her feet and grabbed her pack that had been ready for weeks.

"C'mon, Sam." Oscar stuck his head inside the tent. "I've got us a boat."

Sam quickly stuffed a few last minute things in the bag, grateful to leave the tent for the next gold field hopeful. A wave of men knocked her back against the canvas, dislodging one of the stakes that had held the shelter against the buffeting winter winds.

She ran after Oscar, bounced and wedged amidst the humanity that spilled into the muddy, rutted streets, all headed for the river and the boats that waited to take them to Dawson City.

"Ours is just over there." Oscar pointed to a large, deep well craft rapidly filling with people. "The captain promised me passage as soon as I paid him," Oscar finished as he ran.

"Wait a minute." Sam grabbed his coat sleeve and jerked him to a stop. "You paid the captain?"

"Yes. Yesterday." He faced her and frowned. "Is something wrong? I had enough money from the pictures I've taken of the miners."

Sam felt the world fall out from under her feet. "Oscar, how could you be so stupid? Haven't you been listening the last two weeks?"

"Listening to what?" They stood apart, islands in the flow of humanity.

"To what the others have said about being robbed of their passage money by the captains of these ships. You never should have paid him until we got to Dawson City." Sam shook her head. Poor naive Oscar.

"Well, we won't find out standing here, will we?" Oscar set off again and Sam had to run to catch up.

They arrived at the empty wharf at the same time. Their boat was drifting away around the last bend, laden with miners.

"How much have you got left?" Sam asked without looking at Oscar.

He paused for a moment. "About two dollars."

Sam sighed. Why did everything have to be so hard? "Well, what's done is done and we'll just have to make other plans."

"I'm sorry, Sam." Oscar turned a face so filled with hurt that all Sam's anger drained away.

"Add this to your list of experiences. Now, let's go raise some money."

They walked back toward the tent town, now almost

deserted. At least we won't have a problem finding some-place to sleep, Sam comforted herself. Slogging through the mud, they reached the permanent portion of town, consisting of one hotel, one saloon, a barber shop, and a general store.

"Wait. I have an idea." Sam set her pack on the muddy board porch and pulled out her reporter's pad. "Bring your camera."

She pushed through the saloon doors and was greeted with surprised stares from the few men seated there.

"What can I get you, little lady?" the bartender asked.

"I came to offer you something," Sam replied.

The man with beady black eyes and an elaborately waxed moustache smiled slowly. "And what is that 'something'?"

Instantly regretting her poor choice of words, Sam hurried to recant. "It's not what you think."

The smile left his lips.

"I came here to make you and your customers a business proposition."

Suspicious, he eyed her through dropped lids. "Go on."

"I write obituaries, complete with pictures."

"Obituaries!" His voice carried throughout the room and several men looked up.

"Obituaries. Fine testaments to a man's life, and a picture, to send home in case he encounters some unfor-tunate incident while in the gold fields."

The bartender scratched his head. "Seems kind of morbid, don't it?"

"Oh, no. Paying attention to one's estate is a very modern thing."

"Modern, huh?" He rubbed his chin and glanced around at the nearly empty room. Soon, it would fill up again with more men willing to give their lives and futures to the gold fields, but for now, Sam knew he was worried about business in those weeks in between.

"What's my cut?"

"Twenty percent."

"Forty."

"Thirty-five."

Again he glanced around the room. "All right, thirty-five. Be back here tonight."

Sam glanced triumphantly at a speechless Oscar.

"Sam, you're amazing. Where'd you come up with an idea like that?"

Sam kicked at a clod of mud. "I don't know, it just came to me."

"Have you always been able to do that? I mean, think of things so quickly?" Sam could feel his gaze on her and knew that over the last few weeks, Oscar's fascination with her had deepened. How could she discourage him without hurting his feelings? He was a good man, perhaps a little self-absorbed sometimes, but a decent man all the same. And he'd managed to provide them with money during their layover in Bennett with his photography and never once complained that he did all the work. Now, it was her turn.

"Oh, I could always think my way out of a tight place when I was a child. I just imagined myself looking beyond whatever predicament I was in. You know, like hindsight. And the answer would come to me. That's what I did."

Sam looked out across the Yukon River, now free-flowing except for small chunks of ice. A fistfight had broken out on shore, and two men slugged and rolled in the mud. Standing near them, arms crossed over a scarlet jacket, was Duncan McLeod.

"Sam," Oscar exclaimed as he ran into her back. "Why did you . . . Oh. Him."

"Now what do you mean by that?" Sam turned to face Oscar, scowling toward the river.

"I mean I don't like the way he looks at you."

"How does he look at me?"

Oscar colored. "You know, *that* way."

Sam stifled a laugh and couldn't resist goading Oscar on. "No, I don't. What way?"

"The way a man looks at a woman, Sam. Not the way a Mountie ought to look at a *person* he pulled out of the snow."

"And how should he look at a *person* he pulled out of the snow?"

Oscar pivoted back toward the line of tents, muttering under his breath. She'd apologize later, Sam thought with a smile.

Shouts drew her attention back to the river's shore. The fight was progressing nicely. Both participants were completely covered with thick, sticky mud, yet they slugged on. Duncan stood, nonplussed, watching the men writhing at his feet. Surprisingly, as far as she could see, there wasn't a spot of mud on him.

Giving free rein to the devil sitting on her shoulder, Sam walked down to the waterfront with no idea what she'd say.

"Now that you've got the fight out of you, you both need a bath." With that, one of the men sailed out into the frigid water.

"George, in with you, too." Duncan grabbed the remaining fighter by the belt and collar and lifted him clear of the ground.

"No, McLeod. A man'll catch his death in that water."

"Likely as not, you could use the bath." A loud splash announced the beginning of George's bath. Duncan chuckled and watched the men haul each other out of the water. Muttering curses, they struggled up the hill toward town.

"Inspector McLeod."

Duncan turned, recognizing the voice before he saw the face. It was the voice that had haunted his dreams for weeks, whispering disturbing things. Things he had thought himself too old to dream about. He wasn't a young lad anymore and Samantha Timmets was more than a handful.

A married handful.

They'd parted ways at the summit of Chilkoot Pass, she and her husband to travel on to Bennett Lake and he to stay and relieve some of the men at the summit. Now, the detachment at the summit was to be moved since the collection of duties had been turned over to civilian assessors. And he was assigned to Fort Herchner sooner than he'd expected. Samantha had been the first thing that crossed his mind. God help him.

"Samantha." He used her name because he liked the way it rolled off his tongue. Her eyes were much bluer than in his dreams, her hair silkier, her body curvier. "I thought you and Oscar would be gone to Dawson with the rest."

"Well, we missed our boat. We're waiting for another."

Duncan searched her face for a feature he had failed to memorize, some small thing he could add. "This isn't San Francisco. There won't be another boat along for weeks."

"Well, then. We'll wait weeks."

There was some story here, but it wasn't his business to find out. He'd not dabble in relations between a man and his wife. Even if he suspected no such union existed.

"And how is your husband?"

"He's fine."

Her answer was quick, almost natural. Perhaps he was wrong and they were indeed husband and wife. A flash of jealousy reared its ugly head and Duncan banished the thought. She's a married woman, he kept telling himself.

"Give him my regards." Duncan started away, anxious to leave before she became more firmly implanted in his mind.

"Inspector McLeod." Her hand on his arm stopped him. Even through the red serge he felt her heat, knew the softness of her skin. "Are you going to stay here in Lake Bennett?"

"No," he said after a swallow. "I go back to Dawson City tomorrow. I'm stationed there to secure the shipments of gold."

"Oh?" She raised her eyebrows. "How interesting that job must be."

Tiresome, thankless, yes. Interesting, no. "Aye, it is."

"How do you intend to get to Dawson City, if I might ask?"

By the tantalizing tip of her head, he knew he was in trouble.

"By boat. With some other Policemen."

Her eyes sparkled. "Could my husband and I beg a ride from you? We'd make it worth your while."

He knew he shouldn't ask, shouldn't take the bait. There were con artists and then there were con artists, but Samantha Timmets was in a class by herself. She could disarm a man with those blue eyes quicker than he could with an Enfield revolver.

"And what bargain did you have in mind this time?"

"We'll take pictures. Of all of you and the boat. The town here. Whatever you want. One day history will remember these times and you'll have the pictures to prove you were here."

Duncan crossed his arms. She could have anything she wanted from him. Anything. But she mustn't know that, else he'd be as lost as that poor husband of hers. "It's a matter of record that Inspector Duncan McLeod served in the Yukon Territory in the year 1898. Why would I have to convince anyone of that?"

"Well . . . someday there'll be a woman in your life and she'll be impressed with photographs like this."

"And how do you know there isn't already a woman in my life?"

She actually looked flustered for a moment, then her calm reserve returned. "Then the lovely Mrs. McLeod will treasure a picture of her handsome husband in his splendid scarlet uniform."

Duncan stepped closer and leaned near enough to see the pulse jumping at the base of her neck, visible above the worn flannel of her shirt. He noted with satisfaction that her chest rose and fell in shallow breaths and the tiny pulse increased as he neared. But she met his gaze squarely, giving no hint of her feelings. "I don't need a picture to impress the ladies."

"No, I'm sure you don't," she said and he realized she was unaware that she'd whispered.

"You'll have your ride to Dawson, you and Oscar. Then you'll take any picture I choose. Deal?"

"Deal."

CHAPTER FIVE

"What do you think he meant?"

"How should I know?" Sam muttered, scrambling through her pack for a set of dry, clean clothes. "I don't care what he meant if it'll get us a ride to Dawson City. Where did I put my notepad?"

Oscar reached around her hands and pulled the pad from a side pocket. "Here. We should be going."

"Go outside and let me change my clothes."

She changed into the only skirt she'd packed, coiled her hair up on top of her head, and poked a spare pencil through the bun. Tendrils hung down the side of her face and she smiled at her reflection in the mirror. A little femininity wouldn't hurt business.

The tent town seemed empty compared to the weeks before. Music from the out-of-tune piano drifted from the saloon and up into the cool spring air, straight out into the starlit night. And for a moment, the disturbing memory of Duncan's breath on her cheek floated through her thoughts. She breathed in lungfuls of air so crisp it hurt. Nearby, the cheerful gurgle of the river was fitting background music.

The saloon door swung open and expectant faces turned toward her. She swallowed. The establishment was about half full. She heard Oscar set down his camera equipment.

"I'd like to offer you men the chance to have your obituary written by a professional writer and your picture taken by a professional photographer. It would be a wonderful memento to send home in case of some unfortunate accident in the gold fields, gentlemen. A well-written obituary can be a great comfort to those remaining at home."

Astonished looks passed over the faces staring at her. For the first time, her courage faltered and wavered.

"I'd like mine done." Duncan stepped out from behind a group of men standing at the bar and moved toward her. "And a picture, too."

"Well, if you'll just come over here, Inspector." Sam walked to the bar on unsteady legs and wiped off a clean spot with the sleeve of her shirt, hoping she was hiding her surprise.

He eased himself onto the stool, a slight smile on his face. "Where would you like me to begin?"

"Let me just get some facts while Oscar sets up his camera."

"You're not married, are you?"

Sam looked up. "What?" How on earth could he have known?

"You and Oscar aren't married."

Another lie began to rise to her lips. Didn't they look the loving couple? "No, we're not," she said softly.

"You know that prostitution is illegal." His voice was barely a whisper and Sam glanced quickly at Oscar, who was absorbed in his preparations.

"I'm no prostitute, Inspector McLeod."

Duncan tilted his head and studied her face. "I didn't really think so. Suppose you tell me your story while I tell you mine."

Sam's mind spun. She certainly couldn't tell him the truth and she had to tell him something he'd believe. A small lie this time.

"We're living in sin."

"In sin, are you?"

"Yes. Now, where were you born?"

"On the Isle of Skye. How long have the two of you . . . been together?"

"For a year. Mother and father?"

"Edward and Moira. A year? The two of you don't seem to go together. Are you sure?"

"Well, of course I'm sure."

His eyebrows rose and a smile quirked at the corners of his mouth.

"Maybe not in *sin.* You know we haven't done anything you could classify as *sin.* Not in . . . that way. Year of birth?"

"Born in 1862. So what are the two of you about?"

"I'm running away from a cruel uncle who squandered all my money. Oscar is my best friend, so naturally he came with me. Brothers and sisters?"

"The old cruel uncle story? One sister, Estra."

"It's true. How did you get from Scotland to Canada?"

Duncan's grin widened and Sam felt herself sinking into the pool of lies she had begun. "I came to join the

Mounted Police when I was twenty-one. How did the two of you get here with no money?''

"I had some hidden my uncle didn't know about. How long have you served in the Mounted Police?''

"Where did you and Best Friend Oscar come from? Fifteen years.''

At least she could tell him the truth here. One less thing to remember. "We came from San Francisco. Where did you say was your first posting?''

"Not a very observant uncle to miss the amount of money it would take to travel from San Francisco to Canada.''

Sam looked up from her writing. He wasn't believing a word. How he knew she was lying was a mystery. She was usually so good at this. "No, he was a very bright man, only cruel and self-centered. Wife or children?''

"Have or want?''

Sam looked up again. "Pardon me?''

"Are you asking if I *have* a wife and children or do I *want* a wife and children?'' He smiled, yet in his eyes was a pain, a deep, well-hidden misery.

"Do you have any of either?''

"I was married once a long time ago. Two children. And you?''

"None. I think that's all I need, Inspector.''

"Do you want 'em?''

Sam met his eyes again.

"I beg your pardon?''

"Do you want children?''

"That's a very personal question.''

He shrugged. "Yes, but it's an honest one. I told you my darkest secrets. Now you're obliged to tell me yours.''

"Yes. Someday. Very much. With the right man.''

"And is Oscar there the right man?'' Duncan nodded

to where Oscar lowered the black cloth and picked off a piece of lint.

"Oscar is a dear friend and a kind man."

"You didn't answer my question."

"I am a woman who knows what she wants, Inspector. Someday I will find that man."

He held her gaze for a long, unnerving moment and in a flash of imagination she envisioned making those babies with Duncan, wrapped in his arms, absorbing his strength to give to the tiny life within her.

"Are you going to take my picture?"

"Yes, of course." Sam slid off the stool, grateful to be away from his intense stare, to break this strange connection between them.

"Stand right here." She took his shoulder and positioned him with his back to the bar. "I think a little local color in this would be nice, don't you?"

Duncan glanced over his shoulder to the nude painting that held an honored place over the bar. "Maybe by the door would be better."

He moved out of her grasp. Only then did she realize her hand had lingered on his arm. He yanked down his jacket and stood up straight while men called comments and taunts. He smiled, the smile betrayed by that enticing twitch of his lip. The flash flared and the overpowering scent of sulfur permeated the room.

"I'll just develop this tonight, Inspector, and you can pick up your picture tomorrow morning." Oscar carefully slid the metal plate out of the camera and laid it on a velvet cloth at his side.

"And I'll write up the obituary and have it ready tomorrow." She knew no words would come to her to complete the task. Even envisioning Duncan dead or injured brought a stab of deep pain and an overwhelming sense of loss. Don't be a silly goose, she warned herself. You don't even know the man.

"I think perhaps I'd like you to keep that picture. And the article," Duncan said to her with a smile.

"Why?"

"Call it a memento of your adventure in the Yukon. One day when you're bouncing babies on your knee, you'll pull it out and remember Chilkoot Pass and Duncan McLeod."

Sam met Duncan's eyes again, but looked away from the intensity in them, afraid to believe what she saw mirrored there. "I don't think I want to remember that incident, Inspector. What was the final count of dead?"

Duncan's smile faded. "Seventy-two."

A bone-chilling shiver passed over Sam and she felt death's breath on her shoulders. Until now, the experience hadn't seemed quite real, more like something in a nightmare that nagged at her all day. Yet, standing here, looking into Duncan's eyes, the number made the experience real. Seventy-two hopeful people died on that mountain. Weeks would pass before wives, parents, children would know what happened to their loved ones. Some would never know.

She hated the sudden quiver of her chin. "No, I'd like you to keep these things, Inspector. And remember me." She tucked the notes into her pocket and as she withdrew her hand, Duncan's fingers closed around it.

"You were lucky, lass. There's no shame in being lucky."

Sam stared down at his fingers, weathered and callused. He had a tiny scar on his fourth finger. Heat flowed from his body to hers and Sam wondered if the rest of the room felt the tremors making the very air vibrate. She glanced over her shoulder. Men concentrated on their drinks, or else watched her.

"I know." Slowly, she extricated her hand, immediately missing the feel of his flesh against hers.

He caught her hand again, halting her leaving. "One more question."

"What?"

"What's your real name?"

"Samantha Wilder. Miss."

He smiled softly. "We'll leave in two days. At sunup so we can make the falls before dark." He nodded briefly and was quickly gone, leaving the saloon door swinging behind him.

"Sam?" Oscar's voice stirred the hair around her ears.

"What?" She turned so quickly they almost bumped noses. Hurt filled Oscar's eyes, large behind his glasses.

"You have another customer." He nodded toward a bearded bear of a man.

Sam smiled at the man, who returned a toothy grin. She withdrew her pad and began to write down the details he related, but her mind wandered back to Duncan's face, his smile, his eyes. Loops of writing spilled out from beneath her pencil and she heard herself answer his questions, reply to his comments, but her mind had left with the red serge jacket.

The stench of alcohol and sulfur filled Sam's nose. She held a large glass plate at arm's length while Oscar poured a foul-smelling chemical over it.

"Hold still, Sam, or you'll make me ruin Mr. McLeod's picture." Sam opened a watering eye to look at Oscar. His mouth was set in a grim line.

"You're mad at me, aren't you?" Sam asked, knowing full well he'd deny it. Then she'd ask again. He'd deny it again and round and round they'd go for ten minutes before he'd ever tell her what she'd done this time.

"Yes, I am." He doused the plate with more solution, then took it from her.

"You are?" His quick answer had caught her off guard. "Why?"

Oscar gently set the plate on its side to let it drain, then turned toward her. "You really don't know, do you?"

"I don't know what?"

A slow smile crept across his face as he removed his glasses and pinched the bridge of his nose. "Despite your crooked tongue, you are such an innocent, Samantha."

Sam shifted her weight. It always unnerved her when Oscar called her that. "You're one to talk."

He threw her a sidelong glance and Sam was struck that he really was a nice-looking man, without the thick spectacles. "At least I admit I'm a bit naive. You, on the other hand, would lie to Saint Peter."

Sam sat down on a handy crate. "Well, you know I don't really mean to lie. It's just that it comes in so handy sometimes. They're only little white lies. I'd never hurt anyone."

Oscar smiled and slipped the spectacles back on. "No, Sam. You'd never intentionally hurt a fly. In fact, you'd make a pet of one if you could. I guess that's why I love you."

His eyes never left his work. For a moment, Sam wasn't sure she'd heard him right, the words fell so easily from his lips.

"Oscar ..." She searched for words, but there seemed to be no right way to say what she wanted.

"I didn't mean it like that, Sam. I do love you, but not that way." He turned toward her, a slight smile tugging at his mouth. "God help the man that ever does. God help Inspector McLeod."

"Inspector McLeod? What has he got to do with this?"

"Come on, Sam. You've got a reporter's instincts. Surely this hasn't gone over your head." He transferred the plate from one pan to the next and stood over it, hands on hips.

"What has gone over my head? Really, Oscar. I have no idea what you're talking about." Sam shifted on the crate when a board began to pinch through her clothes.

"He's in love with you. Head over heels, I'd judge. Poor bastard."

"That's ridiculous." Sudden heat poured into Sam's chest and she felt out of control, lost. "We've only exchanged a few words."

"Words have nothing to do with it." Oscar lifted out the plate and held it up to Sam. Displayed on the tin was a perfect image of Inspector Duncan McLeod.

"This is a ridiculous notion and I don't want to talk about it anymore. We have to decide what supplies we're going to buy with the money we've earned."

"You've always taken care of supplies for us, Sam. I trust you to do it again." He stared down at the plate, both hands braced on the bench.

Something in Sam's chest twisted. Guilt? Longing? She couldn't define it. But seeing Oscar there, his shoulders slumped dejectedly, she wished for just an instant she could turn back time and leave him there in his safe, jumbled darkroom in San Francisco.

"I love you, too, Oscar. You're my best friend. My very best friend."

He smiled softly. "You have no idea what those words mean. You think you do, but you don't."

"I don't want to talk about this anymore. Here, take this and go buy what we need. The sooner I'm on my story, the better."

Oscar took the bag of gold dust she held out and dropped it into his vest pocket. "Why don't you finish those plates while I'm gone?" He indicated the stack of unexposed plates they had taken just tonight.

"You be careful. Have you got your gun?"

Oscar nodded and patted his other vest pocket where Sam knew a small derringer lay.

"Make sure you get everything," she called. "We're leaving in the morning."

"Sam, how could I forget that?" Oscar turned and asked, then pivoted and walked away.

"I just thought I ought to remind you," Sam whispered to the night.

Sam awoke with a start, lifting her head off her arms where she'd fallen asleep. Silence filled the night, too much silence. Stiffly, she rose and parted the tent flap. A full moon flecked the river's surface, throwing tiny sparks of light off the water. The tent city was practically deserted. Only a tent or two glowed in the night like Japanese lanterns. A week before, the streets were choked with men even in the wee hours of morning and tents appeared to joust for space along the banks of the river. Now, only the gentle lapping of the water accompanied the stillness of predawn.

Then, a sharp crack broke the quiet. Distant voices

raised in dissent. Another crack and a cry rang out. Sam shrugged and let the tent flap drop closed. Compared to nights past, this was tame.

She turned back to the stack of photographic plates, all developed and sorted. Lifting them into her arms, she made sure her carefully written obituaries were tucked into the pocket. As she reached to push back the tent flap, Duncan burst through, a limp Oscar cradled in his arms.

"Oh my God. What happened?" she asked, moving to the side so Duncan could lay Oscar on the cot. "Oscar. Oh God, Oscar."

Duncan carefully arranged Oscar's arms and legs, then straightened. Sam fell to her knees. His forehead was cool and damp to her touch as she pushed hair away from his eyes. Somewhere along the way, his glasses had fallen off.

"He was shot outside the general store. Probably for the gold dust he was carrying."

"I shouldn't have let him go. I should have gone myself. I always take care of these things." She bit her lip and tried to think.

Duncan stripped off his coat. "Go over to the saloon and have Hank send a pan of warm water, some bandages and a bottle of liquor. Tell him I said the good stuff, not his watered down variety." He reached toward his back and pulled an evil-looking knife from a leather pouch attached to his belt.

Samantha stared down at the red pool growing beside Oscar and her only thought was that he couldn't possibly *have* that much blood.

"Go, Samantha," Duncan chastised gently. Then he gripped her wrist with warm fingers. "He'll be all right. Go."

She fled the tent, running and stumbling across the rutted and gouged ground. When she returned, the front of her shirt soaked with the sloshed water, Duncan was on his knees beside the cot, one hand on Oscar's chest and the other manipulating the knife in a hole in his flesh. For a moment the world swam in a flock of black dots. She shook her head, took a deep breath, and stepped inside. The sickly sweet scent of fresh blood soured the air.

"I almost have the slug," Duncan said with a grunt, then pulled a squashed bit of lead from Oscar's flesh. A fresh spurt of blood oozed across his chest. Duncan reached back and took the basin away from her trembling hands.

"Hold this bandage here, over the wound." He pressed a wad of cloths into her hand and guided it to Oscar's chest, forcing her to press down by covering her hand with his. "Hold it just like that."

She nodded and sniffed back a sob. She wouldn't cry. She wouldn't. There'd be time for that later. Oscar needed her now, her mind clear and working.

"Move the bandage." Duncan uncorked the bottle of whiskey and poured it over the wound. Oscar moaned and turned his head.

Then, Duncan took the cloths from her hand and bandaged the wound, gently lifting Oscar to shove a strip of cloth underneath him and around his chest.

Sitting back on his heels, Duncan watched the gentle rise and fall of Oscar's chest. "I think he'll be all right. He's lost a lot of blood, but he's young and in good health." He turned his dark gaze on her. "What about you?"

Just hearing the compassion in his voice set off a new batch of tears. Her chin quivered even though she clamped her teeth together. "I'm fine," she said, hating the slide and break of her voice.

Duncan rose and pulled her to her feet. "Take a drink of this." He held out the whiskey bottle, an inch or so of the amber liquid left sloshing in the bottom.

Samantha thought to object. She'd never taken spirits in her life, but she took the bottle and downed a swallow. Coughing and sputtering, she wiped her mouth with the back of her hand and stumbled to the door.

Outside, the night was cold and clear, a canopy of stars twinkling overhead. Samantha drew in a deep breath, and willed her nerves to behave themselves even as the whiskey slid sweet lethargy into her limbs.

Duncan stepped out behind her, rolling down his bloody shirt sleeves, his jacket tucked underneath his arm. "I meant what I said, Samantha. I think Oscar will recover just fine if the wound doesn't fester, and I don't think it will. I cleaned it well. He'll be sore for a few days, but in a few weeks, he'll be back to himself."

The whiskey robbed her of the last of her control. Hot tears slipped down her cheeks. She hadn't been the Iron Samantha Oscar believed her to be. Not when he'd needed her the most. She'd dissolved into a pool of doubt and tears, a quivering, sniveling . . . female.

A sudden hiccup burst forth, followed closely by a sob. Covering her traitorous mouth with the back of her hand, she slanted a glance at Duncan, wishing he'd go away so she could sob and snivel in peace.

Instead he stepped closer and tipped her face up with one finger. "Go ahead and cry. You're earned it over the last few weeks, I'd guess."

Again, the soft baritone of his voice seduced away her self-control. She closed her eyes so she wouldn't have to see the satisfaction in his. Poor, fragile woman, flailing around in a man's world, pretending to be self-sufficient and brave.

She caught her breath in surprise when his lips touched hers and he slipped his arms around her back. His kiss was bold, a lover's kiss, not a gentle kiss of compassion. His tongue boldly swept the soft insides of her mouth and he arched his body to press against hers. Warning bells clanged in her head, but her body would have none of the sensible cautioning. She strained toward him, coerced by some unknown force.

Honey-sweet warmth oozed through her and the sudden betrayal of her body made her pull away. Even though their lips parted, he held her for a moment longer, gazing into her eyes. Then, he released her and stepped backwards. Through the thin fabric of his shirt, she could see that his chest rose and fell quickly.

He slipped his arms into the sleeves of his coat, raked back his hair with his fingers, and plopped on his Stetson. "Watch him closely overnight. I'll be by in the morning."

Sam could only nod and wonder if anyone had ever been suddenly struck dumb by a kiss.

Without another word, Duncan strode away toward the faint lights of the saloon, praying his knees wouldn't buckle and pitch him face first into some murky puddle. Never in all his thirty-five years had he ever behaved as he had just now. And never in all that time had a woman excited him to a fever with a mere kiss. He veered away from the boardwalk outside the saloon and stepped into the shadows. With trembling hands he rummaged in his pocket and pulled out his pipe, filled it, and lit the bowl with a match struck against the rough board wall. As he inhaled and savored the sweet taste, he struggled to control the emotions raging through him.

He prided himself on his self-control. Duncan McLeod never succumbed to the base desires of other men. No whores, no liquor. He'd been abstinent since his wife informed him he wasn't needed any longer in his own house, that someone else filled that bill quite nicely. No amount of coaxing or goading from other men had convinced him to engage in an intimate relationship with another woman. To bare one's soul was to reveal weakness. And a woman had a way of stripping naked a man's soul, touching him deep inside.

He blew smoke out in a lazy ring as his thumping heart slowed. What magical force propelled him toward the whirlwind of disaster that was Samantha Wilder? And what would he do the next time her lips tempted him? Samantha Wilder was not the woman for him, no matter what his body said. He had to keep his mind on important matters at hand.

He had to keep his mind on Emily.

CHAPTER SIX

"Samantha?"

Samantha roused from her cot and knelt by Oscar's bed.

He opened his eyes and glanced around the tent. "Where am I?"

"You're in our tent. Someone shot you. Oh, Oscar. I'm so sorry."

She laid her head on his hand. She had no more tears to cry. In fact, she wasn't sure she could cry again for years.

"I knew you'd blame yourself," he said weakly. "It's not your fault. Just one of those things that happens." He tipped his chin down to look at the bandage. "Who dug out the bullet? You, Sam?"

"No," she said, remembering her weakness. "Duncan brought you home and took out the slug."

His eyes flew open wide and he tried to raise his head.

With a groan, he dropped his head back into the pillow. "I found out something, Sam. Something about Duncan."

"What?"

"Those men that robbed me . . . they thought I would have more gold. That's why they shot me. They said Duncan had plenty and surely he'd given you and me some of it. They said he was like that, that he was supporting a whore, too."

The picture of the delicate singer came to mind and the way Duncan gazed at her. Then, she thought of his erotic kiss and wiped her mouth with the back of her hand. Oscar moaned and closed his eyes.

"You'll be all right in a few days." She felt his forehead and found it only warm. Perhaps they would be lucky and he wouldn't develop a fever.

"When does the boat leave for Dawson City?" he asked.

Oh Lord. That was today. In a few hours Duncan would be gone, and with him her best chance of finding out just how much gold dust was being embezzled and how. And she'd miss her chance to find out more about him. She told herself she wanted the information for her story, but another part of her knew better. "Don't worry about that. There'll be other boats to Dawson City."

He gripped her hand and opened his eyes. "But not with a Mountie along for protection. This is the safest way for you, Sam. And the most favorable for your article. Leave me here and I can follow."

"Are you out of your mind? I'm not leaving you anywhere. I'll just have to think of something."

Oscar released her wrist and closed his eyes. "Oh,

Lord, Sam. Please don't think. I can't survive any more of your thinking."

"This time I'll do it right, Oscar. I promise. I'll still get us on that boat. Both of us."

"Inspector McLeod," the young constable exclaimed, extending a hand. "Good to see you again."

Duncan smiled and spread his feet to steady himself on the rocking boat. "Constable Torrey. How's business?" He nodded toward the sheer granite walls to the south. The roar of angry water could be heard in the distance.

"No accidents since last November," Torrey said with a grin. "There's been a crowd past here in the last few days, though, ever since ice break. Are you on your way to Dawson?"

Duncan nodded and leapt onto the river's muddy bank. "Yep. I need McCauley to portage an injured man and a woman around the rapids."

Samantha looked up from her seat in the bottom of the boat. Oscar lay with his head in her lap, fighting the fever they'd feared.

"He's too sick to take the chance and I won't put her at risk," he was saying, his voice barely discernible over the roar of distant water.

Constable Torrey glanced at a gold pocket watch he pulled from his uniform pants. "McCauley's got a rig going around about two this afternoon."

"Guess that'll have to do," Duncan said. "Help me get them inside headquarters."

Constable Torrey and Duncan each caught an end of Oscar's stretcher and carried it to the log headquarters building. A warm fire burned in a stone fireplace to chase away the chill brought on by the swift water churning a fine mist just outside.

"What did you mean by 'portage around'?" she asked Duncan, catching the sleeve of his jacket.

He looked crestfallen for an instant and she knew he was hiding something from her. "This is the head of Miles Canyon. The water ahead is treacherous and fast. We don't allow women or children to travel by boat down the rapids and I'm sure you wouldn't want Oscar to risk the ride. Norman McCauley built a road around the rough water last year to take people and goods down to Canyon City."

Of course she didn't want to risk taking Oscar on the rapids, but oh, what an experience it would be to ride the wild water herself. She'd heard of such adventures, tiny boats washed and tossed while the water thundered in one's ears.

"Stop what you're thinking right now. I'm not going to let you down that river. And that's final." He fixed her with a look that stopped an argument from rising to her lips.

"Inspector?" Torrey asked, poking his head into the tiny room. "Could I see you a moment?"

Duncan nodded and stepped outside. Torrey drew him across the room with a furtive glance in Sam's direction. Her instincts came alive and she strained to hear.

"Are you bringing the customs money back down?" Torrey said.

Duncan nodded. "Yes. As soon as I get to Dawson, I'm to pick it up and bring it down to Dyea."

"Adam McPhail says it's a goodly amount and he's sleeping on the wad every night for fear it'll be stolen out from under him." Torrey leaned closer and Sam loitered by the door, just out of sight.

"He says it's one hundred seventy thousand now."

"A hundred and seventy thousand," Sam breathed. So much money. So much temptation.

"I suppose it is." Duncan laid a hand on Torrey's arm. "And not an unreasonable sum, given the amount of gold passing out of there."

At the sound of boots nearing, Sam hurried to Oscar's bedside and sat down just before she heard Duncan's footfalls in the room.

"I've asked the surgeon to have a look at Oscar. He's passing through on his way to Dawson City."

"He's still hot," she said, placing a hand on his forehead. "Duncan," she said as he turned to leave the room, "what's it like? Running the rapids?"

He paused, studying her. "It's the biggest thrill most people are ever likely to have. Exhilarating. Icy water washes over you and fog keeps you from seeing the shoreline. When the boat leaves the water and lunges into the air, it lands with a shudder that makes you think surely the boards are coming loose."

"You love it, don't you? This life? Here in the unknown?" She hadn't meant to make the conversation personal. The more distance she kept between Duncan McLeod and herself, the safer her future and her heart would be. But secrets lurked behind those incredible blue eyes and her curiosity would not be sated until she knew what they were.

"Yes, I do," he answered simply.

"Me, too. I just want to soak it all in, all at once."

He watched her for a moment longer, an odd expression on his face, then he turned and left the building.

"You're wearing your heart on your sleeve, Sam. At

least play hard-to-get a little," Oscar murmured, his eyes closed.

"How are you feeling?" she asked, leaning over him.

"Worse than hell. I could give you a list but complaining won't do either of us any good." He cracked open an eye. "You're dying to make that trip down the rapids, aren't you?"

"Of course not. You heard Inspector McLeod. It's dangerous and it would be foolish."

"And when has that ever stopped you from doing anything?"

"And besides, I wouldn't leave you to make that dangerous trip on your own."

Oscar caught her hand and pressed it against his chest. "How dangerous can a ride down a log road in a tram be? I'll probably sleep all the way."

"Besides, he's already told me no."

"Poor man. He doesn't know Samantha Wilder doesn't understand the meaning of the word. Nor does she understand the words impossible, dangerous, unadvisable, or insurmountable." He opened his eyes fully and turned his head. "You could wheedle money from a stone. Have another go at him. I'm sure you can change his mind."

"Do you really think so? Would you be willing to let me make the boat trip down? But, who would go with you?"

Oscar laughed, then winced. "I know you love me, in your own way, but you'll always be a spoiled brat. A lovable, spoiled, headstrong brat. Go on. I forgive you your self-indulgence ahead of time so you can enjoy the trip."

"Excuse me," Duncan said, stepping into the room. "Surgeon Colin Fraser is here to examine Oscar."

A tall man with graying hair stepped into the room carrying a small, leather doctor's bag. He sat down on the side of the bed and lifted the bandage to peer underneath. "Inspector McLeod tells me you were shot. I hope the shooters were caught."

Oscar began to relate the tale and Samantha followed Duncan outside to the wide, stone fireplace. A gentle fog had settled on the land, and droplets of moisture dripped off the trees outside. Hands clasped behind his back, Duncan stared through the window.

"I owe you an apology for the other night," he began just above a whisper. "I shouldn't have taken such liberties without asking you first and I'm deeply sorry."

"You are?" she said, then wished her words didn't sound so disappointed. "I mean, I accept and thank you. We were both . . . agitated."

"Yes, indeed. Agitated," he said without looking at her. "I said I was sorry I didn't ask. I didn't say I was sorry I kissed you." He turned toward her, enslaving her with the intensity in his eyes. "You stir me, Sam. More than any woman in many, many years," he whispered. "And I find I'm not sure I can guarantee my behavior if I should find myself faced with a similar opportunity."

"I'd love to have you misbehave at my expense again, Inspector McLeod," she whispered in return, desire making her words bold. She focused her eyes on his lips and remembered the ease with which he'd commanded her mouth. Oh, Lord. What had she just said?

God help him, another word from those innocent lips and he'd sweep her into his arms and have her in some shady, isolated place. Did she realize the effect her honest admissions had on a man? Had no one ever taught her that a lady flirted coyly, using sweet words with no meaning? Did she not know that a lady never admitted to her passion?

He shifted his position and closed his eyes, willing away his body's reaction to her voice, her nearness, her very being.

"You tempt a man to the edge, Samantha," he said with a shake of his head. "Such honesty is bound to land you in trouble some day."

"I believe in honesty, Inspector." She moved in front of him, blocking the view out the window, the distraction that was keeping him from embarrassing himself in public.

He laughed. "Since when?"

She frowned and chewed her bottom lip, her tiny white teeth working mercilessly on the pink skin. "I don't lie about important things. Just things that need a bit of rearranging."

"A bit of rearranging, huh? And how does one know when you're 'rearranging' and when you're telling the truth?"

She shrugged one shoulder. "I think people usually know. They just go along with me because my version is usually better than the truth." She raised her wide, clear eyes to his. "But I never, ever hurt anyone with my . . . exaggerations. And I've never lied to anyone I care deeply about."

"You lied to Oscar."

"That was for his own good. He needed to get out of San Francisco and see the world."

"And you felt it was your duty to see to that?"

"Yes, it was. He's my friend."

"He's more than that, Sam. The boy's in love with you."

She straightened then and sadness flitted through

her eyes. "I know, but he and I have an understanding about that."

"A man couldn't have an 'understanding' with you about love." He wanted badly to touch her, to reach out and stroke the silky strands of hair that framed her face. To cup the roundness of her breast and feel the heated weight against his palm. He glanced toward the door and saw three more Mounties stride around the counter that served as an office.

"With you, Samantha, love would be visceral and real. What you would give, a man would take greedily and beg for more," he whispered. "You wield a strange power that will seduce and enrage. Always be aware of that."

Everything he was urged him to take her in his arms and find someplace private to test that theory. To love her slowly and thoroughly and provide the answers to all those questions in her eyes. But he was not the man destined for that joy, that wonderful release.

She stared up at him, arousal softening her eyes. "Take me down the river with you."

"What?"

"I want to ride the rapids with you."

For a moment he wondered if she was serious or speaking metaphorically.

"Please, Duncan. This may be the only chance I ever get to do anything like this. Please."

"What about Oscar?"

"He says he'll be fine on the tram."

The return transport of over a hundred thousand dollars would be best accomplished with two men along. New replacements had recently arrived at Canyon City. Constable Torrey could be spared to travel with Oscar, he supposed. He looked down into Samantha's face.

She had him wrapped around that tiny pinky of hers, too. He knew he was going to do whatever was necessary to take her on that boat with him. Just as surely as he knew she would, one day, be his undoing.

Cold spray washed over the bow of the boat and Samantha screamed, then laughed. "This is wonderful!" she yelled over the water's roar. "I've never done anything this exciting!"

The boat lunged over the rock and smacked the water with a jaw-crunching impact. Duncan scrambled for a better foothold and gripped the rudder tightly.

Sam's hair was plastered against her head. Tiny, wet tendrils traced down the side of her face. She gripped the sides of the rapid-worthy craft with white knuckles.

A dark shadow of water came into view and Duncan hauled on the rudder to swing them in the other direction. "Look, there's the whirlpool." As they swung a safe distance from the wide swirl, Samantha turned in her seat to watch the mysterious water for as long as she could see it.

"It's sunk many a boat and this has fooled many an experienced pilot." He pointed at the white, churning water only feet ahead.

For the first time since they'd set out, Samantha's perpetual smile faded. "Are you an experienced pilot?"

"Yes, ma'am," he responded as the boat bucked over the first set of rough water. Thick mist obscured both shorelines, swathing them in their own private world of seething water and gray rocks. The tiny scow pitched and yawed until finally they glided into relatively peaceful water.

"Whitehorse is a mile or two down the river," Duncan

said, releasing his grip on the rudder to rub his aching hands together.

"Oh, Duncan. That was just wonderful."

Before he could react, she flew at him with widespread arms, and they both pitched overboard into the breathtakingly cold water. Duncan bobbed to the surface first and looked around for Samantha. She was nowhere to be seen.

He called to her, the nightmare of the situation slowly dawning. She'd only survive a few minutes in the frigid water.

"Duncan! Help! I can't swim!" She surfaced, flailing the water in a panic, her eyes wide.

Duncan dove under and surfaced behind where she went down last. Beneath him in the murky water he could feel the currents of her frantic efforts to rise to the surface. Opening his eyes under the water, he caught sight of her auburn hair flowing freely around her. He reached down, twisted his fingers in its length, and dragged her to the surface. Coughing and fighting, she struggled to get a hold on him. If she did, she'd drown them both, he knew. He ducked under again, leaving her struggling on the surface. He moved behind her, put an arm under her arms, and swam to the shore.

She crawled up on the rocky shore, coughing and vomiting water. Duncan straddled her and held her up with an arm around her waist until she stopped. Then he rolled her to her back.

"Samantha?"

She opened her eyes. "Am I dead?"

"If you are, then I'm an angel."

She coughed again, wiped a hand across her face, then sat up. Duncan plopped down beside her, pulled off his boots, and poured a cupful of water out of each one.

"What happened?"

"You, in your enthusiasm, knocked us both into the water."

She put her face in her hands. "I remember now. I was so happy and the ride was . . . indescribable." She turned then and grinned. "What an adventure."

"Well, you're about to have another one." Duncan pulled off a wool sock and wrung it out.

"What do you mean?"

"I mean that the tram will make the trip far slower than we did. So, unless the boat drifts down to Whitehorse on its own, no one will know we're stranded until Oscar and Constable Torrey arrive. By then, it will be dark."

As he expected, she smiled. "A night in the wilderness. How exciting."

"Are you and Oscar really here to set up a photography business or was that 'rearranging'?"

She glanced away. "Why do you ask?"

"Because, with your enthusiasm for unfortunate circumstances, I'd guess you were a reporter. From some newspaper back east with readers foaming at the mouth for news from the gold fields."

"That's completely untrue."

"Truth?"

"Truth."

Duncan glanced over his shoulder at the thick cluster of spruce and evergreens that crowded close to the river's edge. "We can make a fire up there, away from the wind, and dry our clothes."

Duncan had a fire going in minutes and hung his serge coat and socks on a stick jabbed into the spongy ground. Samantha shed her coat and socks and hung each on another stick. And then they stood there in wet clothes, staring at each other. Water dripped in little circles around their feet.

Duncan shook his head. "We can't stand here like this or we'll catch pneumonia. When it gets dark, the temperature will drop. If our clothes are still wet, we'll freeze."

She nodded silently.

"I'll make you a bargain. I'll undress if you will. I'm wearing clothes underneath."

Again she nodded, her eyes wary. "Me, too. Winter underwear."

Duncan swallowed, remembering the afternoon's conversation and the temptation it had stirred. What strange forces of Fate had decided Duncan McLeod's honor needed further testing?

"I'll take off my uniform and hang it by the fire. There's nothing indecent about a union suit. An unattractive garment, though. I'll cut some boughs of hemlock and you can hold them in front of you. Heat will pass through and we'll be dry before you know it."

"All right."

Duncan sensed her hesitancy. Hell, he was scared half to death he couldn't keep his hands off her. He peeled off his shirt and plunged another stick into the ground to hold it.

She took off her blouse, keeping her eyes on her fingers as she undid the tiny pearl buttons. When she slid the garment down her arms, Duncan willed his eyes away from the soft curves obvious beneath the knit fabric. He hung her blouse beside his shirt.

His fingers fumbled at his belt. He closed his eyes and imagined a cold winter's day, stranded on a field of ice with cold wind whipping icy pellets down his collar as he loosened the buttons and slid the pants down his legs and off his bare feet. When he opened his eyes, he saw that she watched him, her expression guarded.

She undid the buttons on the man's pants she'd worn and slid them down slim, long legs. Thankfully, the union suit was too big and flapped about her instead of delineating her curves. With eyes downcast, she handed him the garment and he hung it with his.

A water-tortured tree trunk from the shore made a dry seat on which to sit; they shared the narrow piece of wood, taking caution not to touch each other. Elbows on knees, side by side, they stared into the fire.

Try as he might, Duncan couldn't keep his mind off Samantha and the thought of sliding that soft knit off her creamy shoulders and down her arms to reveal . . .

"You said you had children. Tell me about them," she asked unexpectedly.

Taken aback, Duncan turned to look at her. "You have a way of going right for the throat, don't you?"

She looked genuinely contrite. "I'm sorry. I was just trying to think of something we could talk about. And," she said with a shrugged shoulder, "I was curious."

"My wife turned me out. Isn't that what you really want to know?"

"Yes, I suppose it is. How terrible. Your heart must have been broken." Her eyes were dark with sorrow when she turned toward him, affording him full view of the curve of her narrow waist as the knit fabric pulled tight.

When she told the truth, she was ruthless. Perhaps lying better suited her after all. "Why do we use that word . . . broken? Torn. Mangled. *Ripped* seem more accurate. I had two lovely children and a wife I adored.

She didn't feel the same and found another more to her liking." He picked up a rock and threw it into the fire. Tiny orange bits floated up into the darkening sky.

"What about your children?"

"She made it clear he was their father now. They were young, a baby and the other just two. In a few years they wouldn't know the difference, she said. All of Scotland wasn't big enough for the two of us, he and I. So I left." What was making him tell this bit of a woman things he'd never told another mortal soul?

"I'm so sorry," she whispered. Her voice, throaty and rough, was a deadly weapon she was unaware she possessed. Over the years, Duncan had learned that heartfelt compassion was a strong aphrodisiac.

"So, what are you and Oscar really doing here?"

She stretched her bare feet out towards the fire, wriggling her toes. Duncan looked away, wishing he were anyplace but here where, with each passing moment, temptation was getting the upper hand.

"Well, you were sort of right. I am a reporter, but for my uncle's paper. He didn't believe I could write a proper story. My job is writing obituaries."

"Ah, hence the idea at the saloon. Very clever."

She beamed. "Thanks. I ran away to escape an evil stepmother."

Duncan cocked an eyebrow in her direction.

"All right, I ran away to get away from my aunt who was determined to marry me off to the next available bachelor."

"That bachelor not being Oscar, I presume."

Sam chuckled. "Heavens, no. Oscar's my best friend." She slanted him a glance. "Truth."

"So, you came up here, unprepared, no money, no

guide, and decided you and Oscar would make your-selves a home in Dawson City?"

"Yes, I guess that's true."

"Amazing."

She was a gritty little seductress, he decided. No mat-ter how foolish the idea was or how lucky both she and Oscar had been, whether they knew it or not, she was gritty. Maybe she did have what it took to survive Dawson City.

CHAPTER SEVEN

As soon as the last trace of sunset disappeared from the sky, the air grew cool, then cold. A breeze, generated by the churning water, drifted through the trees and chilled Samantha's damp skin. The wool underclothes weren't drying as fast as they'd anticipated, especially when the breeze kept the fire leaping from one side of the pile of wood to the other.

She shivered and crossed her arms over her chest.

"Cold?"

"A little."

He watched her for a moment, closed his eyes briefly, then held up his left arm. She scooted over and snuggled against his warm side. His hand settled on her shoulder, cupping the round of her arm. The fire leaned in their direction, warming their faces, and sleep began to overcome Samantha. She nodded, then jerked awake, her cheek brushing against his ribs.

"I'll be right back," he said, then rose and left her for a few minutes. When he returned, his arms were loaded with hemlock branches which he spread at their feet. Then, he sat down on the soft needles and beckoned for her to come and sit by his side. With the warm log to her back and the fire's heat, she began to nod again. Then, sleep claimed her.

She awoke with a start, scattered dreams of rushing rivers and cold waters running through her mind. He was watching her, studying her with an unguarded intensity that sent a strange pressure to her stomach. His hand moved, ever so slightly, fingers toying with a tendril of hair that lay across her shoulder.

She slid her head back, slowly, until she met his eyes, now dark with desire.

"Duncan . . ." Her words drifted away, lost in building anticipation.

"You shouldn't tempt a man so, lass."

"What did I do?"

He smiled and shook his head slightly. "You truly don't know, do you?"

"I didn't mean to do anything wrong."

He raked his fingers through her hair, sending delicious shivers down her spine. "Men are evil creatures, Sam, intent on their own pleasure."

"I don't believe that."

"Ah, but you haven't been alone in the dark woods with one before, have you?"

"I'm not afraid of you."

"Maybe you should be."

"Why?"

He twirled the strand of hair in his fingers. Funny, having one's hair pulled had never seemed an arousing thing. Until now.

"I haven't touched a woman in a very long time."
His voice was almost a whisper, the words edged with
poignancy.

She shifted around until she faced him, the neckline
of her shirt temptingly low, her hair fanned around
her face. He breathed deeply and willed away an erotic
fantasy that involved that hair.

"Tell me about her."

By some instinct, she'd asked the very question, perhaps the only one, that could cool his ardor like a January wind.

"She was beautiful, warm, smart."

"Not so very smart if she left you."

He shrugged one shoulder. "I didn't compare favorably with my competitor," he said sarcastically.

Sam searched his face, his eyes, her probing curiosity
set on ferreting out the details. "She betrayed you?
Intimately?"

He paused, considering his answer. Opening this
wound would likely open an avenue to his heart. Her
compassion would surely be his undoing. "As intimately
as life gets."

Her expression softened. She reached up and stroked
his cheek, soft fingers torturing his skin with their feath-
ery touch. He shivered.

"I'm so sorry. She was a very foolish woman."

She arched up and kissed him, firing again the desire
he thought he'd quelled. He waited for her to break
away, refusing to give in to the urges that bade him take
her in his arms, force open her mouth, and teach her
the melody of love and passion. But she didn't draw
back, and he knew he was lost.

He kissed her lightly, a brush of lip against lip, hoping

that one touch of her lips, one more taste of her, and he'd be cured of this longing for more. He was wrong.

He slid his hand down her arm, stopping even with her breast, wanting to feel the warm mound under his palm.

"Touch me," she whispered. "I want you to touch me."

She begged him for that which she could neither describe nor name, begged from an instinct rooted in innocence. Chivalrous Duncan McLeod slithered away and Duncan McLeod, the lonely man, took over.

His hand slid forward and cupped her softness through the soft knit of her shirt. She inched forward, straining against his palm. He kneaded her breast and she moaned softly against his mouth. She parted her lips, inviting him to invade her again, inviting his tongue to sweep inside, an intimacy he craved with trembling anticipation.

"You're trembling," she murmured. "Are you cold?"

"No, lass," he said. "I'm not cold."

He slipped his hand inside her shirt and the smoothness of her skin nearly sent him over the edge. He pulled back and took a deep breath. He was a randy schoolboy again, afraid of embarrassing himself in his eagerness.

She turned toward him to allow him easier access, pressing against his hand, straining for more contact. He urged her backwards until she lay on the softly whispering bed of hemlock.

"Sam," he whispered against her neck. "You're so soft. So soft."

He leaned over her and unbuttoned the buttons that held her shirt closed, exposing her chest to the cold. Tiny ridges of gooseflesh rose on her pink skin as he pushed aside the fabric to bare her to his sight. She reached up and tangled her hand in his soft curls, bringing his face down so she could torture him with bites and nips.

His hand molded around her and a thumb stroked back and forth across the crest of her breast, sending sharp stabs of satisfaction to her core. He soon replaced his hand with his mouth, an exquisite mouth that tasted her and suckled until her back arched off their fragrant bed and she begged him for a fulfillment she could only sense and not know.

A rough palm slid down her leg, his calluses catching on the knit, making little tugs that marked his progress. He crossed her abdomen with a spread palm and brushed by the area begging to be touched.

"Duncan, please."

"What do you want, Samantha?" he asked in his baritone, made more husky with desire.

"I . . . don't know. Something. Something only you can do. I don't know how I know. I just do."

He buried his face in her neck and nipped at the sensitive skin with sharp little bites. "I wish I could. God, how I wish I could."

She reached for him, reached for the part of him she sensed would give him the same satisfaction as she. He jerked away from her reach.

"Uh-uh."

"Why not?"

"I couldn't bear your touch right now, lass." His brogue had deepened, rolling off his tongue like a song. "It's been a long time since I loved a woman."

He swept past the apex of her legs again and she jerked convulsively.

"What's that got to do with it?" she asked, craving to touch him.

He stilled and breathed into her hair. And she knew their moment was past. "Someday your husband will explain it to you," he said, getting to his feet.

He turned his back and snared his now-dry uniform off the stick and quickly dressed.

"Stay by the fire. I'll be back in a bit," he said and crunched off through the woods.

Samantha pushed herself to her elbows, her heart pounding. The path of his touch across her body still burned with urgency. So, that was the way it was between men and women. And she decided it was worth further investigation.

Duncan stood by the water, the roar of the rapids loud in his ears. He inhaled deep breaths of cold air and wished he could open his body and take the cold inside to cool the desire still coursing through his veins, demanding satisfaction. For a few seconds, he toyed with the idea of returning to her and plunging deep within her soft body until they were both limp with satisfaction. But, that would be dangerous. And . . . wrong. She was young and he had no right to take her innocence, especially when he had nothing to offer her in return.

He scuffed at a river-rounded rock and cursed. He'd actually considered deflowering a virgin he'd only just met. He didn't love Samantha Wilder. No, not at all. She was desirable and soft and he wanted her with lust, not love. And that was wrong. Wasn't that what had cost him his home, his children, and his wife? Lust? Steamy, unbridled sex on a warm Sunday morning? And he'd walked in at an inopportune moment, just as the liaison was coming to a climax. Literally. He closed his eyes, the remembered pain doing what cold air could not. The sounds of his wife's moans, reward for another man's efforts, would forever haunt him.

There was Emily to consider. Dear, fragile Emily. Who desperately needed him, even if she didn't think so. Samantha didn't need him. Samantha could take a straight pin and pack of matches and carve herself out an empire in the Yukon. No, she didn't need him at all. He'd press his suit with Emily as soon as she arrived in Dawson City. He'd offer her his name, his home, his heart if that's what it took to make amends, to set things in his heart back right again. Fragile Emily, who couldn't have stood, much less savored, a ride over the most treacherous white water in the Territories. Fragile Emily, who'd never have survived a cold dip in the Yukon River. And Emily wouldn't have even entertained the idea of making love in freezing temperatures on a bed of crackling hemlock boughs. One day, she'd be the path to his salvation. Once Emily was his wife, safe and cared for, heavy with his child, her sister would see that Duncan McLeod was as much a man as the bastard she'd taken to bed that warm summer morning.

Samantha heard Duncan come back, felt him sit down on the log and add another piece of wood to the fire. She'd put her clothes back on, wrapped her coat closely around her, and lain down on the hemlock bed to sleep. But sleep would not come. Instead, she turned their brief moments together over and over in her mind. His face, the mask of control gone, replaced by raw desire. His mouth, trained and smooth, bringing her to some precipice she longed to plunge over. She opened an eye and saw that he sat with his elbows on his knees, his face buried in his hands.

"Duncan?"

He didn't answer for a few seconds, didn't raise his head. "Sam, I'm sorry. I can't seem to find the words to apologize properly for what just happened."

She scrambled to her knees. Some weird reasoning in her scrambled thoughts said that if he regretted their actions, the seductive memories would disappear from her mind, too. And she couldn't live with that. She always wanted to remember the way his hands played her body like a fine instrument, tuning and stroking to perfection.

"Duncan." She went to him and cupped his hands with hers. "Please, I don't regret what we did. It was wonderful. I've never felt that way before."

"And you shouldn't have." He raised a distressed face from his hands. "Only a husband should see a woman like that. Only a husband should know how to make his wife want him that way, the way you wanted me just now." He pointed to the hemlock bough as if their ghosts still lay there entwined. "And only a wife should know how to bring her husband to . . . How only a touch of her hand can . . ." He struggled for a few seconds, then dropped his gaze to the ground. "We weren't meant to be, Samantha. Not like this."

Her heart plunged into dark depths. He truly regretted touching her. Honestly abhorred the abandon with which she'd offered him her body. He must think her a whore. And why shouldn't he? She'd pretended to be married to Oscar. Lived with him in a small tent for months. Given Duncan's past, surely he thought such behavior immoral and loose and such a woman far beneath his consideration as a lover or a wife.

Long-reserved tears worked their way to the surface. She didn't care that they streamed down her face and made little dark circles on his deep blue pant knees. She didn't care that he stared at her sadly. So, Iron Samantha Wilder was crying. So what? She might just sob before she was through. She'd earned a good cry and she was going to have one. If Inspector Duncan McLeod couldn't stand to see a woman cry, then he'd just have to be miserable. Him with his magic hands and soulful eyes. She wished at this moment that she was back home in San Francisco, safely ensconced in her cubicle, scratching out lovely phrases about dead people.

Samantha was awakened by the distant shouts of human voices. She sat up and found Duncan already gone. She clambered to her feet, her head aching from crying. Her vision blurred, she stared down at the dead fire, puzzled at the warmth that infused her. Then she realized that she sat in a shaft of morning sunlight.

The voices came from the shore of the river. She glanced around for any forgotten possessions, then stumbled to the water's edge. A small boat rocked there in the current, two Mounted Police officers accompanying it. Duncan stood with his back to her, his arms crossed over his chest. One of the men was Constable Torrey, a smile on his face. The other was the quiet doctor who'd attended Oscar. Poor Oscar—she hoped he was all right and not wild with worry.

"Mrs. Timmets," Constable Torrey called. "Your husband is fine. He made the trip well and is resting comfortably at Whitehorse. We've sent a man back to let him know you and Inspector McLeod are safe."

Dr. Fraser studied her face, then smiled sympatheti-
cally. *"Are* you all right, Mrs. Timmets?"

"Yes, I'm fine," she said with as much cheerfulness
as she could generate from her aching head. "I'd like
to wash my face before we go."

She stepped to the edge of the water, knelt, and intentionally avoided Duncan's quizzical glance. The cold
water felt wonderful washing over her tear-saturated
skin. She buried her face in a handful of the bracing
water and then stood, wiping away all traces of her
sorrow with the sleeve of her coat.

"We can leave anytime," Constable Torrey said,
glancing from her to Duncan.

"I'm ready to go as soon as possible," she replied
and climbed into the boat without aid. The three men
climbed in behind her, Duncan seating himself at the
front after pushing the boat off the shore.

The short ride to Whitehorse was tense and she
heaved a sigh of relief when the clustered town came
into view. When the boat docked, she scrambled out
and headed for the one-story building where Oscar
awaited her.

"Samantha. I was so worried."

Samantha threw herself across him, careful not to
press against his wound, and fought down a new crop
of tears.

"How are you feeling? Was the tram ride awful?" she
asked, disengaging herself from his tangled sheets and
wiping away tears.

Oscar frowned slightly, squinting for the loss of his
glasses. "I'm fine, but you look like the very devil. Were
you hurt?"

"No. Just a little tired, I guess," she said, diverting

her eyes from his all-too-knowing study. "What about the tram ride?"

"Trying to assuage your conscience for putting me in a wagon and having the time of your life shooting the rapids?"

A stab of guilt twisted her until she saw that Oscar was struggling to keep a straight face.

"Oh, it was wonderful, Oscar. So exciting. The water was so cold and mist covered the river until you couldn't see either shoreline. It was just like drifting along in a cloud."

"Well, I don't remember much of the tram ride. Seems Dr. Fraser slipped me a healthy dose of laudanum and I slept the whole way." He frowned again. "But something happened out there, didn't it?"

"Well, I almost drowned. Inspector McLeod pulled me out of the water, though. The boat capsized. That's why we were stranded overnight."

Oscar squinted at her again and she wondered if everything she and Duncan had done showed on her face for the world to see. Did Oscar know that her heart still hammered at the memory of Duncan's touch? Or that her heart twisted when she remembered his confession about his wife? Or that tears sprang anew when she remembered that he didn't want her?

"Sam?"

"Yes?"

"Are you sure you're all right? Should we have Dr. Fraser take a look at you?"

"I'm fine. Now I have to find someplace to dry all my things. I think I have enough money to buy us passage all the way to Dawson City."

"Do you still want to go, Sam? Truthfully."

"Of course I want to go. You don't think I'd come this far and then back down?"

"No, but I'm wondering if you're reconsidering your original mission here?"

Sam faltered. Oscar simply knew her too well. It was unnerving to have someone else make perfect sense of one's jumbled thoughts. "The embezzlement. No. I'm still convinced it's going on and I intend to find out who and how."

"What about Inspector McLeod?"

"He's still suspect, of course. As is anyone else who handles the gold."

Oscar crossed his arms over his chest and winced slightly. "Are you sure about that?"

"Of course. Why? Don't I seem sincere?"

"You race pell mell through life, Sam, not stopping to think before you leap. Your whole life is fueled by your latest crazy notion. There's more to life than that."

"Like what?"

"Like marriage. A home. Babies. A career you love. Friends. Lots of things."

"Oscar, we talked about this—"

"I'm not referring to me, though heaven knows I wish I were. I'm speaking of Inspector McLeod."

"Oh posh, Oscar." She sprang up off the bed, wishing she could fly out the door and avoid Oscar's finely honed questions she was sure he had carefully planned.

"He's in love with you. I know it. He knows it. We're both waiting for you to realize it and accept that you're in love with him, too."

"That's ridiculous. Why, he has a lover that sings in the saloon back in Lake Bennett. I saw him there watching her." She flung out her arm and paced to the tiny window that looked out on bobbing boats and swift water. "She's tiny and delicate and . . . perfect."

"And it makes you mad as hell, doesn't it?"

"No, it tells me that his type of woman is someone with all looks and no brains."

"Quite unlike you, of course, who's all brains and no looks."

"I didn't say that. I don't want to get married, Oscar. This arrangement of ours is as close as I ever want to get."

"This arrangement is a lie, Sam. A front to allow us to investigate men who by reputation have been honest and upstanding and have earned that reputation by fighting cold, floods, disease, and bullets. We're here simply on your idea that if somebody has a reputation for goodness, there must be some dirt someplace. We have absolutely no proof that anything dishonest is going on."

"We have the interviews we've already done. And the article in the *Bay Star*. And those rumors we heard in Bennett."

"All circumstantial, as I'm sure you well know."

"There's a story here. I know it."

"Are you running *to* Dawson City or *away* from Aunt Sophia? There's a difference, you know."

Sam turned from the window and studied Oscar. He looked so frail amid the quilts, his body skinny and bony. He was right. Most of her schemes were crazy and ill-considered. But not this one. This one she felt in her bone marrow. "Why this change in attitude?"

"Because these fine men have nursed me faithfully

and kindly and I have received nothing but care and consideration at their hands."

"I didn't say they were all stealing, I just said somebody probably was." She sounded like a whiny child, even to her own ears.

"Probably? We've traveled halfway across a continent on that?"

"Well, you didn't object when I talked you into this."

"That had more to do with who was asking than with why we were coming."

Sam turned away. Outside the window, Duncan strode along the shore, hands clasped behind him, occasionally lifting his head to gaze off across the dark water. What would it be like to quench the desire she'd seen in his eyes? To bear his children or rub his back at night? To lie in his arms and finish what they'd started? To explore that wonderful mystery just beginning to unravel for her?

The din of rumbling wagons, barking dogs, shouting men, and braying mules was deafening.

"Isn't this wonderful, Oscar?" Sam asked, hat in hand and arms outstretched. Dawson City was every bit as loud, colorful, and sinful as she'd imagined. Wide banners strung across the street advertised steamer passages to the gold fields of Bonanza King and the Eldorado in ten days. Another advertised LAUNDRY DONE OVERNIGHT — 10 CENTS. And as far as she could see, small white tents squatted on marshy, damp ground. The stampeders had arrived in Dawson City in droves.

"We have to see to lodging right away," Sam commented and trudged toward a hotel billing itself as The Gold Nugget.

"Original name," Oscar said as they walked up to the desk.

A clerk came out from behind a curtain and looked down his long nose at them. "May I be of service?" he asked in a cultured voice, carefully pronouncing each word.

"We'd like two rooms, please."

He turned to survey a network of pigeon holes on the back wall, then selected two keys. "That will be one hundred fifty dollars for the week."

"Let's go, Sam." Oscar caught her arm and tugged.

"No, wait." She pulled her arm loose. "If we find a place to set up our business within the week, can we get a refund if we move out?"

The clerk regarded them for a moment. "I believe that can be arranged. After all, someone will want the rooms."

"We can find an empty shop, I know it," Sam whispered as they trudged up the stairs, Oscar's photography equipment rattling at their side. "We'll move in there and get some of our money back. At least for now we'll have a soft bed and a bath." She inserted the key in her lock and the door swung open to reveal what she now considered to be luxury. She placed her pack on the double bed and bounced on the mattress for a second before she flopped backwards and sighed. "This is heaven, Oscar. Try it."

He shuffled to the next room and she heard the bed squeak. Smiling, she closed her eyes. They were finally in Dawson City and it was everything she'd imagined. As soon as they'd set up a shop, she'd start her investigation. The Mounted Police had sent reinforcements, she'd read in a paper on the steamer from Whitehorse.

Now their number was nearly a hundred, and Fort Herchmer had been expanded.

She rolled over onto her side and gazed out the window. Somewhere in this crowd, Duncan walked the streets on patrol. He'd taken the same steamer as she and Oscar, but he'd kept their contact to a minimum. And when they docked at the Aurora Dock in Dawson City, he'd said a simple good-bye and melted into the waiting crowd. She wondered if she'd ever see him again.

Oscar's cautioning crept back into her thoughts. Was she racing through life? Was she missing something by not settling down with diapers and dishes? No, she decided. There was too much world out there to see, too much to experience, to devote her life to one man's comfort. Unless, of course, that one man was Duncan McLeod, whispered a traitorous voice.

No, she scolded, springing up from the bed to pour a basin of water from the flowered pitcher. Duncan was a distraction to avoid at all costs. She splashed water on her face and looked up into the mirror while the droplets fell back in the basin. Her skin was rough and peeling, sunburned from her days on the icy heights of Chilkoot Pass. Freckles, once carefully lightened with lemon juice, now rioted across her cheeks. No, she couldn't begin to compare to Duncan's songbird.

Did he touch The Canary the way he'd touched her that night? Did he kiss her the same way, tasting and savoring her? Did his hand drift down her delicate skin to brush forbidden areas?

Sam jerked away from the mirror and yanked her shirt out of the waistband of her skirt. She looked down at the tattered and torn material. New clothes were high on her list of things to buy as soon as possible. Now that they were in town, she couldn't run about in the pants she'd worn for so many miles. Dejectedly, she sat on the edge of her bed and glanced at the sunset. She supposed she had to eat supper. Otherwise, she'd crawl between the clean sheets and sleep until noon. And dream about absolutely nothing.

CHAPTER EIGHT

Dust motes floated in a sunbeam that quivered and danced. Sam drummed her fingers on the counter, then toyed with a stack of papers.

"I can't stand another minute of waiting," she said and Oscar poked his head out of a curtained cubicle in the back of the store.

"What?"

"Nobody's coming. We've been here for a week and you've only taken two pictures."

"There's another shop at the end of the street. They're better established, better known. It'll take time for us to win some of their customers away."

"Maybe we should take the camera and go down to the dock." She whirled, the idea snapping her mind into gear. "Take pictures as people get off the steamer. 'My dear, I arrived safely'." She made a frame with her fingers and held her hands up to the light. "We could even make a sign for them to hold with those very words. What do you think?"

Oscar stared at her, a soft smile on his face. "You never cease to amaze me. When does your mind rest?"

"Never, I hope. Oh, Oscar. What a romantic place this is. So many people from so many different places."

"Only you would think muddy streets and widespread cases of typhoid were romantic. What is the good in those, Miss Sunshine?"

He shuffled over to a rickety bookcase and rearranged his dwindling supply of photography plates.

"Aren't you happy here, Oscar?" She climbed down off the stool and moved to his side.

"I'm happy wherever I am as long as you're there," he answered with a shy glance.

"Why, that's the sweetest thing you've ever said to me." She pushed his hair back off his forehead and saw a flash of darkness in his eyes. "What's wrong?"

He sighed and turned to face her. "You really don't know, do you?"

Sam shook her head. "No."

"I love you, Sam. I always have. And not in a brother-sister sort of way, like you think. But the way a man loves the woman he wants to be his wife. Would you, Sam?" He dropped to one knee. "Would you be my wife?"

Stunned, Sam could only gape down at him. Her Oscar there on one knee, asking for her hand, asking permission to do what Duncan had done . . .

"Oscar," she began, taking an involuntary step backwards.

When he looked up, his eyes were sorrowful, resigned, and he slowly clambered to his feet. "I've dreamed for years of doing that." He bent down to brush off the knees of his pants. "I'd always hoped the answer would be different."

"Oh, Oscar, I—"

"You don't have to explain, Sam. You're in love with Inspector McLeod. It doesn't take an idiot like me to figure that out. I had held out hope, though, if I finally confessed," he smiled at her softly, "you might find just a little love there for me."

"Oh, Oscar. I do love you, but—"

"Not the way you love Duncan."

"I don't love Duncan."

Oscar smiled sadly. "Yes, you do, but I can well imagine you're too stubborn to admit it to yourself. So, we'll all roll around in this until you come to your senses and accept the fact."

"I don't want to lose you. You're my best friend. I don't know what I'd do without you. We've been together forever. It's just that, well ... I just never thought you were *serious* all those times you said you loved me. I just thought ..."

Oscar put his arms around her and drew her against the chest she knew so well. Tears welled and spilled over her lids.

"Don't cry, Sam. You won't lose me. Nothing will ever separate us. I'll always be here for you and you for me. We made a pact. Remember? When we were kids?"

"I remember," she blubbered. "I'm so sorry, Oscar."

He cupped her face and lifted her chin with his thumbs. "No more tears, all right? That's out of the way and now we can go back to being who we are. Pact?"

"Pact."

"Mr. Morgan gave me ten dollars for that last set of pictures. I bought a new bag of cornmeal." He released her and stepped away, seemingly done with the embarrassment between them.

"How much?"

"Ten dollars."

Food was so expensive. And scarce. Hordes of stampeders had poured into town in the last three weeks. With the overcrowding had come disease—the Mounted Police hospitals were nearly full. She looked at Oscar as he turned back to his straightening. His clothes were tattered and faded. He was usually immaculate about his dress. To go about so was truly a sacrifice. She couldn't let them starve, but the stampede of business she'd envisioned hadn't materialized. So, there was only once choice left.

"I dunno, Charlie. She's mighty skinny. The gents might think them ribs'd poke 'em to death."

"I ain't intending this one for a whore. Just an appetizer for the real women. Look at that hair. The color of copper. Don't do a man no harm to dream a little 'fore he gets the main course." Perched on the edge of the stage, Charlie Benton held his ample stomach as he laughed.

Gertie swished over to Sam, petticoats rustling with every step. "Can you dance, honey?"

Sam stared at her. Well, she could waltz, but that hardly seemed like what the saloon patrons would want. She twisted and wriggled a little, sending poor Charlie into another fit of laughter.

"They'll think she's got lice, Gertie, with all that switching around."

"Come over here, honey." Her face caked with makeup, Gertie took her arm and pulled her to her side. "Now, what the men want to see is for a woman to swing her hips. Like this. See?" She undulated her lower section and held her hands over her head. "Hold your arms up, too. Makes your titties stick out."

"My what?"

"Your breasts. Bosoms."

"Oh." Sam tried it. Sure enough, it worked. "Are you sure this is what the men want? Looks kind of uncomfortable, don't you think?"

"They ain't interested in comfort, honey, 'lessen it's theirs. They're only interested in one thing when they come through those doors. And with these here moves, you're promising it to 'em."

Gertie dropped her arms and put her hands on her hips. "Try this." She thrust her hips forward and around in a circular rotation.

Sam tried to follow, but ended up sending Charlie off into another gale of laughter that almost toppled him onto the floor.

"Honey, have you ever made love?" Gertie stopped her gyrations and placed both hands on Sam's shoulders.

Sam colored. "No."

"Well, when you do, you grind your hips around like this. Gives your man and you more pleasure. Smooth like, round and round. Round and round. The men in the audience want to imagine that's what you're doing to 'em."

Sam could only stare, stunned into silence. Maybe this wasn't such a good idea after all.

"Iffen you don't stop that, Gertie, me and you are going to have to go to the back room," Charlie said with a grin and a lifted eyebrow.

"You and me ain't going nowhere, Charlie Simmons.

Don't pay no attention to him. You know, Charlie, we could bill her as The Virgin. Teach her some of these dances. It would drive the men wild to get to the girls upstairs."

Charlie rubbed a beefy hand over his chin. "Yeah, I can see how it would."

"How much?" Sam asked.

"A hundred dollars a week."

"A hundred and seventy-five."

"A hundred seventy-five!" Gertie and Charlie said in unison. "Out of the question."

"I'll learn what Gertie just showed me."

"A hundred fifty."

"Done."

"Be here at two o'clock this afternoon so Gertie can teach you," Charlie finished with a sneer. "Might just sit in the front row myself."

Oscar had blustered and fumed—he'd even cursed when she told him her latest idea.

"You'll not whore yourself out," he'd exclaimed, pacing the floor, his hands rammed down in his pockets.

"Of course I wouldn't do that, Oscar. Don't be ridiculous. I'll just be the . . . appetizer, they said."

His face reddened until she thought he'd explode like a tea kettle left too long on the stove. "I don't want you being anybody's . . . appetizer. You go down there this second and tell them you were out of your mind and you've thought better of the deal."

"No, Oscar. I won't. It's good money. I'm not doing anything wrong. And, besides, we're broke. I got us into this and I can do this to help out. For heaven's sake, Oscar. Who could possibly be there that we'd know?"

* * *

Sam scratched at the stiff lace forming the low neckline of her red satin gown, then hauled it back above
her cleavage. Lord, she felt as if she'd burst from the
garment any moment.

"Leave it alone, honey. The men want a little peek.
They can guess the rest." Gertie yanked the dress back
down and shifted her around until two pink mounds
of flesh bulged up from the nest of ivory lace.

Voices were beginning to hum from the other side
of the curtain. Sam parted the tattered drapes and
peeped out at the rapidly filling saloon. A layer of smoke
already hung about the room. Men, miners mostly, sat
around bare tables, their clothes ragged and dirty. But
she'd bet every one of them had a pocket or a bag or
a box full of gold dust. Gold dust destined for Fort
Herchmer, to be left under the care of the North West
Mounted Police. Tomorrow, she promised herself, she'd
find some way in and do some snooping around.

The outside door opened, allowing the yellow light
of sunset to spill across the floor. A slim, feminine silhouette filled the space. The room hushed and heads
turned. The unmistakable outline of a Stetson-hatted
Mountie followed her.

"Damn," Sam muttered and snatched the curtains
closed.

The piano tinkled out a few bars of a tune.

"That's your cue, Sam," Gertie hissed from behind
her.

The piano player repeated the introduction. She
couldn't make her feet move.

"Get out there," Gertie shoved her through the curtains and onto the stage. A chorus of whistles went up and her music began. She avoided looking at faces and instead focused her eyes on the back of the room, at the dirty streaks on the windows set against a dying sunset.

She lifted her hands over her head and closed her eyes. Gertie had instructed her in plain language how a woman's body accommodated a lover, how to move one's body for the pleasure of a partner. She concentrated on those instructions and imagined her body moving with Duncan's, imagined that they lay on a soft bed of spring grass. That he touched her as he'd touched her that night.

She combined her thoughts with the ballet lessons her mother had insisted upon, twirling across the stage on her toes, liking the way her skirts billowed out around her.

His hands would grab handfuls of the soft sheets they lay on and she would moan softly. She would be a consummate lover, driving him past his point of control, past reason. He'd bury his face in her hair and beg for mercy, but she'd grant him none. Not until he was hers and the delicate Emily was a distant thought.

She made a last pass across the boards and ended in a graceful curtsy. She peeked open an eye. The room was deadly quiet for a breath, then deafening applause erupted. Sam stood and looked straight into Duncan's angry blue eyes. He stood inches away, both hands planted on the edge of the stage.

"What the hell do you think you're doing?" His voice carried over half the room and the applause died to a few sporadic claps.

"I'm trying to make a living," she answered between clenched teeth. "Now go away."

"Not until you come down from there this instant. What's gotten into you?"

Sam snatched her wrist out of his grasp and stepped back. The applause resumed. She smiled at the crowd and accepted their praise with a bow.

He was furious. Well, good. She was glad he was mad. In fact, she wished steam were rolling out of his ears. Who did he think he was that he could march in here and tell her what to do? Especially with The Canary on his arm.

"Do it again!" The audience stomped their feet. Bert at the bar shot her a fearful glance and lunged to protect his glasses from tumbling off a shelf.

"Tomorrow night, boys," she said over the din, and drifted backwards on raised toes until she passed through the split in the curtain.

"I'll raise your salary to two hundred a week if you'll do that every night," Charlie said, his face sweaty and his eyes glazed. "Word'll get around and they'll pack in here tomorrow night. I better see to some more hooch." He waddled away, wiping his forehead with a dirty handkerchief.

"You did just fine," Gertie said with a hand on her shoulder. "Charlie'll pay good now. Ask for another twenty-five."

"Twenty-five more dollars?"

"Yeah. He'll fork it over. I thought he was going to have a stroke watching you through the curtains."

"Samantha!"

She recoiled as Duncan's footsteps thumped across the stage. "Can I see you a moment, please?" he asked, his voice once again low and controlled. "Alone?"

"You can use Charlie's office, honey," Gertie said with a glimmer in her eyes. "So, Inspector. Got your

britches hot, did she?'' Gertie swept him up and down
with an experienced glance, then sashayed off, a chuckle
drifting back over her shoulder.

Duncan took her elbow, led her into the small room
just behind the bar, and shut the door. ''Do you have
any idea what you just did to every man in that room?
Where'd you learn to do such . . . things?''

Sam smiled slyly. ''Were you one of those men?''

''Don't change the subject.'' He paced to the window
and lifted a torn and faded curtain.

''What bothers you the most, Duncan? The fact that
every man wanted me or that you did?''

He stopped pacing and faced her. ''You're an innocent, Sam, so you don't know. Men who've been alone
for months and haven't seen a woman in longer can't
stand much of that pressure. It's dangerous to taunt
them like that.''

Sam smiled secretly when his gaze strayed to the low
neckline of her dress. ''No, it's not. Because right now
they're clambering to get to the girls upstairs. That was
the whole idea.''

Duncan shook his head slowly. ''How on earth did
you get involved in something like this?''

''I'm gathering information for a story on the saloons
of the Yukon.''

''You could have asked me. I can tell you everything
you want to know about saloons in the Yukon.''

''Can you tell me what it's like to be a dance hall
girl?''

''Use that vivid imagination of yours and stay off the
stage.''

''I did use my imagination.'' She stepped closer and

liked the color that appeared above his collar. "Gertie taught me the ... moves and I added the rest. Do you know what I was imagining?"

Duncan's anger faded from his eyes, replaced by something more dangerous that sent a shiver down her spine. "No, and I'm not sure I want to know."

She stopped when her satin shoes touched the polished leather of his boots. "Gertie told me to use my body like I was making love. So, I closed my eyes and imagined you and me ... making love."

His eyes drifted closed briefly. "Don't tease me, Sam. Not like this."

"I remembered that night in the woods and how much more I wanted from you," she continued, emboldened by the flash of desire in his eyes.

He put an arm around her waist and pulled her firmly against him. He lowered his head as if to kiss her, his lips a breath away from hers. "You shouldn't be talking like this, Sam. You don't know what you're doing, what you're flirting with. That night shouldn't have happened."

"But it did, Duncan, and it has made me wonder what would have happened if you hadn't stopped. And my vivid imagination, as you called it, sort of filled in the gaps."

"I don't want you to do this again."

"You don't have a say."

"Please, Sam. You don't know men. You don't know what they're capable of. Sure, some of them will stampede upstairs, but there's others that won't. They'll come after you."

"Posh. Why would they be interested in me when

there's a stable of experienced women waiting upstairs?''

Duncan's eyes softened. "You have no idea the gifts you've been given, do you?''

She could only stare up at him. What was he saying?

"You make a man think dangerous thoughts, Samantha Wilder. Promise me you'll remember that." He released her and stepped away, arousal in his eyes.

"I promise."

He started for the door.

"Do you think dangerous thoughts about me, Duncan?''

Duncan paused with his hand on the doorknob. "Yes, God have mercy on me. I do.''

The last warbled note of Emily's song bounced off the rafters before the room burst into applause. She accepted with a modest bow of her head before she stepped back through the curtains.

"Pardon me," she said, jostling against Sam. "Oh, you're the dancer.''

"Yes, I am." Close up, she was lovelier than Sam remembered. Doe eyes filled the narrow face edged with fine wisps of hair. So delicate. So feminine. No wonder Duncan loved her.

He'd watched Emily's performance from the audience, hanging on every note, his face soft, filled with love. The way she wished he'd look at her. She'd only been a dalliance, she decided, having heard the word someplace. Emily was the woman he wanted to marry.

"Your dance was very lovely," Emily continued without a trace of sarcasm in her words. "You've studied ballet." Her words were perfect and carefully chosen, as if she'd just stepped out of a finishing school.

"Yes, as a child."

Emily smiled. "And you've adapted your steps to suit the surroundings."

Sam grinned. "That's a lovely way to put it."

"My mother thought I should sing in the opera and sent me to London to study. I, too, have adapted to fit my surroundings."

Despite the hatred she'd have loved to harbor, Sam found she couldn't dislike the gentle woman before her.

"Duncan was very angry that you were dancing here."

"Well, Inspector McLeod is concerned that I might be hurt by some of the customers."

"Yes, he is a very considerate man. So kind."

Sam narrowed her gaze. She just had to know what was between these two. "Have you known Duncan long?"

"Oh, yes. Since we were children. He has asked me to marry him many times."

Her words fell like a cannonball. But before Sam could put her brain back in gear, Duncan parted the curtain and placed himself between them. "We should be going, Emily. We'll walk Miss Wilder home."

"I don't need to be walked home, Inspector Mc-Leod," she snapped, hating the intimacy his words to Emily had suggested.

"It's my duty to make the streets of Dawson City safe, and you on the loose, Miss Wilder, is a risk to the Yukon Territory."

Sam could only bristle under his words. Thoughts, other than that he intended to marry The Canary, simply would not materialize. So why had he kissed her, touched her that night? Had it all meant absolutely nothing to him? Her bravado fled and she was suddenly very, very tired.

"Yes, I'd appreciate it if you'd walk me home. That way I'll be safe from the hordes of sex-starved men waiting for me in the alley."

"You've only been here a few hours and already your language is lewd."

"I'm saying the same thing you did in Charlie's office. And there's nothing lewd about my language." Sam picked up her shawl, snatching it out of Duncan's grip. "I can dress myself."

He gently placed Emily's wrap across her shoulders and held the door open for them all.

"Good night, Gertie," Sam called over her shoulder and Gertie shouted something unintelligible from the back.

The saloon was still full of patrons, even though it was well past midnight. A full moon traced lacy patterns on the churned, muddy street, casting an ethereal beauty over the crowded, dirty town.

"I love the north," Emily said, pulling her wrapper tighter around her. "It is such an exciting place. Not like the Isle of Skye. Don't you think so, Duncan?"

Duncan pulled his pipe out of his pocket, filled it, and lit it with a match scratched against the bottom of his shoe. "I don't know. Home could be pretty exciting at times."

They launched into a discussion of some childhood event, shutting Sam out, so she focused her attention on the rough boards beneath her feet. How odd that they were both from the same place in Scotland. Besides odd, what did it mean?

"I beg your pardon. Are you The Virgin?" A young man suddenly stepped into her path from a shadowy alleyway.

Sam jumped, startled, and saw Duncan move Emily from between them with a gentle nudge of his forearm. One hand drifted down toward his revolver.

"Yes, I am."

The young man reached out a trembling, dirty hand and took hers. "I wanted you to know that I'm a virgin, too."

Duncan's tobacco smoke floated around them, reminding her of his prediction about desperate men.

"Well, I think that's very honorable." She cast Duncan a sidelong glance. He cupped the bowl of his pipe in his palm and watched.

"But I'm reckoning not to be come Christmas and I was hoping you could be the first . . . Miss Virgin."

Duncan coughed and Sam turned her back on him. "Well, Mr. . . ."

"Andy Simmons, ma'am."

"Well, Mr. Simmons. I don't really do that . . . sort of thing. I'm just a dancer, you see. Now, there's a whole lot of ladies there that would take care of that for you."

Andy shook his head. "No, I don't want no whore. I want a lady virgin to be my first. And there ain't no virgin whores, 'ceptin' you."

Sam cast a backward glance at Duncan. He crossed his arms over his chest, his pipe tightly clamped in his teeth. Emily's eyes were huge.

"Now, Andy. Like I said, I'm not a whore. I just dance. Someday you'll meet some nice young lady and the two of you can learn together."

"Do you reckon?"

"Yes, Andy. I reckon."

"Well, you looked like you knew what you was doing."

"It was just a dance."

He shuffled his feet. "I sure was hoping . . ."

"Good night, Andy." Samantha stepped around him and headed off down the sidewalk, knowing that Duncan followed, laughing around his pipe stem.

CHAPTER NINE

"Me and my brother Tom staked this claim three years ago and you're gonna let this bastard waltz in here and take it away from me?" Wilton Adcox shook his fist in Duncan's face.

"You didn't file the claim, Wilton. You know you have to file at the claims office for it to be legal. I've told you that myself." Duncan shook his head. "You're a stubborn man."

"I wouldn't try that if I were you," Mike Finnegan said, laying his revolver across Wilton's forearm as he reached toward the leather holster on his hip. "Shooting Inspector McLeod wouldn't be the smartest thing you did today, lad."

"It ain't right and you know it, Mountie. Ain't right to take away a man's land that he's sweated and grunted over." Wilton eased his arm back down by his side.

"I agree and I did a thorough investigation before

coming out here. Mr. Wooten's claim is legal, filed, and recorded. You never bothered to follow the laws, you and Tom, even though you knew them well."

"The Yukon's a big place and still a man can't get away from people a-pushing and a-shoving him around. I don't hold with no paper making a place belong to a man. Oughta be the work he puts into it. Any damned fool can fill out a paper."

Duncan sighed and wished he were doing anything but this right now. Separating a man from the land he's worked and sacrificed for didn't set well, but the law was the law. And Wilton and Tom Adcox believed they were above it. Alex Wooten, on the other hand, knew the power of laws and had been cunning enough to look into that fact and file the claim himself. Now, what was done was done and Wilton and his brother were the legal owners of a new claim fifteen miles away in Gold Creek. They'd have to start all over again, but at least they hadn't come away empty-handed for their stupidity.

"Here's the paperwork for the new claim."

Wilton took the folded sheaf of documents and tossed them on the ground. "The land at Gold Creek's mined out. Any fool knows that."

"Superintendent Steele looked into this land himself. It has the potential to be as good as you have here. Better."

"What the hell do a bunch of Mounties know about gold-bearing land? You know how to pan, Inspector? Or how to build a sluice?"

"Mining's not my business. Seeing that claims are legally filed is."

Duncan turned and walked back to his horse, feeling the hairs on his neck rise at turning his back on Wilcox.

Finnegan glanced back once, but Wilcox kicked at the papers and went into his cabin.

"We're not done with that one," Finnegan said, swinging up onto his horse's back.

"No, I'm afraid we're not." Duncan settled into the saddle and wished he didn't have a ten-mile ride back to Dawson in front of him.

"Tom nor Wilton don't take kindly to any interference."

"No, and in this case I don't much blame them for being furious."

"Still and all, they can be dangerous when they're riled."

"I'll worry about that when the time comes." He turned his horse back toward the trail and hunched his shoulders against a sudden chill that swept down from rocky heights.

"You wouldn't be having any special reason for hurrying back to Dawson City, now would you?" Finnegan's eyes danced with mischief.

"No, except for the fact that it's going to rain before dark."

"Maybe you're figuring on paying Charlie's another visit."

Duncan glanced at Finnegan and grinned.

"Made quite a figure of yourself last night the way me and the rest of the detachment heard it."

"What exactly did you hear?" He guided his horse around a huge felled tree.

"Oh, just that you ordered Samantha Wilder off the stage after she did an . . . unusual dance."

"Unusual is right. She damned near set the place on fire."

"And upright Inspector McLeod along with it."

"There's nothing between Miss Wilder and myself except friendship."

"Is that why you lie awake at night counting the rats that run across the beams?"

"I'm going to marry Emily."

"Ah, has the lass had a change of mind?"

"No. She hasn't said yes yet. But she will."

Finnegan dropped the subject and let peaceful silence again fall between them. Sweet, delicate Emily, with her soft eyes and gentle ways. Duncan remembered her as a child when he'd gone to court her sister. Long, straight, dark hair. Perfectly groomed and perfectly mannered. So different from stormy, passionate Elizabeth.

No, he wouldn't remember tangled sheets and tasting the saltiness of Elizabeth's skin. He wouldn't remember stormy nights and making love in the minutes before dawn. Or the days his babies were born into the world, red and screaming. He'd concentrate on Emily. Tranquil, like an afternoon by a gentle river. Within her arms he'd find his manhood again, the confidence Elizabeth had ripped from him. He'd miss passion, but compromises must be made.

But try as he might, passionate thoughts always emerged wearing Samantha's face. Hers was the face amid tumbled sheets. Hers was the face beneath him, eyes closed in ecstasy. Never Emily. No, Emily was a prize to be won, the tool of his revenge. He'd prove Elizabeth wrong and Emily would have a home. And as always, a prick of guilt accompanied the small wash of satisfaction.

His thoughts wandered to Samantha and as clearly as last night, he could again see her writhing on the stage. He hadn't the heart to tell her that she'd looked utterly ridiculous to all but love-starved miners. She thought she held those men in her hand, held him there, too, breathless and panting for her.

And she was right.

He'd spent all night wanting her and talking himself out of loving her. And most of him had listened. But not all. Not the parts that remembered the sweet weight of her flesh balanced in his hand or the boldness with which she'd tried to bring him the same pleasure as she. She'd be a willing lover, warm and eager. But no more passionate women for him. Life with a delicate beauty like Emily was more to his liking.

He wondered if he'd ever come to believe that lie.

"Superintendent Steele." Sam held out a white-gloved hand and smiled her brightest smile.

Moustached Samuel B. Steele rose from behind his massive desk and reached across to take her hand in his large one. "Miss Wilder."

Surprised that he knew her name, Sam plunged on. "I am recently arrived in Dawson City and wondered if I might be afforded a tour of your lovely fort."

Steele frowned slightly. "That's an unusual request, one I can say I've never received before. Do you have some particular interest in Fort Herchner?"

She drew in a breath, careful not to let her fear show in her eyes. He was sharper than she'd anticipated. "Why, yes, I do. I've read so much about the Mounted Police that my curiosity overcame me."

Steele smiled and looked down at his desk. "Miss Wilder, prostitution is a profession that is frowned on by the police. I will admit we have not been very suc-

cessful in controlling it, but I don't feel I should pro-
mote—''

"I am not a prostitute, Superintendent." She worked
up a tear or two and dabbed at the corners of her eyes
with a handkerchief. "I'm deeply wounded that you
have listened to idle gossip. I thought you a more honorable man than that."

Instantly contrite, Steele rounded the desk. "I beg
your pardon, Miss Wilder, but from your ... performance last night ..."

"I'm a classical dancer, trained in some of the finest
ballet schools in San Francisco. I was merely expressing
in my dance the loneliness that I felt from the men in
the room."

"And a wonderful dance it was," he countered
quickly. "I merely wanted there to be no misunderstanding—"

"There isn't and I do forgive you your mistake. I
observed such horrible living conditions on my trip into
Dawson that I wondered if the fine men who keep us
safe had adequate quarters and food. I do have some
connections in San Francisco and thought—"

"We provide our men everything they need, Miss
Wilder, but I would be honored to give you a tour, if
you would still like one."

"Oh, yes. I would indeed." She snapped open her
purse and dropped the handkerchief inside, hoping
Steele would take the action as a cue she had forgiven
him.

He called to a young constable just passing by his
open doorway. "Constable Harper, would you be so
good as to give Miss Wilder a tour of our fort."

Wide-eyed and tongue-tied, Constable Harper obviously knew who she was. The flamboyant reputation she

seemed to have acquired overnight was already beginning to chafe her.

"Yes, sir," he managed to croak, yanking down his tunic.

They strolled through the long log building that housed the men's barracks. Eyes followed her as she passed through, noting that a large number of men either lounged on their bunks or slept. Three shifts of men were now seeing to the safety of Dawson City. And three shifts of men guarded the gold.

"I understand that your brave men are responsible for thousands of dollars in gold. How unnerving that must be for them."

"Yes, ma'am, but we're quite up to the task," he said, pride in his voice.

"Still, it must weigh heavy on a man's mind. Do you suppose I could actually see the gold?" She stopped and turned all her charm on him.

"Well, I don't know."

"Please, Constable. It would be so exciting."

When he still seemed hesitant, she played her ace. "Perhaps you could come and see me dance tonight? I'd love to see you in the audience." She moved a step closer and his neck reddened.

"I don't suppose it would hurt anything." He led her to a small log building set away from the others. "This was the powder magazine 'til we got so much gold. Then we put it in here with guards posted." Sam glanced at the two men standing guard, but neither acknowledged her, staring straight ahead at the distant forest.

"William, open the door and let Miss Wilder have a look."

The guard on the left cast a glance at his partner.

"Oh, if it's too much trouble . . ."

William leaned over, pulled a key from his pocket, and unlocked the padlock. The door swung open to reveal piles of cloth bags. The floor sparkled with tiny golden bits as sunshine crept inside.

"Christ," she swore under her breath. She'd expected a lot but this amount was amazing. How on earth did they keep up with so much and how did they ever get it out of the Territory without being murdered?

"Oh my," she exclaimed, returning to her adopted persona. "That will make quite a few baubles, won't it, Constable?"

Constable Harper swung the door closed and the guard locked the building again.

"Well, this has been wonderful." She offered the Constable her hand, which he took and kissed gently. "I'll be looking for you tonight." She smiled coyly, then turned and walked away with as much sway to her hips as she could manage without toppling over onto her face.

Oscar crouched behind the tree, the rope dangling in his hand. A shaft of morning sun seduced him into drowsiness as the rough bark of a cedar dug into his back. In the small clearing around a stump, a rabbit nibbled at tender, green shoots of grass.

He struggled to keep his eyes on the noose lying a few inches left of the feeding rabbit and prayed the animal would see fit to step into it. They'd eaten corn-meal mush for so long, he didn't think he could ever eat corn again. Food had grown scarcer as more and more stampeders had flooded into Dawson City. Eggs were eighteen dollars a dozen and a can of oysters was an incredible twenty-five dollars. Game in the surrounding hills had been hunted to depletion and the Mounted Police had convinced several hundred stampeders to move down river to the better supplied community of Fort Yukon.

His head hit the tree with a soft thump. Alerted, the rabbit paused in its browsing, its tiny nose wiggling as it sniffed the air. Then, it hopped to the left, one tiny foot in the noose, and stopped again, stretching up on its back feet.

"Look how perfect God made the rabbit," a soft voice whispered in his ear. "Aren't they amazing creatures?"

Convulsively, he jerked the rope. The noose closed harmlessly and the rabbit scampered away. He turned and looked into Emily's delicate face. Scrambling to his feet, Oscar brushed off his ragged pants.

"I'm so sorry I startled you," she said, her large, expressive eyes mirroring her smile. "And I probably ruined your supper, too, didn't I?"

Oscar shook his head. "I'm not sure I could have gone through with it anyway."

She wore a dress that would have gone better on the evening streets of San Francisco, a long, filmy garment topped by a sheer wrapper she held around her shoulders. The intrusive shaft of sunlight that had lured him into sleep lit her hair with dancing highlights. She was beautiful, the lines of her face reminding him of paintings of angels in a cathedral. An orchid growing in a garden of marigolds. She had no more place here than he did.

"You're Mr. Wilder. I saw your wife dance last night. She's a very talented lady."

"Sam?" he responded before he thought. "Ah, yes, she is. And you're Emily, Inspector McLeod's ... friend."

A soft smile crept across her face. "Yes, his friend."

Oscar longed to touch her and see if she was as smooth and fine as the Dresden china she reminded him of.

"I'm actually Duncan's sister-in-law . . . once upon a time, anyway."

"The inspector is married?" Oscar frowned. Sam had left out that small bit.

"Not any longer. He was married to my sister many years ago. Since I came here from Scotland, he has appointed himself my guardian."

So, the Inspector was an experienced man, knowl-edgeable in the ways of love and women. A shaft of jealousy pricked him. He couldn't even hope to offer Sam that.

"You're his sister-in-law?" That would explain his con-stant hovering around Emily, he supposed. Oscar won-dered if Sam knew that was all there was between them? Part of him wanted to rush and tell her, to see her beam in pleasure. But another, darker part of him wanted to cling to that bit of information, a feeble effort to hold back what he knew was inevitable. "Have you been in Canada long?" he asked.

"A year or two. I wanted to see the wonderful Territor-ies. The descriptions are so vivid in the newspapers back east."

"What brought you to Dawson City?"

She shrugged and lifted her gossamer wrap higher on her shoulder. "I followed Duncan here. There was work, singing in dance halls. I could earn a living on my own and allow him to look after me, too." She laughed, the sound tinkling through the sunlit forest. "He refuses to believe that I am perfectly capable of looking after myself. He feels some sort of responsibility to me, but I think perhaps his motives are not quite so noble as he believes."

She sat down on a rotting stump before Oscar could snatch off his coat and offer it as protection to her dress.

"My sister deceived Duncan, left him for another man, the son of a baron. She took his children away, his life. His pride was hurt. I believe he sees in me a means to recover that pride by proving her wrong."

Oscar sat down on the ground at her side, intrigued that she would reveal so much intimate information to a man she'd just met. She certainly didn't seem a gossip, so what was her purpose?

"Sam's not my wife," Oscar blurted.

"She isn't?"

He shook his head. "We're just very good friends. We work for a paper in San Francisco. She wanted to come to the Yukon." He paused, tempted to unburden himself completely, but his loyalty to Sam was stronger. "And she talked me into coming with her."

"You must be a very good friend," she replied with a soft smile.

He shrugged and studied the patterns in the dead leaves.

"I had suspected as much."

"How?"

"You and she seem to be exactly what you are— soulmates in a sense. But not romantically."

"Well, if it were left up to me, things would be different. But Sam is Sam and, well . . ."

"Ah, so you are in love with Sam, too?"

Oscar picked up a twig and traced a jagged path in the dark soil. "I've never wanted anybody but Sam. She's always been there since we were children. I always thought it was meant to be. But I have to admit that being married to Samantha Wilder would probably kill most mortal men."

"She's in love with Duncan, isn't she?"

Oscar's head snapped up. "Head over heels, if I'm any judge."

She gazed off into the morning shadows. "And he is in love with her. I can see it in his eyes and he denies it too vehemently when I bring up the subject." She leaned down and touched Oscar's shoulder. Tingles shot up his arm straight to his heart, then tumbled into the lower regions of his body. He nearly groaned out loud from the sensation.

"It is up to you and me to see that they find each other." She tightened her grip. "Very soon Duncan will need her as he has needed no one in a long, long time."

Oscar frowned and wondered if Sam was right and Duncan was about to be caught in illegal activity. "Why?"

"That I cannot tell. But know that when the time comes, he will need her."

Oscar wanted to pursue the issue further, but Emily's hooded expression said the subject was closed.

"And do you love Inspector McLeod, also?" What could have emboldened him to ask such a question? He cringed beneath her wide-eyed gaze, his neck reddening.

"As a brother only," she said with a slow, inviting smile.

Rain pelted Duncan's oilskin coat and dripped off the brim of his Stetson as he rode into Eldorado. The small, ramshackle town hosted a single street and clustered, lopsided buildings. Swamped with a flood of miners in the last two months, a city of tents had sprung up on the surrounding hillsides. The Yukon River and her tributaries were full and a spring flood was feared. With little regard for safety, tent homes clung to the muddy banks of the encroaching streams.

The streets were oddly quiet, despite the deluge of rain. Few people walked the rickety boarded sidewalk and only one or two rain-weary horses stood with heads bowed in misery at hitching rails. The one saloon in town, George's Dead Dog Saloon, seemed to be earning its name today as the interior remained dark.

Duncan swung down, mud oozing up around his booted ankles. He looped his reins around the rail and stomped up onto the sidewalk, kicking clods of mud off the boots. He took off his hat and slung persistent raindrops off the brim, then walked into the saloon. Only one man sat at a table, nursing a drink.

Odd, thought Duncan. "Where's George?" he asked the bartender, wiping lethargically at the rough board bar.

"Sick," the man answered with elaboration.

"How so?"

The bartender shrugged. "Injuns say it's the water. I reckon it's typhoid."

Duncan's blood chilled. Assistant Surgeon Richardson had already warned the residents of Dawson City that an epidemic of the dreaded disease was imminent. Sanitary conditions were horrid. Garbage littered the streets and the contents of chamber pots were flung out upper floor windows without regard to their final destination. Conditions in the adjoining mining communities were equally bad. Including Eldorado.

"How many are sick?" he asked.

"Most of the town. A bunch of missionaries are trying to look after who they can at their place to the east."

"I'm going back to Dawson City for help. Have you been sick?" Duncan asked.

The bartender shook his head. "Nope. I don't drink the water. Don't drink nothing but whiskey." He reached underneath the counter and produced a glass of dark liquid. "I seen typhoid wipe out a whole village of Blackfeet once. And I seen this time coming when the woods filled up with tents and the streets filled up with filth."

Sam stepped out of the dance hall and into the pouring rain. Pulling her hood up over her head, she hurried down the walkway toward the hotel. The splatter of galloping hoofbeats made her step into the recess of a doorway and look up. Duncan galloped past, his horse's hooves throwing up sprays of water and mud.

Her curiosity piqued, she watched him turn into the gates of the fort, ride up to Steele's headquarters, and dismount. He banged briefly on the door, then hurried inside the dark building. She must be crazy, she thought, as she stepped into the muddy street and started toward the fort. But then whatever was afoot must be urgent, and might lead to a good story. Heaven knows she'd gotten nowhere with her investigation. If there was any scandal going on, no one was talking.

She nearly ran nose to nose with Duncan when he barreled out of Steele's now lit headquarters.

"Sam?" he said, his muddy boots sliding as he stopped quickly. "What are you doing here?" He gazed down at her from beneath his soggy hat, water dripping off the soaked oilskins and his moustache.

"I saw you ride in."

"And you couldn't resist finding out what was going on?"

"Yes."

He smiled and touched her shoulder. "Go back to the hotel. It's nothing that would interest you."

Didn't he know that was the very thing not to say to a reporter? "Has there been a murder? A robbery?"

"No, Sam. It's typhoid. In Eldorado."

Her face blanched. "Typhoid?" A ravenous beast that consumed young and old alike.

He started toward the storeroom where Constable Harper had shown her the gold and she kept pace at his side. "What are you going to do?"

"I'm taking some supplies and going to offer what help I can. Finnegan and Harper are coming with me. We can't spare any more men from here." He stopped at the door and turned to face her. "Don't drink any water, Sam. Richardson says it lives in the water."

She thought of the glass she'd dipped from Gertie's bucket just before she left the dance hall.

He pulled a key from his pocket and unlocked the door. The two rain-soaked guards didn't give him a glance as the door swung open and he stepped nonchalantly over the bags of gold dust.

"Let me go with you," she called into the dark room, suddenly fearful for him.

"No," he said, handing a bundle of bandages to one of the guards.

"I can help. I'd be two more hands."

"No." He disappeared back into the dark and she heard the scrape of wooden crates being moved.

"Duncan," she said with a hand to his arm when he reemerged, "I've done this before."

"Done what?" he asked, then instructed one of the guards to bring his horse.

"Nursed."

He chuckled. "Now why don't I believe that?"

"I have. I swear. There was an epidemic in the red light district in San Francisco once and the ladies' auxiliary tended them."

He handed out several more packets, which the constable stuffed into Duncan's saddlebags, then he locked the door back.

"I'm sorry, Sam. I don't have the time to believe one of your tall tales." He turned to go, but she caught a handful of his wet coat.

"Wait. All right, I didn't do it myself. But my mother did. And I remember sitting on the steps when I was supposed to be in bed and listening to what she came home and told Father. It haunted her, Duncan, and I remember perfectly everything she said. At the time I thought she was having quite an adventure." She tightened her grip. "I at least know what to expect."

He looked down at her a moment longer, then leaned closer and kissed her gently. "No, lass. I want you to promise me you'll stay here. I want to know that your smiling face'll be waiting for me when I get home."

She gazed up at him, her mind whirring, searching for the words to convince him to let her go. Somehow she knew—she just *knew*—that if he rode out into the dark night she'd never see him again.

"Promise me, Sam." He shook her shoulder.

"I promise," she murmured.

CHAPTER TEN

Oscar, Have gone to Eldorado with Duncan. Please don't worry. Will return safely. Promise.

                                        Sam

She folded the note and slid it under Oscar's door. Not a sound came from the other side. Straightening, she tiptoed to her room and hefted her pack onto her back, then slipped out the door and eased it shut behind her. If she hadn't raided the hotel's linen closet, she wouldn't be carrying thirty extra pounds, she thought as she crept down the stairs, cringing in dismay at every board that creaked.

The rain had abated but dark clouds scuttled across the moon. Now, where could she get a horse? she wondered, looking up and down the deserted street. Down near Charlie's, a lone horse stood, head down. Staying to the wooden sidewalk as much as possible, she reached the animal and ran a hand across its wet neck. It raised its head and she realized it was a mule.

"Hello, girl," she said, circling the beast. "You want to take me to Eldorado?"

The mule wore a soggy saddle with a soaked blanket roll tied behind. Sam glanced over her shoulder to the top floors of Charlie's. Some patron had talked one of the girls into letting him spend the night in her bed. Sam tied her pack on behind the saddle, leaving the blanket roll conspicuously in a straight-backed chair nearby, then swung up into the saddle and headed east out of town.

Dawn broke with drizzling rain as Sam came into sight of the bedraggled settlement. As in Dawson, the street was a quagmire. Building sides were splashed with a fine layer of silt and acres of sodden, muddy tents dotted the surrounding hillsides. But not a soul walked the once-busy streets.

She drew the mule to a stop and assessed the miserable sight before her. Where was the best place to get information? She glanced down the street until she spotted George's Dead Dog Saloon. She'd heard Charlie mention the name.

She dismounted in front of the saloon and walked in, her long coat slapping soddenly around her legs. The place was deserted. Tables and chairs were arranged neatly and the bar was clean and orderly. "Hello," she called and received no answer.

A single piece of paper lay on the board slabs that served as the bar. *Closed on account of typhoid. Take what you need only if you need it,* it read.

She picked up the note and a chill ran down her back. Where was everyone? And especially, where was

Duncan? What had possessed her to do this foolish thing, placing herself in such danger? The answer immediately surfaced. If she hadn't followed, Duncan would die. Her irrational fear was as simple and unshakable as that. There was no rhyme, reason, or logic to her decision and she refused to look past the premonition that had haunted her days and nights. She was supposed to be here. Divine intervention, maybe. But her heart had spoken louder than her reasoning.

The scuff of boots at the door made her whirl. Duncan stood there in the gray dawn light, his sleeves rolled up and his hair disheveled. Somewhere, he'd abandoned his coat. Mud splattered his pants and his boots.

"Sam." He closed his eyes for a moment and she braced herself for a tongue lashing. "Thank God you're here."

She moved closer and saw that his skin was a sickly shade of gray. "Are you ill?" she asked, reaching out to touch his forehead.

"No, just tired. There were Jesuit missionaries here before, looking after the sick. They just left." He shrugged. "Rode away without a backward look. Probably scared to death." He focused his eyes on hers with an effort. "There are so many sick, Sam. So many dead. I don't have enough hands." He held out his palms and stared down at them as if bewildered.

"When was the last time you slept?" She moved still closer and raked fingers through the dark hair over his ear. He practically swayed on his feet.

"I don't know. Two days. Maybe three. Just catnaps beyond that."

"Where're Finnegan and Harper?"

He jerked his head. "Down there. Near the end of town. We've set up a hospital of sorts."

He stared at her blankly, as if thoughts simply would not coalesce.

Sam set down her pack. "I've brought some more linens. We'll work in shifts now that there're four of us, two to a shift." She took his arm and steered him toward the door. Suddenly, he stopped.

"I came here for something."

"What?" she asked.

"Whiskey. I came for whiskey. Richardson said to pour whiskey over everything the sick ones touch."

Sam grabbed as many bottles as she could fit into her pack, then led Duncan down the sidewalk to the building he indicated.

The stench was overwhelming.

Sam gagged and put a hand over her mouth. All manner of human odors circulated around her. "The first thing we have to do is get these windows up," she declared and hoisted the nearest window sash.

"You'll give 'em their death of cold," Finnegan said from his seat by a cot where he mopped a patient's brow.

"They'll smother to death first from this odor," she muttered and flung up another window.

"Now to bed with you," she grabbed Duncan's sleeve, "and you." She poked a finger at young Harper. "Finnegan and I will do what we can. We'll wake you up before dark."

"There's no beds left," Harper said, staring at her as vacantly as Duncan.

She glanced out the open window to the Dead Dog. A second row of windows looked out above the first. Rooms for whores. Who, if they had any sense, would have skedaddled at the first whiff of sickness.

"Come with me." She dragged the two exhausted

Introducing Ballad,
A LINE OF HISTORICAL ROMANCES

*A*s a lover of historical romance, you'll adore Ballad Romances. Written by today's most popular romance authors, every book in the Ballad line is not only an individual story, but part of a two to six book series as well. You can look forward to 4 new titles each month – each taking place at a different time and place in history.

But don't take our word for how wonderful these stories are! Accept our introductory shipment of 4 Ballad Romance novels – a $23.96 value – ABSOLUTELY FREE – and see for yourself!

*O*nce you've experienced your first 4 Ballad Romances, we're sure you'll want to continue receiving these wonderful historical romance novels each month – without ever having to leave your home – using our convenient and inexpensive home subscription service. Here's what you get for joining:

- *4 BRAND NEW Ballad Romances delivered to your door each month*
- *30% off the cover price with your home subscription.*
- *A FREE monthly newsletter filled with author interviews, book previews, special offers, and more!*
- *No risk or obligation...you're free to cancel whenever you wish... no questions asked.*

Passion-
Adventure-
Excitement-
Romance-
Ballad!

*T*o start your membership, simply complete and return the card provided. You'll receive your Introductory Shipment of 4 FREE Ballad Romances. Then, each month, as long as your account is in good standing, you will receive the 4 newest Ballad Romances. Each shipment will be yours to examine for 10 days. If you decide to keep the books, you'll pay the preferred home subscriber's price – a savings of 30% off the cover price! (plus shipping & handling) If you want us to stop sending books, just say the word...it's that simple.

A $23.96 value – **FREE** No obligation to buy anything – ever.
4 FREE BOOKS are waiting for you! Just mail in the certificate below!

BOOK CERTIFICATE

Yes! Please send me 4 Ballad Romances ABSOLUTELY FREE! After my introductory shipment, I will receive 4 new Ballad Romances each month to preview FREE for 10 days (as long as my account is in good standing). If I decide to keep the books, I will pay the money-saving preferred publisher's price plus shipping and handling. That's 30% off the cover price. I may return the shipment within 10 days and owe nothing, and I may cancel my subscription at any time. The 4 FREE books will be mine to keep in any case.

Name _____

Address _____ Apt. _____

City _____ State _____ Zip _____

Telephone (____) _____

Signature _____

(If under 18, parent or guardian must sign)

All orders subject to approval by Zebra Home Subscription Service.
Terms and prices subject to change. Offer valid only in the U.S.

Passion...
Adventure...
Excitement...
Romance...

llɪ..lɪ..lllɪ...llllɪlɪlɪ..llɪɪ..llɪ.ɪ.ɪ..llɪlɪ..lllɪ..l

BALLAD ROMANCES
Zebra Home Subscription Service, Inc.
P.O. Box 5214
Clifton NJ 07015-5214

PLACE
STAMP
HERE

men the short distance to the saloon, and up the stairs. Sure enough, there were two vacant rooms. Not one scrap of personal belongings remained behind.

Harper fell across a bed in one room, put an arm over his eyes, and didn't move again. Sam steered Duncan to the second room. He turned in the doorway to look at her. "Are you truly here, or am I dreaming?"

"I'm here," she said softly.

He frowned. "Why did you come? Didn't I tell you not to?"

"I guess I don't take orders very well."

He studied her for a few seconds. "This isn't the Samantha Wilder I know."

"Well, this is the one you haven't met yet."

"Why did you come, Sam?"

Did he want a soul-purging confession? She sensed he at least wanted her to confirm something he suspected. Fear leapt out from behind the Brave-Sam persona she'd invented on the way here and snatched away all the pretense that stood between them. "I knew," she began in a quivering voice, "that if I let you ride off without me, I'd never see you again."

"Sam," he said softly, took a step toward her, then stopped. "You have to go home, Sam. I don't know what I was thinking letting you stay this long. I must be out of my mind."

"I thought you were glad I was here."

"I'd have been glad to see another pair of hands no matter who they belonged to." He rubbed a hand over his face. "I didn't mean that the way it sounded."

"I know you didn't. Now, get into bed."

He sat on the edge of the mattress. Sam knelt and took off his boots, smiling when she saw that one sock hosted a hole large enough to allow two toes to escape.

He stretched out on the bed and sighed, seeming to melt into the mattress.

Sam started to step away, but he caught a handful of her skirt. "Stay. For just a minute?"

She sat down beside him on the bed and shoved an errant curl off his forehead. He caught her wrist and nipped at the tip of one finger, sending chills racing up her arm.

"You're like a balm to my soul, Sam Wilder." He cupped the back of her head in his hand and brought her lips to his. Even as he kissed her, the rapid breaths of great emotion brushed by her cheeks. When she drew away, he blinked quickly to hide a hint of moisture. "No one's worried about me . . . in a long time."

Fatigue had stripped him of his reserve and bared his soul for only her to see. Strong, proud Inspector Duncan McLeod lay before her, a mere mortal man. She leaned down and kissed him again, savoring the softness of his lips, his warmth. Then she laid her cheek against his and threaded her fingers in his dark curls. "I love you," she whispered. "You deserve to be worried about."

Somehow Sam and Mike made it through the day. The first time a patient vomited on her shoes, she promptly went outside and lost her lunch. After that, she viewed each experience with detachment, as if she were floating above her own body, watching as another Sam cleaned patients racked with diarrhea and fever. By dusk, they were both stumbling from fatigue and more than a little lightheaded from the odor of copious amounts of whiskey poured over hands, pans, clothes, and sometimes patients.

Adhering to Assistant Surgeon Richardson's directions, they used the spirits liberally.

Not until dusk settled in did she have the time to step outside and reflect on her confession to Duncan. In fact, she hardly viewed it as a confession at all, considering he hadn't heard a word of it. The moment her lips left his, she realized he was asleep. But it had been the truth then and was the truth now. She couldn't remember when she'd fallen in love with him. Somehow, through some miracle of the human spirit, he had worked his way into her heart, edging past all the barriers her conscious self would have thrown up in defense. But there he was, firmly ensconced. Now, she asked herself, what would she do about it?

As dark drew a curtain over the ravaged town, Sam ran an arm across her forehead and wondered if she could stumble two more steps. Then, as if she'd conjured him, Duncan appeared.

"Do I smell like a whore?" he whispered in her ear, coming up behind her.

"Oh my, yes, you do." She turned around and pressed her wrist to her nose. "But anything is preferable to the odors in here." He was freshly shaved and drops of water still glistened in his hair. Water. He'd used water. Her thoughts spun, remembering Richardson's cautions. Typhoid lived and spread in water, he believed.

"I found an abandoned bar of soap in one of the rooms," he said with a smile, looking nearly like his old self. "Can't say I'd want to use it all the time, but the images it calls to mind . . ." He grinned at her.

There was a new intimacy between them, quivering on the air, unseen. He smiled and she recalled the feel of his lips. He stepped to the side, asking about a patient, and she observed and noted how every inch of his body moved. Oh, she was smitten, all right. Sometime during the last two months, Cupid had thwacked her with a hammer instead of piercing her with an arrow.

Dawn hung at the window like a silken curtain, a dull graying of the sky, devoid of color. Sam rolled over and opened her eyes. Two sparse chairs beneath the window were fuzzy shapes against the receding night. She should get up, she knew, and relieve Duncan and Harper at the hospital, but she remained for a few minutes, contemplating. She was in love with a man she didn't know, a man silent and closed and mysterious. He'd swept into her life and grabbed away the purpose she'd traveled a thousand miles to pursue. Missing gold dust seemed very unimportant now and San Francisco very far away.

A soft splash of water interrupted her thoughts and she knew without turning over that Duncan was in the room. How or when or why he'd come in, she didn't know. A thrill of excitement danced through her.

The faint odor of rose soap swirled around her and a methodical scrape, scrape, scrape. Another soft swish of water. He was shaving. A sweet warmth poured through her. Something about a man shaving, she mused with a smile. An intimate act, unguarded. She turned over softly, feigning sleep, one eye peeped open.

Shirtless, he stood at the bowl and pitcher, lowered suspenders making dark swoops against the legs of his pants. One hand held his cheek taut while the other scraped away with a straight razor. Why had he come to her room when Finnegan lay asleep in the other with a bowl and pitcher just as usable as hers? Did he have intentions other than merely shaving, or was this his attempt at an intimacy between them, an easiness he couldn't voice nor act on in public.

She watched, mesmerized, as he picked up a piece of cloth and wiped away traces of soap. Here they were, together, alone, inappropriately attired, in the middle of a life-and-death struggle. And he shaved with as much aplomb as if he'd been in his own quarters.

He put the cloth down and looked over at her. Did he suspect she watched him? He hesitated a moment, then walked to the bed and looked down at her. Surely, he knew she was faking. The mattress sagged with his weight and the rough fabric of his pants scrubbed against the thin batiste of her pantalets. She lay out from under the covers in the warm room, bare to his assessment.

Fingers lifted her hair, toying with the strands, much as he'd done that night by the fire. She rolled over and looked up into his eyes. "Hello."

He smiled. "Hello. Sleep well?"

"Uh-huh."

He glanced lower. The thin material of her chemise would do little to hide the pink of her breasts in adequate light. But here in the dawn, she was hidden.

Would he touch her again, cup her flesh with his warm hand? Caress her as she craved him to?

"I'm sorry I intruded. Finnegan's asleep next door and I thought I'd have a quick shave before you woke up. Since there's no water in there."

He was lying. She'd put the water in there herself last night before she went to bed. He was telling an outright lie. Honorable Duncan McLeod. She wanted to grin from ear to ear and bounce on the bed with joy. But given the fact that such unannounced actions would probably frighten him to death, she decided against that course of action. He wanted her and he'd come to see if she wanted him.

And if Gertie's information was correct, Lord, did she want him.

Her desire must have shown on her face, because she knew the moment he changed his mind. The warmth went out of his eyes and his gaze darted away. He started to rise, but she caught his arm.

"Don't go."

He looked down at her fingers coiled around his forearm. "It's wrong, what I'm thinking."

"No, Duncan. It isn't wrong." She tightened her grip.

"These things . . . we've done. A man shouldn't feel this way . . . about a woman he's not pledged to."

His words stung, but she knew he'd not meant them as a slight to her, but to the woman who'd wronged him so long ago.

"Pledged or no, love must come first. She didn't love you, or she'd have never let you go."

He recoiled from her, emotionally and physically, leaning away, straining against the grip she held on his arm.

"Let her go, Duncan."

"You've no right . . . you didn't know her."

Sam sat up, aware that with the increasing light, her chemise hid nothing from his eyes. His reaction was human, she surmised, but his defense of his wife grated on already sensitive nerves. "No, I didn't. But I know you and I know that you'd have loved her with your last breath if she hadn't driven you away." She pulled his arm toward her, hoping the rest of him would follow. "Let me try to fix the parts of you she broke."

She met him halfway across the distance between them and his eyes slid closed as she kissed him. His lips yielded beneath her urging and she swept the interior of his mouth as he'd done hers and wondered if his knees had turned to jelly, too.

He followed her backwards to lie beside her, the odd scent of rose soap clinging to his skin and hair. The old mattress beneath them groaned its disapproval at the added weight.

"I promised myself I'd never lie with another woman when Elizabeth left," he said softly, trailing a finger across her collarbone. "If only lying with them and loving them didn't become so intertwined."

Sam rolled to her side to face him, his breath stirring the tendrils of hair at her temples. "But with you, they're one and the same, aren't they?"

He watched her for a moment, their breaths mingling in the small space between them. "Yes, they are."

Had she become a wanton since leaving home? Had she so completely abandoned her mother's conservative teachings? Or was it lust, pure and simple, that tempted her to cup him and feel him press against her palm as she'd struggled to press against his touch? Or did she just want to see his eyes soften in desire and know that that change was wrought by her hand?

She coasted a finger along his ribcage, taking note of every ridge and hollow, stopping at the waist of his pants. "What do you want, Duncan?"

He rose up on one elbow and leaned over her, driving her to her back to stare up into his face. Her heart began to hammer as he braced a hand on the other side of her head.

"I want you to look at me this way every night, lass. And I want to know that I'm welcome in your arms. But I can't promise you my heart, Sam, because I don't have all the pieces. Don't you see, you can't give away something if you don't have all the pieces."

By the end of the statement that had begun as a seduction, his voice had taken on a note of desperation. He truly wasn't over Elizabeth and maybe he never would be. Their love, however misguided, had produced two children and a bond, whether wrought of love or misery, that apparently stretched halfway around the world.

She captured his still-damp cheeks between her palms. "You'll always be welcome in my arms and in my bed. And I don't care how that sounds, that's what I mean. But it's only big enough for you and me, Duncan. There's no room for Elizabeth."

By the time the rain abated, Eldorado was all but deserted. Those not afflicted with typhoid moved to uninfected settlements and those stricken either recovered or died. Sam left the fifth day after she arrived, riding home to Dawson City on her stolen mule. Constable Harper accompanied her, promising to straighten out the confusion over the mule if the original owner protested. But by the time they reached Dawson, the population had more to worry about than one mule. The epidemic had moved downriver.

Three hospitals established by the Mounted Police were full to bulging with patients. Sam Steele had levied strict guidelines about garbage and human waste disposal. And through it all, stampeders continued to pour into the area and the business of mining gold dust went on uninterrupted.

Sam eased open the door to their shop, allowing sunbeams to skitter in ahead of her. Through the darkroom curtains, she could hear Oscar rattling plates and bottles.

"Oscar?" she called, bracing herself for the scolding she was sure would follow.

He parted the curtains and stepped into the light, wearing the frown she expected.

"So, you're back."

"I'm sorry if you worried."

He shook his head slowly. "Of course I worried, Sam, but then I'm also amazed. You did a courageously unselfish thing."

His sarcasm stung, but she supposed she deserved it.

She dropped her pack onto the floor. "I couldn't let him go alone. I knew if I did, something terrible would happen."

Oscar only nodded his agreement. The door opened and Emily swept in. Oscar smiled and warning bells clanged in Sam's head.

"I've come for my picture," she said softly and bestowed a gracious smile on Sam.

Who was this woman with only a first name who gathered hearts like summer flowers? Was she so unsatisfied with having Duncan's heart that she wanted Oscar's as well? Sam rubbed the spot between her eyes that was beginning to ache.

"Sam, could you help me?" Oscar asked, taking Emily's hand and leading her over to a large, fan-backed chair. Wondering briefly where Oscar had found such a piece of furniture, Sam helped him set up the camera, then watched as he gently positioned Emily's hands, holding her fingers for a second or two longer than necessary.

Oscar was in love.

The same cupid that had clobbered her had apparently done likewise to Oscar, rendering them both sense-less. They were in love with two people who shared an odd attachment to each other. It wasn't a triangle of love, it was a rectangle of misery.

The flash flared, immortalizing Emily's angelic smile and filling the room with cough-inducing sulfur smoke. Oscar switched plates, lovingly repositioned Emily, and ignited the flash again. When he was finally done, she rose from the throne-like chair.

"Sam, could you come to my room tonight?" she asked. "There's something I'd like to speak with you about."

Was she going to ask for Oscar's hand in marriage? Was she going to warn her away from Duncan with thinly veiled threats? Various wild scenarios flashed through Sam's thoughts. "Of course," she answered.

"Come after your performance tonight."

Sam cast a glance at Oscar, but his face held no clues.

CHAPTER ELEVEN

The crowd that looked up at Sam from the edge of the stage was sparse. Besides an epidemic of typhoid, the Yukon River had overflowed its banks and boats now paddled up and down the streets of Dawson City. Fort Herchmer was flooded and the Mounted Police slept only on the top bunks in their flooded barracks. The whole town was on edge as the death toll mounted; typhoid seemed an unwelcome, permanent guest.

Sam breathed a sigh of relief when she stepped backwards through the curtains to sporadic applause.

"I'm shutting the bar down early," Charlie said, lumbering past. "People ain't doin' nothin' but sittin' and not drinkin'."

Sam stepped out into the summer night and picked her way down the muddy sidewalk to the hotel. In the lobby, Emily waited, her hands demurely crossed over her knees as she perched in a ragged upholstered chair.

"I thought you might try to avoid me," she said, rising as Sam closed the door behind her.

"No. Why would I do that?"

"I can sense that you're nervous about tonight."

Sam tilted her head and took another look at the woman before her. What, exactly, was her game? She seemed to have no ambition, no friends, no plans. She simply drifted from one day to the next. And she also seemed to have some strange hold over Duncan. "I'm curious, not particularly nervous."

Emily delicately lifted her skirts and started up the stairs. "You're a strong woman, a woman who knows her own mind."

"Yes, I believe I am."

"And you are in love with Duncan."

Sam stopped on the first landing. "Look, if this has something to do with Oscar—"

"No," she said, taking Sam's elbow to urge her to continue. "I would rather discuss this in my room."

Emily opened the door and motioned Sam to precede her. Sam stopped dead in her tracks when Duncan raised his head and looked into her eyes. He sat on Emily's bed, elbows on his knees, his hands clasped together. His eyes darkened and he frowned. "What's this about, Emily?"

Sam glanced from one to the other. Had they conceived of this meeting to torture her? Were they going to confess their undying love for each other in front of her? Was Oscar invited, too, so that his heart might be shattered along with hers?

Sam stepped back a step. "Look, I don't know what's going on here, but I can already tell that I want nothing to do with this, so if you'll excuse me." She whirled to leave.

"Sam, please stay. Please," Emily implored. "I can't do this without you here."

She stopped with her hand on the doorknob.

"Duncan needs you."

Sam turned and looked at Duncan, but he was staring up at Emily, a mixture of amazement and anger on his face.

Emily walked over to the table and took a folded envelope from her reticule. She moved to stand in front of him, the letter clutched in her hand. "Duncan, Elizabeth is dead."

Duncan paled visibly and swallowed. He threw Sam a quick glance, then stood and walked to the window. Raising his shoulders, he flexed his back as if a fist had landed between his shoulder blades, then looked down at the floor. "How?"

"Murdered, most likely, by Rob McDonald's hand. The official report says she slipped over a sea cliff and fell to her death."

Duncan didn't stir, didn't signal he'd even heard her words. Sam stood rooted in one spot. How she longed to go to him and slip her arms around his waist, to slide around in front of him and pull his head to her shoulder. But Duncan was not a man easily comforted, she sensed. Especially when the pain was this deep.

He breathed out slowly, loudly, as if he'd held his breath and his chest was about to explode. Sam wanted to be anywhere but here, witness anything but this soul-wrenching blow. Is this why Emily had invited her? Was there some perverse reason she should witness his pain?

"My girls?" he asked softly.

"McDonald's turned them out. Said the last thing he wanted was two brats to raise."

"Where are they?" He turned around, abject misery

in his eyes. Sam took a step forward, drawn to him by some unseen force.

Emily looked deep into his eyes. "They're on their way to you. Here. They'll be in Dawson City by Friday."

"Here?"

She smiled. "Yes, Duncan. They're coming to you."

He shook his head. "How did you know what had happened? How?"

She held out the letter. "Lizzy's written to me since she was old enough to write. It took a long time to convince Sarah to defy her stepfather."

He took the letter with trembling hands and gazed down at the script that looped across the parchment as if it were some rare and priceless document. "You've had contact with my girls. You knew about their childhoods. What they played. What they dreamed. And you never told me. Why?" His voice quivered and Sam wished she could melt into the floor rather than add to his distress. Who was Emily that she could hold such power over him? His mistress?

Emily sat down on the bed in the spot he'd deserted. "We started looking for you ten years ago. Elizabeth didn't live with Rob long before she found out the kind of man he really was. But you'd disappeared into the great American forests and only Fate led me to you this last year."

"Did he strike her?"

"Yes."

Duncan swallowed again. "Did he strike the girls?"

"I don't think so."

He opened the letter and walked over to the window.

"Perhaps I should go," Sam said, edging toward the door.

"No," Emily said with a shake of her head.

Duncan let the arm that held the letter dangle at his side as he stared at his own reflection in the dark glass. "Thank you," he said softly, "for watching after them."

"No one could have convinced Elizabeth that Rob was the man we all knew him to be."

"I certainly couldn't and God knows I tried that morning," he said softly. "I should have written to them, should have tried."

"Rob was a predator, selfishly guarding his victim. He wouldn't have let a single missive of yours into their hands. You know this, Duncan."

He put a hand over his eyes. When he raised his head, he was smiling. "My girls will be here Friday. I wonder what they look like. I only remember them as wee babes."

Emily threw Sam a glance that sent shivers all the way to her toes. Some terrible thing hung in the air. What she'd just heard was nothing to what she was about to hear, she sensed, and the reason she'd been asked here.

"There's something else."

His smiled faded.

Emily rose, took his hands in hers, and gazed up into his face. "About five years ago, there was a fire. In the stables. Sarah was playing there. She was burned."

"How badly?"

Emily rotated his hands until she had them firmly in her grasp. "She can't walk. She lost a leg."

He jerked his hands away and stalked to the window. "Dammit," he swore softly, his voice breaking on the last syllable. Then, he whirled and stalked past them. Sam caught a glimpse of tears on his cheeks as he passed her.

They heard him clomp down the stairs, heard the

door below close. Sam sank into the chair, her energy spent.

"I had hoped he would turn to you," Emily said softly. "He needs someone to love him again."

"And you thought that should be me? I thought he loved you."

Emily laughed. "No, Duncan never loved me. Oh, he thought he did when we met again in Edmonton. He courted me shamelessly with flowers and sweet words and proposals of marriage. But he never loved me."

Sam's head spun and her heart sank. Duncan McLeod was a wounded man, a man whose heart would never be the same, who hoped to replace the woman he'd lost. She could have no future with such a man. Feeling her own tears sting the backs of her eyes, Sam rose to go, wishing for the privacy of her room and a soft pillow to cry into.

"My sister was a whore, a woman who took her passion anyplace she could find it except in the bed of the husband who offered it freely."

"Your sister?"

Emily looked up. "Yes, Elizabeth was my sister."

Sam sat back down.

"Duncan fancied himself in love with me the moment he laid eyes on me again. At first I was flattered and gave his court some consideration," she said with a smile that set Sam's teeth on edge.

"But then I realized that he saw Elizabeth in me, a way to exonerate himself, to prove to her and himself that he was a desirable man and that she was a fool." Emily shook her head sadly. "By that time, Elizabeth was well aware of the mistake she'd made."

"Why didn't she leave this Rob McDonald and find Duncan?"

"The circumstances of their parting were too . . . intimate, too final for her to beg or expect his forgiveness. She knew when she closed the door of their cottage for the last time that she closed the door between their hearts. She was too proud to grovel at his feet . . . as she should have."

Sam stood up again. "I should be going. It's late." She moved toward the door and opened it. Emily put a hand on her forearm.

"If he comes to you, remember all I've said. Take him to your heart, Sam."

"He won't," Sam said with a backward glance. "Now that she's dead and a ghost, he'll never be rid of her."

Incessant pounding awoke Sam. She threw back the quilt, trotted across the cold floor, and opened the door, expecting to see a white-faced Oscar there with news of some disaster. Instead, Duncan stood in the hall, the faint odor of whiskey wafting around him.

"Oh, Lord," she breathed and stepped back to let him in.

"I've had a little too much to drink." He sat down in a chair facing the fire and balanced his hat on his knee.

Sam threw on some wood and coaxed a feeble flame back to life.

"But I'm not drunk."

"No, of course you aren't."

He raked a hand through his thick, dark curls. "I've come to apologize to you." His brogue had thickened with the application of liquor. "We shouldn't have aired our dirty laundry in front of you. I don't know what Emily was thinking, including you."

His words hurt. He hadn't wanted her there, hadn't wanted her comfort or concern. She moved around behind him and sat down on the bed. He didn't turn, continuing to watch the leaping fire.

Why was he really here in her room at midnight? Sam wished that he found her so irresistible he couldn't stay away from her. However, she knew the answer wasn't as simple as that. He was looking for vindication, for assurance that he was still a man and still a man worthy of love. He ran a hand through the back of his hair, disturbing the indentation put there by his hat band.

"Elizabeth's leaving me was . . . a nasty affair," he began, "and one I don't talk about."

"You don't owe me an explanation. I'll pretend I never heard any of it." *And you can go on pretending you don't need anybody.*

He rubbed his fingers back and forth across his forehead. "Maybe you can, lass, but I cannot."

Sam slid off the bed, put on her wrapper, and moved around in front of him. He looked up at her slowly, as if moving his head was painful. She dropped to her knees and rested her arms on his legs. "What do you want to tell me, Duncan? Do you want me to know all the story? Do you want to tell me how she broke your heart and that you haven't been able to put the pieces back together?"

He stared at her with his dark eyes, eyes filled with pain and confusion. Hurt pride and embarrassment. Would she ever be able to work past that hard shell he'd built up around himself, one he crawled out of only when he chose?

"She was my wife," he said as if that explained it all. "The mother of my girls. We'd promised to love each other forever and I intended to keep my end of the deal."

"But she didn't keep hers."

He looked away from her face and back at the fire. "I came home one morning and found her with him. Naked, both of them. Joined. In our bed." His throat worked convulsively. "She'd meant all along to leave with him, she said. She'd only wanted one more time ... with him ... there where we—" His jaw clenched, tightening the skin across his cheek. "She hated me for being a poor man. She'd always wanted more, more than I could give. I gave her children. I gave her a home, food. I gave her my love. But it was never enough."

Sam took his hands in hers. "She left you, Duncan. She made the decision to leave, not you. You take too much guilt upon yourself for this."

"My Sarah's been burned, maimed for life. All because of her ... and him."

The wells of despair in Duncan McLeod's heart were bottomless, Sam thought, looking into his tortured eyes. She wedged herself between his knees and cupped the back of his head with her hand. "If you continue to carry this anger, it will eat you from the inside out," she said, bringing his face closer. "Do you understand?"

Firelight reflected in the centers of his eyes, now grown large and black in the dim light. He leaned forward, then paused, his lips close. Then, he captured her mouth in a rough kiss that gentled when he reached down and hauled her onto his lap.

He was an experienced lover and she was an innocent, but she knew that tonight she would be his teacher.

A big hand cupped her breast, gently squeezing, and he kissed her again, pressing her head back against his forearm. When he lifted his mouth, she slid out of his lap and stood on the small hooked rug in front of his chair. So what if he saw the devious Elizabeth when he looked at her. And so what if his arousal was for a ghost and not her. She'd seduce him, if that's what it took. She'd use the imagination with which she was so generously endowed and make him forget the woman who'd thrust a knife into his heart.

Hadn't she taught herself how to climb an icy mountain and dance erotically before a room full of men? Then she could teach herself how to seduce a man.

She raised her hands to the buttons of her nightgown and undid each one with deliberate slowness, keeping her eyes on his, holding his gaze. When the garment hung open, she slipped it over her shoulders and allowed the soft fabric to drift down, across her waist and over her hips to pool on the floor at her feet. She stood naked before him, the fire heating her from behind and his stare heating her from the front.

"Come to my bed, Duncan, and I'll make you forget." She held out a hand and prayed he wouldn't bolt and run for the door.

He scanned her boldly, taking in every inch, before he leaned over, set his hat on the floor, and stood. He took her hand and rolled her fingers intimately in his. "I have no promises or guarantees to give you."

"I don't care about promises. I know what I feel in my heart and what I see in your eyes."

"Are you sure, Sam? Because if you aren't, say so now."

"I'm sure," she whispered.

He cupped her hips in his hands and pulled her against him, letting her know her efforts had not gone unnoticed, while his teeth nipped tiny ridges on her bare shoulders.

She led him to the side of her bed and worked loose the buckles on his belts. They clattered to the floor and she began on the brass buttons of his tunic. Finally loose, the jacket hung open and Sam circled around him and slid the garment off his shoulders and down his arms, removing it with what she hoped was maddening deliberation. She hung it on one bedpost.

"I've had this daydream for weeks now of seeing your jacket hanging at the foot of my bed," she said as she fingered the buttons of his white shirt. He looked down and smiled for the first time while she undid the tiny circles of pearl and dropped it at her feet.

She slipped her fingertips underneath the waistband of his pants and smiled when his stomach contracted at her touch. He was uncomfortable having her undress him. He felt out of control, off balance. Good, she wanted to keep him that way.

With her thumb, she flicked open the top button of his pants and then each other one in succession. Sliding her hands inside to fan out across his narrow hips, she forced the garment down his legs, skimming his bare skin with the palms of her hands, resisting more intimate touches.

He looked shaken and unsure as she put a hand to his chest and forced him to sit down on the bed. Then she knelt, removed his boots, and pulled his pants off. She padded away to hang her second trophy on the other bedpost. As she turned back toward him, she marveled that six months ago no one could have convinced her she'd be here, in the Yukon, naked as the day she was born, blatantly seducing Inspector Duncan McLeod.

He rose to meet her, confidence restored to his expression. He drew her arms around his waist, pressing against the entire warm, hard length of him. He rested his chin on the top of her head and sighed deeply, as if cleansing his soul. "You're a hard woman not to love," he said into her hair.

He snatched back the quilt, scooped her into his arms, and then laid her in the soft nest of sheets. A hard knee on the mattress made the springs groan and then he was stretched out beside her. Sam had initiated and controlled the seduction to this point, but there was now no doubt who would control the bed.

He leaned over her, one quivering forearm braced beside her ear. His lips captured hers again in a bruising kiss as one hand slid down her hip, across her abdomen to touch the area he'd only teased before.

"Oh," she sighed. "Duncan . . . what?"

"Shhh," he cautioned, trailing kisses down her chest to the crest of her breast which he took in his mouth and tormented with his teeth.

Sam clutched the tops of his shoulders, squeezing, squeezing as fire burned a path down her body to pool in a warm reservoir where his hand rested.

"Love me, Duncan," she begged. "Please, love me now."

"Not yet, lass. You're not ready."

She looked up into his face and saw doubt resurface.

"It's been a long time." He hesitated, struggling with words. "I don't want to disappoint you."

Gertie said to tell a man if it was your first time, Sam remembered.

"I haven't done this before, so . . . I'm not sure what to expect," she finished.

He skimmed fingers through her hair. "Ah, and you're offering pearls before swine, lass."

She gripped his forearm, felt the muscles tremble.

"Don't you say that about the man I love." She smiled up at him. "I love you, Duncan. You and all your ghosts."

His body ached mightily, throbbing with want of the woman beneath him. He couldn't remember ever being this aroused. Never with Elizabeth. Never in any dream or fantasy he might have entertained. And he was sure he wouldn't last two seconds once her softness closed around him.

She said she loved him. Did she? And did he love her in return? The temptation to give her the answer she expected poised on the end of his tongue, but he bit it back. He wouldn't be dishonest with her and right now, he couldn't think at all.

She reached down between them and touched him, nearly sending him over the edge. He jerked away. "No . . . or I'll embarrass the both of us."

She frowned, not understanding, and reached for him again, this time closing her hand around him. He moved over her and she shifted to open herself to him, arched up, driven by some instinct. She was soft and maddeningly eager as skin slid against skin. But he stopped when he reached the barrier of her innocence.

"Gertie says it won't hurt much," she murmured before he could put together a fit comment.

He kissed her gently, looking down into her sweet face, then plunged through the barrier and felt his body explode within her. Deep moans racked his body as spasms of release rippled down his body and into hers. He dropped his head to her chest and wished he could disappear into the mattress.

"It's all right," she whispered, combing through his hair. "It's all right."

He raised his head and looked into her understanding eyes.

"It wasn't supposed to be like that, was it?"

"No," was the only word he could conjure at the moment.

"Is this what you meant when you said it had been a long time?" She locked her ankles behind his back, holding him captive inside her.

His body stirred within her and he tried not to let the surprise show on his face. But she was quick to notice and smiled slowly, like a milk-sated cat. "Can you do it again so quickly?"

"You ask too many questions," he growled, silencing her with a kiss. Lord, how her mind could churn and he could barely remember his name. She hugged him with her body, timed to perfectly coincide with his thrusts. He thought to beg her to stop cooperating, to just lie there before he humiliated himself again.

She was born to love a man, eager and willing to share in the joy. And he knew he'd want more of her now that she'd reawakened him to passion. He'd suffer untold humiliation in her presence, wanting her with an intensity that would strain both his dignity and his patience.

She'd closed her eyes, angling her body to match his. He bracketed her waist and slid his hands up her ribcage, across the mounds of her breasts, up the insides of her arms to entwine his fingers with hers. Pinning her hands to the mattress, he kissed her gently, then quickened his pace to plunge them both over the precipice on which they'd teetered.

She moaned against his lips, a heart-wrenching sound that wrung the last ounce of passion from him before he rolled away from her to lie on his back and wonder if he was dead. Pent-up regret and anger had poured, along with his seed, into her slim body. And for the first time in fifteen years, he breathed a deep, satisfied sigh.

She was on him in a minute, astraddle his hips, her eyes bright, rattling off questions. No virginal aches or regrets for Sam Wilder.

"Oh, Duncan, that was . . . indescribable. Will it be like that every time? Can you do it three times in a row? Did I do things right? How could you tell I was a virgin?"

He clamped a hand over her mouth. "Give a man a chance to find his brains again, lass."

Her eyes softened and her warm tongue flickered out to lick his palm. "I love you," she said when he moved his hand away.

And he did love her. Breathlessly. Endlessly. From this second on, he'd need her with the same desperation as he needed air. But those words. Those binding words so quickly cast away, discarded. An unreasonable suspicion arose in his mind. If he declared his love, it might disappear again, as it had on a misty summer morning long ago.

He closed his eyes, hoping to hide his confusion from her. No such luck.

"You're afraid to tell me, aren't you?" she said, one hand in his hair, her hips threatening to kill him with their enthusiastic wiggling. "Well, you can't fool me any longer. I know you love me, else you wouldn't have done . . . what we just did. You're not a man to take advantage of a woman."

She pried one of his eyelids open with a gentle finger and peered at him with her sparkling blue eyes.

"You don't leave a man any hiding places, do you?"

"Nope," she said with another suggestive wiggle and an impish smile.

"Stop that. I'm an old man and you'll kill me yet."

"No, you're not."

He chuckled and cupped her breasts. "And you're an insatiable young vixen."

"Hmmm. A vixen." Mischief glinted in her eyes.

He tumbled her off him with a gentle shove and sat up on the edge of the bed. Her nails traced paths down his back and he closed his eyes as his skin rippled with sensitivity beneath her touch. Had he been aware he'd missed this so, this intimacy with another being? Complete abandon without structure or confines? No, he'd stored that disappointment away with the rest, this Pandora's mix of emotions that he kept under lock and key inside him. Lust. Anger. Need. Desperation. The deep ache for the touch of another hand. All held at bay.

One of her breasts rested heavily on his arm while she leaned over him, tormenting the shaggy hair over his ear, seemingly fascinated with twirling the ends around her fingers. An old married couple, frolicking in bed on a rainy morning.

The thought was terrifying and shocking in its blatant reality, chasing away the last remnants of his soft, fuzzy joy. Marriage. Commitment. Laying one's soul upon the altar of sacrifice.

He glanced down into her grinning face. A rust smear across her thigh was the only evidence of her lost innocence, a precious gift she'd given willingly. A matching stain arced across his abdomen. He was marked by her, both in body and heart. Making love to a woman with such wild abandon was something he didn't take lightly. But baring one's body and baring one's heart were two very different things.

CHAPTER TWELVE

Duncan wondered how many nights he'd marked with a crackling fire and a lit pipe. He packed tobacco in the bowl and leaned forward to light it with a bit of kindling fished out of the fireplace.

A soft cloud of smoke rose to circle his head and he leaned back in the chair. The night was retreating, driven away by a relentless graying of the sky. Behind him, Sam slept, curled in her bed like a kitten, one shoulder bare, her hip making a smooth curve beneath the colorful quilt.

He'd answered relentless questions about a man's anatomy and the finer points of lovemaking until she fell asleep in mid-question, her head burrowed onto his shoulder. When she was finally silent, he'd admired her by the golden light of the fire. She was so tiny and so wiry. Gutsy. Aggravating. Endearing. And she'd wormed herself a permanent place in his heart. She hadn't asked

again for a confession of love and he adored her for
that. He'd left her bed a few hours ago, put on his pants,
and spent the rest of the sleepless night staring at the
fire.

He'd always made it a point not to dig too deeply
into what he thought. Introspection often led to second
guessing and doubt could get a man killed. But now,
alone with only his pipe and the fire, he was forced to
consider the condition of his heart.

The first layer was covered with guilt. He'd just made
passionate, wild love to a virgin he wasn't married to,
hadn't proposed to nor had spoken to of commitment
or responsibility. They'd come together in this coupling
out of mutual need. Not a fact he was proud of, he
decided, now that his ardor had cooled and a lurking
soreness was setting in. But he wouldn't change the last
few hours for all the fine morals in the world.

Secondly, just how did he feel about the bundle of
questions and unpredictability tempting him from the
tousled bed? He loved her. The answer came with swift
assurance. He couldn't imagine a day, let alone a life,
without her.

Thirdly, just what did he do about these revelations
his mind was uncovering? She could be with child. At
this moment, his baby could be growing inside her. Icy
blood suddenly filled his veins. Funny how those sorts
of truths get pushed to the back of the picture, he told
himself. He took his pipe out of his mouth and a spot
between his eyes began to throb. A baby. A chance to
experience what he'd missed with Lizzy and Sarah. He
smiled down at the carved bowl, scarred and burnt, and
imagined a little Sam running around, all legs and arms
and curiosity. With her mother's beautiful blue eyes.

"You know you love her, old man. What's the matter

with you?" he asked the floor, his elbows propped on his knees.

He glanced over at her, a soft silhouette in the quickly lightening room. Soon, he'd have to find some way to get out of the hotel without being seen, without fueling the gossip fires. And this magical time between them would be over.

The bed was soft and warm as he slipped in beside her, his suspenders catching on the bed frame. He didn't dare take off his pants, else they'd be here come midday. He slid a hand underneath the quilts and felt the silkiness of the warm skin on her bare hip. He caressed the fullness of her buttocks and up along the soft dip of her waist.

"I don't really need the words, you know," she whispered and opened her eyes to stare straight into his. "I can see it in your eyes."

Duncan swallowed, caught off guard by her honesty . . . and her ability to see straight into his heart.

"I'm not the ninny I sometimes appear to be." She caressed his cheek. "I wouldn't have given myself to you if I wasn't sure last night that you loved me. And that I loved you. And that we will each continue to feel this way."

She scooted closer until her head was on his shoulder, her lithe, naked body pressed against his. "I've never been one to subscribe to convention, Duncan. If this is what you can give me, I'll gladly take it with no questions asked. And if something else should come of our time here," she paused, pinning him with a sincere gaze, "we will deal with that if and when the time comes."

Her logic, devoid of hysterics or regrets, was nearly as shattering as her surprising passion had been last night. In a matter of seconds, she had his pants off. The sun was full up and the floorboards in the hall groaned with passing guests as she teased him to arousal.

Duncan sat up in bed and she scrambled onto his lap, wrapping her legs around his waist. He lifted her hips and impaled her, surprised at both his own prowess and her stamina.

"Oh, God, Duncan," she said, leaning her forehead against his shoulder. "Can we do it like this?"

"Yes, lass. We can," he breathed into her hair.

"Sam?" Oscar's voice came at the door, accompanied by a sharp rap. "Are you all right?"

Sam put a hand over Duncan's mouth. "I'll be along in a bit. I'm not feeling too well this morning." Then she stifled her own giggle with her other hand.

"It's not typhoid, is it? Do you have a fever?"

"No, I don't have a fever."

"You're giving me one," Duncan whispered into her hair, intrigue heightening his passion.

"Well, I'll run along then. Should I look for you at the shop later?"

"Yes, Oscar. I'll be along later."

His steps receded. Duncan lifted Sam a little higher and pushed her down on him deeper until they both found release, she with her head thrown back in undisguised ecstasy and he with his face buried in her neck.

The morning sun was warm on them as they lay, sated. "You're so beautiful," she said, accompanied by one of her beaming smiles.

The heat of a flush crept up his neck and set fire to his cheeks as she chuckled softly. "You're blushing. Has no one ever told you you were beautiful?"

"I feel like a damned fool, blushing at my age." He rolled over onto his back and put an arm across his eyes. "And no, no one's ever told me that."

"Well, I shall. And often."

"You're set on torturing me, aren't you?"

Warm fingertips spider-walked down his arm. "It'll never be just exactly like this again, will it?" she asked quietly.

"I suppose not exactly like this." He turned his head so one eye peeked out. What was she about now?

Duncan watched her face, knowing the assurance she wanted, the guarantee she deserved. But he couldn't promise her a future. Not yet. Not until his daughters arrived and he convinced himself he could live with the tragedy of their lives.

"Tom, why did Inspector McLeod leave here with an armload of firewood?" Oscar propped a foot on the bottom edge of a crate and glared across the counter at the hotel clerk, as he stuffed a sandwich in his mouth.

"I dunno," Tom muttered. "He said something about it being green wood and likely to start a fire. Said he'd bring back some seasoned wood in its place."

"Hmm. And how did he know about this wood?"

Tom swallowed and for an instant Oscar thought he'd choke on the huge bite, but it slowly drifted down his skinny neck. He shrugged. "Beats me. All's I saw was him coming down this morning toting the wood."

Oscar pushed away from the counter, a mixture of emotions swirling in the pit of his stomach. Sam had come into the shop looking disheveled and distracted, her lips swollen and pink. An hour later, Inspector McLeod left the hotel, his arms full of perfectly good firewood. A cover for mischief if he ever saw one, Oscar thought. He'd thought Sam's voice sounded a little odd from behind her room door this morning.

They'd spent the night together. That was the only logical explanation. Oscar stepped out into the street and toed a pile of dried horse manure, sending it scattering in all directions. Well, he wasn't sure how he felt about that. It was sinful, of course, but he'd had the same thought himself a time or two. And when was it a sin anyway? At the thinking or at the doing?

Sam could get pregnant and God bless the child whose mother was Sam Wilder. He smiled, imagining a little Sam. Yes, God bless her. She'd be beautiful and exotic and rare. And tough and tenacious and aggravating. Just like her mother. And Sam would be an outcast. Would McLeod own up to his responsibility if Sam conceived?

He wondered, as he scuffed back to his shop, if he should say anything to Sam. Should he confront her? After all, he'd been her conscience for years. Or was this territory too private? A matter too deep to be reasoned with words. Yes, he believed it was.

The tiny bell over the door tinkled as he walked in and Sam jumped.

"Oscar, you scared the wits out of me." She swiped a hand across her forehead and tried to concentrate on the paper in front of her.

"You're jumpy today." He waited for her answer.

After a pause, she slanted him a glance. "So?"

"It's just not like you, that's all."

Sam put down her quill and turned toward him. "Out with it, Oscar."

"Did you sleep with Inspector McLeod?" The words had just rushed out, uncensored. He recoiled from his own brashness and wished he could call them back.

Sam's expression didn't change . . . either for the better or the worse. "Yes, I did."

He hadn't expected so honest an answer and the words washed over him like a swift wind.

"I love him." She picked up the quill and turned it, thoroughly inking her fingers. "I know all the things you're going to say." She raised her face. "But I love him, Oscar. And last night might be the only piece of him I ever have."

The anger and resentment Oscar expected to feel didn't materialize, only a sad compassion for her obvious pain. And as he stared at her, he realized they had become two different people since leaving San Francisco. Two mature, seasoned people. Soulmates, bound in friendship. "You want him to love you and he can't."

She shrugged one shoulder. "He loves me, he just can't admit it. Not out loud, anyway. Not with words. And I told him I didn't care about confessions."

And at that moment, Oscar realized Sam would never be his, that his path was destined to take a very different turn.

The bell over the door tinkled again and two muddy men stomped inside.

"May I help you?" Oscar asked.

"Yeah. I'm looking for the newspaper lady that come up from San Francisco."

Sam slid off her stool. "That's me."

The men glanced at each other. "Could we talk to you in private?"

Oscar frowned, but Sam ushered the two men to the far corner of the store. "Now, what can I do for you?" she asked.

"We heard you was looking for information on gold getting stold from the Mountie fort."

Sam looked from one to the other. How could they have known that? "And what if I am?"

"Well, we got what you want."

"Where did you hear about me?"

"We heared it in Charlie's last night."

Who had she told? Gertie. She'd vaguely questioned Gertie about any rumored gold thefts.

"What's your price?"

"What's it worth to you?"

What was information damaging enough to ruin lives and reputations worth? And did she even want it anymore? Kiss by kiss, she'd lost sight of her goal here in the Yukon. She had no job to go home to, no sure future here. The doubts she'd kept at bay all night surged out to envelope her.

"Twenty-five dollars."

"Make it fifty."

"Thirty-five."

The men exchanged glances again. "Done."

Sam walked back over to her desk and pulled her reticule out from beneath the counter.

"What are you doing?" Oscar asked with a frown.

"They know something about the missing gold," she said as she rummaged for the money.

Oscar clamped a firm grip on her upper arm. "You don't even know if any gold *is* missing."

She dumped the entire bag out on the desktop and scraped through the articles until she found the money. "This is the chance we've been waiting for." She gripped the gold coins in her palm.

"How do you know they're not lying?"

"I don't, but I'm willing to take the gamble."

"Don't do this, Sam. You're going to regret it." He squeezed her arm. "Please, Sam."

She pulled her arm away. "I came here for a story

and here it sits. I'm not going to pass up the chance to
finish what I started."

Oscar glared down at her. "What's happened? A few
minutes ago . . ."

"This has nothing to do with Duncan."

"Are you sure?"

A niggle of doubt wormed its way into her confidence.
"What do you mean?"

Oscar looked over her head to the morning traffic in
the street. "Sometimes the things we love won't bear
up to close scrutiny . . . in the light of reality, so to
speak."

Sam narrowed her eyes. "Do you know something
you're not telling me?"

"No, but just how deep do you want to look into a
man like McLeod, a man with a tragic past and lost
years behind him? Let things lie, Sam, and take the man
for what he is today."

"Duncan would never do anything wrong. This is just
a story, a very important story. One that guarantees me
a future in the newspaper business."

But as she walked back toward the two men, an uneasi-
ness chased away her contentment.

The steamer *Victoria* nudged the Aurora dock,
belching thick columns of black smoke as its paddle
wheel churned the gray water. Dawn and an overnight
rain had thrown a pristine sheen of moisture over everything, hesitant droplets quivering in the morning sun.

Duncan swallowed and ran his moist palms down the
legs of his blue uniform pants, his calluses catching on
the yellow stripe. Deck hands wrestled a gangplank out
and dropped it onto the shore right at his feet.

"Pardon, Constable," the man said and hurried back onto the ship.

Soon, passengers began to pour off, their baggage in hand. Somewhere among the crowd were his girls, now nearly grown women. He wondered what they looked like, having only his image of them as sleeping babies. Emily had insisted he meet them alone, assuring him they would recognize him, but he suspected their only clue to identity would be his scarlet jacket.

A dark-haired young woman walked to the edge of the gangplank and looked out over the crowd. Duncan held his breath and started to raise a hand when a young man in a threadbare suit dashed across the plank and swept her into his arms.

Duncan released a shaky breath, closed his eyes, and shook his head. "Damn," he swore in a whisper.

"I beg your pardon."

He looked up into eyes he knew so well—his eyes.

"Would you be Duncan McLeod?"

She was tall and lithe, delicately graceful. Dark waves of hair were held in check by neat, silver combs.

"Lizzy?" He barely forced the word past the boulder in his throat. Blinking, he drew in a quick breath as his last image of her flooded his mind. A dark cherub child, asleep in her bed, a thumb in her mouth, her skin smooth and alabaster. Innocent wisps of hair fluttering with her gentle breaths.

A moment of insecurity flashed through those eyes, eyes harder and more worldly than they should be at sixteen. Was she suffering the same shock as he? Did she see herself mirrored in him?

"I'm pleased to meet you," she said, extending a slender hand.

He gripped her hand, wishing he could draw her into

his arms. She'd been so soft as a baby, soft and warm nestled in his arms. Slowly, she extracted her hand.

"You look exactly as Aunt Emily said you would."

"I do?"

She nodded. "Precisely. She did an excellent job of describing you."

So cold. So . . . old. Where was the bubbling personality he remembered? Where was the exuberance of youth? Beaten down by abuse? He wouldn't let himself think that. If he did, he'd be on the next ship to Scotland to kill the bastard McDonald like he should have done fifteen years ago.

"Where is Sarah?" he asked, struggling for every word.

Lizzy turned away and he fought the urge to grab her arm and haul her back, never to let her leave his sight again. She returned in a few minutes, pushing a wheelchair.

Sarah was as light as Lizzy was dark, with eyes the shade of a Scottish sky—her mother's eyes—and hair the color of the sun. She'd only been a babe that last day, asleep with the remains of her mother's milk circled on her pink mouth. His gaze dropped to her legs. One small foot in a buttoned-up shoe stuck out from under her skirts. Quick, hot tears stung his eyes and tightened his throat.

He leaned down, but Sarah was even less enthusiastic with her greeting, giving him a small, polite hug. "Hello, Father."

Lizzy scanned the crowd, clutching her wrap around her shoulders. "Where is Aunt Emily?"

Duncan moved behind the chair, but Sarah leaned back and stopped him with a hand on his arm. "Lizzy does that."

He backed away and tried not to let the admonition hurt. After all, he reminded himself, he was a stranger to them, the man who'd left them behind to endure Rob McDonald. "She's waiting for us at the hotel."

"Are we going to stay at a hotel, Lizzy?" Sarah asked her sister, ignoring him.

"Yes, that's what Aunt Emily said."

"This place smells funny," Sarah said as they reached the main street. Deep, muddy ruts slashed the length of the street. Cursing his lack of thought, Duncan wondered how on earth he was going to get the chair across.

Lizzy watched him with an aloof air—measuring, judging his fitness as a father, he imagined. Why hadn't he thought of this particular detail during his sleepless hours last night?

"Good morning, Inspector McLeod," Sam's sweet voice called from across the street.

She stood holding the handle of a pushcart filled with boxes, two wide planks laying at her side. "I was just about to lay myself a path over to Boswell's store so I could roll this cart. Would you be so kind as to help me manage this? And then we can both stay out of the mud."

He could have kissed her right there—if he could have reached her. Obviously, she'd seen his plight from her studio a few doors down and decided to rescue both him and his pride.

"Of course," he responded, stepping down into the muddy street.

Duncan laid the wide boards across the worst of the ruts and wheeled Sam's cart across first. "There's not a damned thing in these boxes," he whispered as he pulled the cart onto the makeshift bridge.

"I know. But it worked, didn't it?"

He pulled her cart up beside the wheelchair and Sam smiled down at his children. "And who are these lovely ladies?"

Lizzy and Sarah stared back at her with guarded expressions. "These are my daughters, Lizzy and Sarah. This is Miss Samantha Wilder. She's a writer and a photographer."

"I'm very pleased to meet you." She shook each one's hand. "What do you think of Dawson City so far?"

"It smells bad," Sarah said.

"It's dirty," Lizzy responded.

"Well, you must have your father bring you to my studio sometime. My friend and I have lots of pictures of the gold fields and the miners."

"Our stepfather said only gluttons would give up their homes and families to look for gold and that gluttony is a sin." Lizzy tipped up her chin and threw Duncan a look that begged him to challenge her.

Duncan shook off a shudder of anger. "Many of the people that come here have nothing in life except the pursuit of a better future."

"Then perhaps they should have put their faith in the Bible instead of worldly riches." Her eyes, so like her mother's, flashed open hostility, baiting him.

Duncan took a deep breath, aware that Sam watched him with concerned eyes, puzzled at the venom in Lizzy's words. "Perhaps we are both right, then," he said, hoping to quell an argument.

"I have to be on my way," Sam interjected. "Maybe you can come by sometime and see my pictures anyway."

"Of course we can. Thank you for the invitation, Miss Wilder," he said, hoping his eyes conveyed the depth of his gratitude.

Lizzy started forward with the wheelchair, carefully positioning the wheels onto the boards.

"They're beautiful, Duncan. I can see you in them."

"You can?"

She chuckled softly and took the handle of her cart away from him. "Now go on along so they won't see me wrestle this cart back across the street in a few minutes."

Duncan led Lizzy and Sarah down the sidewalk to the hotel where Sam and Oscar also had rooms. He'd taken two rooms there himself until he could figure out what to do. The girls certainly couldn't stay with him at Fort Herchmer. This had all happened so suddenly, he hadn't had time to sit down with Superintendent Sam Steele and work out the details.

Emily was waiting for them in the lobby. Even though they'd exchanged letters for years, she and her nieces had never met. As they hugged and conversed, he was glad for the opportunity to step back and watch them all, to allow his mind to come to grips with the fact that Sarah was the image of her mother.

Hair, blond and fine, lay in golden coils around her head. Her eyes were the shade of a stormy sea, huge in a narrow, delicate face. Old, painful memories rose, but he quickly pushed them away. That part of his life was over. Over and done. He had two beautiful daughters to get to know and a warm, passionate woman to learn to love. There was no more room for regrets.

"What do you mean you're going to Lake Bennett for a month?"

Emily carefully pulled on her white gloves and picked up her carpetbag. "I have a month-long singing engagement in a saloon there."

"And you're just going to leave me here with the girls?" Duncan stood in front of her door, blocking her exit, all the while thinking how ridiculous he was behaving. After all, they were *his* daughters. But the thought of being solely responsible for two near-women he hardly knew in a town like Dawson City ... "You can't leave me, Emily. You got me into this."

Emily laughed and stepped up to him. "You got yourself into this, Duncan McLeod. They're *your* children. They're not dangerous criminals or savage Indians. They're almost grown women."

"That's the part that worries me. I don't know anything about daughters, Emily."

She pushed him out of the way, then patted his shoulder and smiled. "If you get into trouble, go get Sam."

"Sam? What does she know about children?"

"Probably very little. But I'd wager she knows a lot about being a young woman."

Emily opened the door, then paused and turned to face him. "Sam's good for you, Duncan. You're a different man since you've let her love you."

He wondered at her usage of the word *love*. Did she mean emotionally or physically? And did she know that their love was about as physical as it could get?

"I don't know what to say to them, how to treat them. So much time has passed."

"They're wonderful, generous children, Duncan. And you're a compassionate, kind man. You'll learn to love each other. Just be their father. And remember, children can sense dishonesty."

"You're leaving me with them on purpose, aren't you?"

Emily smiled. "This is for your own good." She set down her bag and touched his arm. "Remember that

Elizabeth was all they had to cling to, however pitiful a
comfort that might have been. She was their mother
and they had no memories of you at all. I've tried to
make you come alive in my letters, but now the fleshing
out of the real Duncan McLeod is up to you. This is
one battle you're going to have to fight on your own.''

CHAPTER THIRTEEN

Evening mist swirled up from the Yukon River, filling the aspen grove with a ground-hugging fog.

"Are we almost there?" Sam whispered, eyeing her companion.

"Yep, almost there." Wilton Adcox pulled back a low-hanging branch and held it for her to duck underneath. Then he motioned her to the side and indicated that she should hide in a thick grove of young spruce and aspen seedlings.

The soft slap, slap of oars broke the reverie of the still night. Somewhere beyond the curtain of fog, a boat keel scraped on river-tumbled rocks, then beached. Soft footfalls, cushioned by the damp leaf litter, moved past them. Mumbled greetings were followed by a brief conversation.

Sam peeped out from behind her curtain of foliage. Two men stood near the river's edge, ghost-like in the thick fog, face-to-face, engaged in conversation. They were dressed in ordinary clothes—nondescript shirts, jackets, and pants—nothing to identify them as Mounties. On the ground lay several bags, suspiciously like the ones she'd seen in the Fort Herchmer storehouse.

She squinted in the murk, hoping to make out a face. What if it was Duncan? The thought made her draw back. Did she want to know if it was? Of course she did. She was after the truth. Wasn't she?

"How do you know they're Mounties?" she whispered. "They could be anybody."

"They're Mounties, all right. They ain't gonna wear them scarlet jackets when they don't want to be seen," Wilton added.

Something thudded hollowly, echoing against the river bank. She peeped back around the tree. They were loading the bags into the boat. Rocks scraped again as the boat moved from its mooring and disappeared into the fog.

She waited, crouched, until the footsteps passed her by in the opposite direction, fading into the distance.

"They come here two, three times a week," Wilton whispered. "Boat comes up the river, they load it up, and it's gone."

"What do you think they're doing with it?"

"Stealing it, a'course."

"I know that, but why?" Part of her thrilled to have her long-held suspicions verified, but another part of her quaked. Did Duncan have anything to do with this? And if he did, what would she do with the information?

They made their way out of the woods and back to the muddy, rutted road that lead to Dawson City. Oscar and Duncan would be fit to be tied if they knew she was tramping around in dark woods with the likes of Wilton Adcox.

"What are you gonna do now?" Wilton asked as they trudged down the worn road.

"I'm going to gather more information before I do anything."

"How much more proof you gotta have?" he asked, a note of irritation in his voice that set a warning bell to ringing in her head.

"A good reporter never writes an exposé based on one incident."

"Writes a what?"

"An exposé. An article the exposes a wrong."

"So how many more incidents do you need?"

She slanted a glance at her companion and wondered just what he was getting out of helping her. Adcox wasn't the kind of man to help out of the kindness of his heart. He was up to something, all right, but he also knew the right kind of carrot to dangle in front of her.

"You leave the sleuthing to me and just keep your eyes open."

Duncan laid aside his fork, steepled his fingers, and surrendered to the knot in his stomach. Across the tiny table, Lizzy picked at the plain meal of beef and potatoes. Surely the ordinary fare paled in comparison to the meals Rob McDonald's kitchen had produced, he thought with a twist of bitterness.

"Do you not like the beef? I could order you something else," he offered.

Lizzy looked up, a haunting sadness in her eyes, eyes that looked into his soul and wrested out a carefully packaged pain he'd thought he'd put to rest. "It's fine. I'm just not hungry is all."

Sarah was doing little better, chasing an errant potato with her fork, making little effort to catch it. He wanted to ask them a thousand questions, to extract every detail of their lives since the morning they were snatched away from him. But there was a wall between them, a wall of time and anger and misunderstanding only patience could tear down.

"Why didn't you come back for us?" Lizzy asked abruptly and laid down her fork.

Duncan glanced around the cafe at the scattered diners, hardly the place he wanted to pour out his heart. He had no easy answers. "I wanted to, very much." He looked down at his plate, not seeing the uneaten food, seeing instead a sunlit morning when the world wobbled off its axis and spun off into madness. "Rob McDonald was a powerful man and your mother was set on having him. I was young and intimidated by McDonald's influence." Duncan shrugged and looked up into Lizzy's face. "I was a coward."

"Yes, you were," she said without either compassion or anger. "Mother said you were."

Duncan slid his eyes closed and absorbed the blow. Only a fool would stage an argument with a dead woman, and with her death, Elizabeth had become all-powerful in Lizzy's eyes.

"You want to know about her, don't you?" Lizzy folded her napkin and laid it in her lap, followed by her clasped hands.

Weeping inside for his daughters' lost childhood, Duncan swallowed and braced himself for the double brunt of pain. "Do you want to tell me?"

She studied his face and he forced his eyes not to glance away under her scrutiny. "Yes."

Sarah looked at her sister, her eyes wide, as if she'd broached some unspoken agreement between them.

"She talked about you a lot." Lizzy squinted her eyes, studying him. "She said she'd been a fool to ever leave you."

Duncan fought to keep the surprise out of his eyes.

"She told us all about you even before Aunt Emily started writing to us. She always said that someday you'd come and get us."

Regret surged through him. Had they waited then, imagining him coming to their rescue?

"But I knew you wouldn't."

The words, dipped in delicate, deadly poison, lodged in his heart. "And how did you know that?"

"Because you're smart enough to know that Rob would have had you killed if you'd set foot on his property."

A sixteen-year-old body harboring a fifty-year-old soul, Lizzy gazed at him with an eerie, accepting calm. Duncan looked away, down at the checked figures on the tablecloth, and tried to make some sense of this duality of anger in Lizzy.

"Mama always said we'd have to come and live with you one day. She said that one day Rob would get angry enough to kill her."

"Is that what happened?" He expected blinding fury to rise up and engulf him, but he felt only regret, regret at a life wasted.

Lizzy shrugged. "No one knows or ever will. It will always remain between them."

And with that statement, Duncan shrugged off Elizabeth McLeod's ghost. She would live on in her daughters but no more in his heart. Past was past and done was done. His babies were here, safe with him. Now the task that lay before him was to restore their youth to them.

"Tell me about yourselves," he asked, shifting the conversation.

They glanced at each other, secrets he could only wonder at passing between them.

"What do you like to do? Where have you been?"

The anger in Lizzy's eyes mellowed into sadness before she fixed him with her sedate stare. "Rob wouldn't allow us off his estate. Mother insisted that we have a tutor and we did sometimes."

"I rode a horse once," Sarah offered, her eyes brightening for a moment.

How, then, had these two children spent their childhood? How had they passed fifteen years without knowledge or passion or wonderment? A cold hand closed around his heart at the imagined empty hours and the slow, methodical smothering of imagination.

"Did you read?" At least Elizabeth had seen to their education and their world would have been broadened by the printed word. Books would have furnished some escape.

"There were no books in the McDonald house, except the Bible. Rob burned them all," Lizzy said in her maddeningly calm voice. "As he should have," she finished. "They were full of sinful things."

An invisible fist punched Duncan in the stomach and he almost coughed with the blow. Was McDonald a madman, then? Had he treated them like hostages or prisoners?

"Why would he burn the books?"

Again, the sisters exchanged looks. "We had a book

once," Lizzy said. "Mother found it in the attic and brought it to us. It was a book of plays by a Mr. Shakespeare, she said. We took it down to the edge of the stream where we could hide. We found a story about two young people in love. Sarah was Juliet and I was Romeo. We read the parts and acted it out, but Rob had followed us and saw what we did. He said we were horrid, sinful girls and the devil would take us for sure. That night he burned every book in the house. I can see now that he was right."

"It was such an awful big fire," Sarah chimed in. "The whole courtyard was ablaze."

Cold, sinking horror filled Duncan. Elizabeth had taken to bed the very devil himself, a monster whose mind was full of the demons he feared. Stomach roiling, Duncan eased back in his chair. His first thought was to take the next steamer out of the Yukon and slaughter McDonald in the fashion he deserved. But his responsibility now was to undo the damage done to his daughters. He hadn't followed Elizabeth that day. He hadn't stormed the gates of the McDonald fortress and demanded his children back. In his pain and shock, he'd allowed Elizabeth her freedom.

"It wasn't so very awful there," Lizzy said. "Sometimes Rob was gone for months and then we had wonderful times with Mother."

What was this strange duality in his daughters, this ill-placed loyalty for the man who'd stepped into his place? Did they feel some gratitude to the bastard for his support? Or, in their childhood guilelessness, had they grasped at any man to call Father? Even one that apparently abused them?

"Was he . . . cruel to your mother?"

Sarah jerked a tattling glance at her sister, a glance

filled with fear and dread, but Lizzy maintained the cold shell she'd built and met his eyes steadily, relaying silent information she should have been too young to know. "Rob was a man used to getting his way." She chose her words carefully. "He didn't like to be challenged."

Her eyes said she'd been witness to more than she should, knowledgeable of things about her mother no child should know. He glanced at Sarah. Her eyes were wide and dark and the possibilities of what they might have seen rioted through his mind in a succession of increasing eroticism.

"Will we live here with you now or do you intend to send us off to school?" Lizzy asked.

I'll never let you out of my sight again. "Yes, you'll live here with me. I haven't worked out the details with my superintendent, but eventually we'll have a home of our own."

There were a thousand questions in their eyes. They barely knew him, knew nothing of his habits or personality. The only man they'd ever known had robbed them of their childhood. Perhaps he *should* send them off to school, try to provide them with the education they'd missed. But as soon as the thought took form, his heart discounted it. Their place was at his side. Formal schooling would have to take second place to learning how to take joy in living.

Sarah returned to tormenting the potato. "Is Miss Wilder a good friend of yours?"

So, the feminine intuition was working perfectly. "Yes, she's a friend."

The girls glanced at each other again, another chapter in this silent conversation going on between them.

"She seems very nice," Lizzy said.

"Yes, she is."

"Do you have a wife?"

The question nearly jolted him out of his chair and he realized he'd told them none of the basics of his life. What other misconceptions did they harbor about him? Had their tender minds conjured a female Rob McDonald, a wicked stepmother to haunt their lives? "No. I've never remarried."

"Are you thinking about marrying Miss Wilder?" Sarah blurted despite a dark, warning glance from her sister.

Duncan allowed the question to slither over and around him to lodge in his heart. "No. She's just a friend." So, he'd taken to lying, too. Somehow, at this moment, he couldn't confess his complex feeling for Sam, couldn't let them know there was a competitor for his time and attention. That could come later.

Lizzy looked up at him from beneath dark lashes and he knew at that moment that she knew far more about the intimate side of life than any sixteen-year-old should.

In the early morning stillness, Sam crept down the hall, cringing with every floor board that protested softly under her bare feet. She passed Oscar's door safely and three more, including Duncan's daughters', until she reached his. A polished number 7 hung crookedly on the dark wood. Her fingers gripped the brass doorknob and she hesitated, seized with an inopportune attack of conscience.

She was going to seduce him again. No manner of lies she could concoct for her own peace of mind would cover that intent. She wanted him with an intensity that was frightening and distracting, robbing her thoughts and disturbing her nights. And no matter how she dressed it up, there it was in its naked glory.

He hadn't come to her, hadn't asked for her hand on bended knee. He hadn't said he loved her, hadn't forced himself to formulate the words. He hadn't even said he wanted her. But she knew he did. And she knew he needed her now, maybe more than he'd ever need her again. Emily's prophetic words drifted out of the recesses of her mind.

The knob turned easily in her hand and the door swung open, surprisingly unlocked. Pausing to let her eyes adjust to the darkness, she stopped just inside the door and the sweet odor of pipe smoke surrounded her.

He was silhouetted against the moonlit window, sitting in a chair, his sock-clad feet propped up on the windowsill. The outline of the briarwood pipe held in his teeth lay stark against the outline of a rising moon.

"Close the door, lass," he said softly without turning around.

She let the door click shut and padded across the floor to his side. Still, he didn't look away from his observation of moonrise.

"You shouldn't come here, Sam."

She laid a hand on his arm, longing to run her fingertips through the dark fur on his bare chest. He flinched almost imperceptibly under her touch, as if he'd been expecting and dreading the contact.

"I was worried about you . . . and your daughters."

He took the pipe out of his mouth and brought his feet to the floor, interrupting the solid yellow line the stripe on his pants formed in the semi-darkness. Half-turning, he looked up into her face. "You've come for more than that."

She stared into his eyes. "Yes."

He leaned over and laid his pipe on the floor. Then he cupped an arm around her hips and pulled her onto his lap. "You've come to corrupt what's left of my morals, haven't you?"

She smiled at the sparkle in his eyes. "Yes, indeed."

He snugged her shoulder and cheek against his chest and propped his feet up again, cradling her in his lap like a child.

"Have you ever sat and regarded the wonder of the moon?" he said, his breath brushing against her temple while one hand cupped her breast, lazily stroking as if they'd sat like this every night for years.

"No, I suppose not," she replied and ran her fingers through the hair above his ear.

He captured the errant hand, kissed her fingertips, then rolled her slim fingers with his large, blunted ones. "Neither have my girls. And they've never been held in someone's arms, safe and warm."

There was an odd quiver to his voice and a quickening of his breathing. Her own pulse increased. What horrors had his daughters brought him? What ghosts to haunt his guilt-laden heart?

"He denied them the simple pleasures of childhood. Kept them locked away. Abused Elizabeth for them to—" He stopped and swallowed. The fingers that held hers trembled slightly.

He was fighting for control, both of himself and his life. She couldn't offer him advice. She had none. She could only offer him love.

She wiggled upright and buried her face against his neck, inhaling the muskiness of his hair and the clinging odor of his tobacco.

His hand wandered down to cup her bottom and pull her hip tighter against him.

"I should have gone after them."

The whispered statement hung in the air, pregnant with regret.

Sam waited for him to continue, but he didn't, his chest rising and falling erratically. "Whether you should have or not, Duncan, you didn't. What's past is past. You have them here with you now. You can start fresh." She rubbed her cheek against the prominent rise of his chest and his grip on her tightened.

He leaned his forehead against her, burying his face in her hair, his throat working convulsively. "I love you, Sam."

Fear and anguish had wrested the confession from him. Sam leaned away and cupped his cheeks in her hands. The calm facade he wore as easily as he wore his scarlet uniform had disappeared from his eyes. Instead, fear and unrequited desire resided there.

"And you know that I love you," she said with a smile.

He blinked as if in surprise. "You say that so easily."

She examined his eyes again. He didn't think he was worthy. "It is easy. I love you and that's that."

She'd expected a smile and got none. "Do you want me to say that I love you despite the mistakes you've made? Despite the fact you allowed a madman to raise your children?"

He flinched and turned his head. She caressed his whiskered cheek and turned his head back to face her. "Do you want someone to forgive you? Then, I do. I forgive you for being young and inexperienced and addled by hurt."

"I should have gone after them," he whispered in a

choked voice. "I should have moved heaven and hell to get to them."

"But you didn't."

"No."

"Are you going to punish them and yourself for the rest of your lives for that mistake? Do penance until you're an old man?"

He looked away, out the window to the watchful moon. "There's not enough penance in the world to return what's been taken away from them."

"No, there's not. The only thing you can give them is yourself. They don't care about the past, Duncan, not in the way you think. They only care about the future and getting to know the wonderful man their father is."

They sat in companionable silence for a time and watched the moon take dominion over the sky. Then, Duncan shifted her in his arms, holding her as if she were a child, smiling down at her.

"How did you get to be so wise?"

"I'm not so wise. I just make a lot of mistakes. If I hadn't learned to forgive myself, I'd have gone crazy with guilt long ago."

He smiled and brushed away a strand of her hair. Then his hand wandered down the length of her cotton gown and slipped beneath. "Tell me why you came here tonight."

"Because I want you to make love to me."

He knew why she came, yet he needed to hear the words, needed affirmation that she desired him. He kissed her, a light brush that hinted at hidden and barely controlled passion. "When you do tell the truth, you're brutally honest, aren't you?"

His hand, warm, broad, rough, found her sensitive area and stroked her. She gasped and looked up at him.

"Surprised?"

"No . . . I mean, yes." She closed her eyes. What he was doing to her had to be illegal . . . or something. She'd never have imagined a man's hands could give so much pleasure.

"You're a curse on my morals, Sam Wilder."

Her body seemed to have a mind of its own, arching to meet his touch, aching to be filled by him.

"I want you . . . inside me," she gasped, gripping his shoulders, all her attention and thoughts seemingly concentrated on the motion of his hand.

"This will have to do, love," he whispered. "If I go inside you tonight, I'll get you with child. Don't ask me how I know, I just do. I won't have you disgraced, and yet, God help me, I can't stay away from you."

She shifted in his arms, desperate to touch him, to give him the same pleasure, but he clamped his arms down and kept her from turning.

"No, love. Don't touch me."

Weak with the passion climbing within her, she fought to put together an argument and couldn't. His mouth covered hers and his touches quickened. Shards of light and joy exploded within her and he swallowed her moans with his eloquent kiss.

She drifted back down and opened her eyes. He stared down at her, unveiled hunger in his gaze. "I want another child, Sam. A baby. With you. Marry me, Sam."

She wriggled to sit up and he moaned as she brushed against his arousal. "Oh, Duncan. Yes, of course, yes."

"But not now."

Sam stared up at him, her joy dampened. "Why?"

He set her gently on her feet, rose, and stepped to the window where moonlight bathed his bare shoulders. "Because I'm asking you to be a mother to two daughters nearly your own age, two daughters I barely know. And they deserve to have all of me for a time. And I can't tell you for how long."

She couldn't argue with his reasoning, nor the fairness of his statement. Lizzy and Sarah *did* deserve his undivided attention. And to bring a new wife into their already tenuous relationship might further distance them from their father. Duncan was right, but that fact did nothing to quell the disappointment edging through her.

She wanted his name and a place in his bed more than anything—a surprising truth given that had been the very thing that she'd run away from. But most of all she wanted the unfettered intimacy they'd shared before. Naked bodies and naked souls, joined. No excuses. No false pride. No lies.

"The answer is still yes." She came up behind him and wrapped her arms around him, resisting the temptation to touch him more intimately.

"Aren't you going to kiss me to seal the bargain?" she said, circling to face him.

He brushed her lips with a chaste kiss and she feigned an exaggerated pout.

"That'll have to do, lass. I've taken enough from you already."

"You took nothing. I may have been a virgin, but I wasn't a stupid one. I knew what I was doing." She tipped her head. "But if your mind is made up . . ."

"It is."

She smiled at him. "Then I'll spend my time planning our wedding night."

CHAPTER
FOURTEEN

Intrigued by the crowd gathered outside Brown's Mercantile, Sam paused in her trip to work to wiggle through the bodies until she stood before the wide plate glass window. A group of women pressed their noses against the glass and peeped underneath the gold scrolled letters. Sam cupped her hands and leaned forward to peer into the darkened interior. Duncan stood dead center of the lady's clothing section, a pink calico dress pressed against his chest, a yellow one dangling in the other hand. Deep in consideration, he apparently had no idea he was attracting a crowd.

"Excuse me," Sam muttered and worked her way to the door.

"If you were sixteen, which one would you want?" he asked, looking up at her approach.

Sam glanced at the garments, each at least two sizes too small for Lizzy. The pink one bore cavorting lambs and the yellow one was blinding with bright buttercups. Casting a glance at the crowd outside the glass, she took his elbow and urged him forward to another section.

"Neither. They're both abysmal." She took the dresses away from him, then dived into another rack, emerging a few seconds later with a dress of soft blue. "Now this is more like it."

Duncan frowned. "That's a grown woman's dress."

Sam held it against his chest. "Lizzy is a woman."

"Isn't the neckline a little low?"

"No lower than most of mine."

Duncan cocked an eyebrow. "That's what worries me. I don't want some young buck thinking the same things about Lizzy that I think about you."

Sam laughed. "She'll love this. Now for Sarah." She dug through the rack a second time and emerged with a soft ivory, delicate roses entwined around the neck.

"How about one of those first two for Sarah?"

"She's fourteen, Duncan, not four."

"So what's the unwritten law here? How old is too old for lambs?"

"I'd say six or seven."

"Hmmm. And buttercups?"

"Eight at the most."

His dark eyes sparkled with mischief. "I can imagine you wearing lambs and buttercups. In fact, I can imagine you wearing nothing at all."

Sam stepped closer and looked up into his face. "I shouldn't think you'd have to overwork your imagination for that one."

He glanced around the store quickly, then kissed her, hauling her closer, crushing the dresses between them. "I've missed you," he whispered.

"Me, too."

He released her, allowing his fingers to glide over the indentation of her waist, as if reluctant to give up the contact between them.

"How are your daughters adjusting?" Sam stepped a discreet distance away, the effects of his touch sinking low in her belly.

The sparkle left his eyes and he looked down at the dress. "They're angry with me, angry with the world. Rightfully so, I suppose."

"They've learned hard truths too early. But they'll come around. They only need a little time." She touched the blue dress and smiled. "Are you resorting to bribery, Inspector McLeod?"

"Yes, and anything else that'll erase Lizzy's stiff upper lip."

"Then at least make it worth your while." She plopped two pairs of white kid leather shoes in his arms and took his elbow, steering him to the cosmetics counter.

"He'll have one of those." Sam pointed to small bottles of cologne water aligned carefully behind the glass case's front.

"Good God, Sam. I don't want every man in Dawson City sniffing after my girls."

Mr. Brown set the bottle on the counter and looked at Sam with a wry grin.

"Sarah, no. But Lizzy's old enough for some innocent flirting."

Duncan looked so stricken that Sam had to laugh. "You've never asked me how old I am," she said, turning to face him.

"No, I suppose I never thought—how old are you?"

"I'm twenty, four years older than Lizzy." She raised

her eyebrows in a pointed reminder of what a difference could be wrought in a woman in four years.

His face blanched and he swallowed. "So I had better prepare myself, is that what you're telling me?"

Sam winked at Mr. Brown, who chuckled out loud. "That's exactly what I'm telling you."

When Sam was done, Duncan's arms were full. He spilled the contents onto the counter. "Orin, I'm going to owe you all of next month's pay."

Orin Brown licked the end of his pencil and scribbled away. "I know you're good for it, Inspector. Leastways, I know where you live."

When Sam and Duncan stepped out onto the sidewalk, the crowd of observers moved away with studied nonchalance, titters of laughter drifting back over their shoulders.

"There's a long line, you know," Sam said, strolling down the sidewalk toward the hotel.

Duncan frowned. "What kind of line?"

"The one made up of eligible females waiting to marry you."

"Well, they better find another line to stand in. I'm already taken." He slipped an arm around her waist and ignored the stares they received. "Do you think they can tell I'm aching to have you?" he whispered, leaning closer.

"I think if you don't stop breathing in my ear that way, they're going to know for sure."

He laughed a soft chuckle she felt rather than heard. She loved sparring with him and his quick wit, but buried in the humor was a deep longing. He'd awakened in her a desire that went deeper than air or water or food. And she wanted more of it. More of him. But he'd made his position plain. She'd have to apply patience to her ache.

"Let me fix supper for you and your daughters," she said suddenly, stopping in front of the hotel.

"You can't cook. Especially not in a hotel room." He nodded toward the false-fronted structure behind him.

"I can, too, cook and there's a kitchen of sorts in the studio. Oscar's been fixing it up. We can't live in the hotel forever."

Duncan pushed his hat back and scratched his head. "I suppose it might be a good thing. Give them a good range of the food here in Dawson—worse to worst."

"I'll take that challenge, Duncan McLeod. Tomorrow night. At six."

"Six it is," he said with a wink.

Oscar fanned the smoke with his hat. "You're going to burn the whole building down, Sam. Did you check to see if the stovepipe was clogged before you started?"

Sam glowered at him and swiped at her cheek. "No, because I thought *you* had."

"I told you the stove wasn't ready."

"When did you tell me?"

"The other day. When you obviously weren't listening."

Sam yanked open the window, grabbed Oscar's hat out of his hand, and fanned the smoke outside. "Well, maybe I wasn't."

"You've been awfully distracted lately," he observed, and Sam slowed her smoke-waving.

She glanced at him and plopped down in a chair by the table Oscar had rummaged from someplace. "Duncan's asked me to marry him," she said, sneaking a glance at Oscar, dreading his reaction.

He stared down at her, then smiled slowly. "That's wonderful, Sam. I assume you said yes."

"Oscar—"

He held up a hand. "No need for excuses or apologies. I saw this coming."

"I said yes."

"When's the wedding?"

Sam swallowed and a small frown played across Oscar's face. "He wants to wait until things are more settled with his daughters."

"I see," he said with a nod. "And did you agree?"

She fidgeted under Oscar's assessment, knowing he'd see far more than she wanted. "I guess I'm just impatient. He's right, of course. He needs time with them, time to get to know them again."

Oscar squatted down in front of her and took her hands in his. "He's a good man, Sam. I can't think of anyone I'd rather lose you to."

"I'm so sorry."

Oscar shook his head. "No need. You were right . . . of course. We were never intended to be husband and wife. Had we been so foolish as to marry, I'd have lost my best friend." He squeezed her fingers. "A wife, I might be able to afford to lose, but best friends are irreplaceable." He grinned at her and stood. "Try not to burn down my studio."

"Where are you going?"

Oscar stepped away and lifted a valise he'd placed on the floor. "I'm going to Lake Bennett to see Emily."

Sam turned and hooked an arm over the chair back. "Emily?"

"I've been seeing her for several weeks now. We have quite a bit in common, I've found."

Sam smiled. "And I thought you were going there for supplies."

"I was . . . but not totally," he finished with a crooked grin.

"Good luck," Sam said, scrambling out of the chair to throw her arms around his neck.

Oscar patted her back and returned the hug. "And good luck to you, too. Duncan's going to need it."

The faint odor of burning food drifted out as Duncan opened the door to the photography studio. Oscar and Sam had done wonders with the small space. Now, an elegant chair sat before a painted background and a short white column waited for some patron to lean an arm across it and pose for a portrait. But there were no singed walls and no smoke boiled from the door in the back of the shop. "Hello?" he called, poking his head inside.

"Duncan? Come in," Sam called.

Duncan held the door for Lizzy and Sarah, then stepped inside himself. Mingled with the scorched scent were the intriguing odors of Oscar's developing chemicals. Sam bustled out from behind the partition, pristine in her simple cotton dress, wearing no evidence of a culinary disaster.

"Hello again," she said, directing her attention first to Lizzy and Sarah.

They glanced at each other as if seeking permission to respond. "Hello," they said with small smiles.

Sam turned her attention to Duncan. "Good evening, Inspector McLeod." Her eyes were warm and welcoming and he longed to yank her close and bury his face in the ironed cotton scent of her dress.

"Thank you for having us, Miss Wilder."

"Supper will be ready in a few minutes." She beckoned them through the door and as they stepped in, Duncan stopped and shook his head. She and Oscar had managed to create a home in the cramped quarters.

Although it was just one room, the area contained all the comforts Oscar needed, as he'd moved from the hotel. A small bed sat in one corner, cheerful flowers in an old liquor bottle on a table—one of Sam's touches, no doubt. A kitchen filled the other side, complete with a wood-burning stove, its pipe poking through the wall. A table set for four dominated the center of the room, with more wildflowers bobbing from a Red-Eyed Jack bottle.

"You've done wonders here."

Sam lifted a pot lid and stirred the contents, the motion giving an intriguing wiggle to her backside. "Oscar did most of it, really. He said living in a hotel was keeping him from his work." She laid down the spoon and turned. "Find yourselves a seat."

Lizzy and Sarah immediately sat across from each other. So they could continue their maddening silent conversation, no doubt, Duncan surmised. He eased into a chair at the end of the table.

Sam buzzed around the table, filling plates, pouring water into cups, finishing by turning the flower arrangement a hair to the left before she slid into her chair.

Duncan tasted a spoonful of the stew and lifted an eyebrow in Sam's direction. She avoided his glance by keeping her eyes on her own plate.

"This is very good."

"Thank you, Inspector. Lizzy, would you like a biscuit?'' Deftly avoiding his eyes, Sam lifted the towel-covered plate and held it out.

Lizzy selected a biscuit and Sam turned to Duncan. "Inspector?"

He shook his head and her glance darted away. "In fact, this is delicious. What's your secret?"

She waved a hand in the air. "Oh, a little of this and a little of that. Sarah, would you like some butter? I found a lady east of town who brought a milk cow with her. She came to Dawson City on a steamer, though, and didn't attempt to climb the pass."

Duncan glanced at the stove. Peeking out from behind the stove was the edge of a charred cloth. A small piece of blackened biscuit lay just behind the left leg.

"You must have worked on this meal all day. What do you think, girls?"

"It's very good," Lizzy said, keeping her eyes on her plate.

"Your dresses are lovely," Sam rattled on.

"Thank you. Father picked them out for us," Lizzy replied, casting Duncan a glance. "But we know you helped him."

"Well, maybe just a little," Sam replied.

"He said he wanted to buy us dresses with lambs on them but you wouldn't let him," Sarah blurted, happily digging into her meal. Duncan's breath caught in his chest. That was the first comment she'd made without first obtaining that silent approval from her sister. From the corner of his eye, he gauged Lizzy's reaction to her sister's small rebellion. But Lizzy concentrated on her plate, neither looking up nor responding.

"There's a dance and social Saturday night at the church. Would you girls like to go?"

Duncan nearly choked on his food, narrowing his eyes at Sam. All manner of men would flock to such an event to ogle whatever decent young ladies were foolish enough to exhibit themselves in such a manner.

Sam ignored his warning and plunged ahead. "I understand there'll be armloads of flowers and food and if the weather holds, the night should be beautiful."

Lizzy sneaked a glance at her father, taking him aback with her silent and hesitant question. He glanced at Sarah, who was openly begging with her sea-gray eyes.

"Miss Wilder, would you like to accompany us?"

"I'd be delighted, Inspector."

When the meal was finished, Lizzy pushed Sarah's chair to the front of the studio to look at the collection of pictures Oscar had taken since their arrival.

"Did you think I wouldn't recognize Mary Turner's stew?" Duncan whispered in her ear as he dropped a kiss on the back of her neck.

"I was hoping you wouldn't," Sam said, turning around. "After I charred mine, I had to get supper someplace."

Their lips inches apart, Duncan was tempted to devour her right there with her back against the still-warm stove. If his daughters weren't in the next room, he'd entertain the idea of making love to her on the sturdy table.

"Help with the dishes?" he offered instead and stepped a safe distance away.

Once the dishes were done and dried, Sam launched into a lengthy presentation to Lizzy and Sarah on Oscar's work, describing in detail the photographic procedures, their pictures and how and where they were taken. Eyes large, both girls listened raptly, their attention completely absorbed with Sam's prattling.

Duncan sat down in the fan-backed chair and closed his eyes. Her words bounced off him, but the sweet singsong of her voice lulled him. Laughter broke the tirade and he opened his eyes to see all three women giggling, Lizzy with a hand over her mouth. What nonsense was Sam spinning now? he wondered, rejoicing in Lizzy's ability to enjoy whatever tall tale it might be.

He pulled out his pocket watch and checked the time. Midnight would come soon and he had details to manage before he reported for duty.

"We should be going," Duncan said, reluctant to break up the camaraderie developing between Sam and his daughters.

"I'll walk along with you," Sam said and hurried to secure the shop.

Stars blinked out of a clear sky as they walked down the still-busy main street. Saloons were doing a brisk business as miners were still pouring into the gold fields. But Sam's hand on his arm was all that was important, that and the fact that Lizzy and Sarah strolled at his side, safe and maybe happy. Happier, at least, than they were in their former life.

"We're going to our room," Lizzy stated when they reached the hallway of the hotel. Then she and Sarah exchanged another meaningful glance, went inside, and closed the door.

"Do you suppose they left us out here on purpose?" Duncan asked, stepping closer.

Sam backed up until the cool wooden panels of her door lay against her back. She fumbled for the knob and closed her fingers around it. "Want to come inside?"

The answer was in his eyes and Sam was grateful for the support of the sturdy door.

"No, lass. Can't trust myself behind closed doors with you."

"I'll leave the door open."

His eyes darkened and drifted closed for an instant before he snapped them open again. "Right now, I'm not sure even that would protect you."

She enjoyed her passion the same way she enjoyed a sunlit day or the glass of beer he once saw her sneak at Charlie's—without guilt or regrets. Beneath this seemingly haphazard life she led, lay carefully orchestrated plans to nurture and care for the people she loved. Yet, embedded in her generosity was a vulnerability to those that would harm her. And this flaw gave rise to a sense of protectiveness in Duncan that defied all that would bring her unhappiness—even himself.

"I'm not sure I want to be protected. In fact, life as a scarlet woman seems interesting—as long as it's you that's besmirched me." She moved into his arms as easily as if she'd been born for this one purpose. Rising up on tiptoe, she pressed her lips to his, seducing his mouth if she couldn't have the whole of him.

"Your kisses could kill a man," he said, breaking the embrace when most of him took a vote and decided to open the door and throw her across the bed.

"I was serious about Saturday night. The dance and supper will be perfectly proper. The girls would love it."

"I'll think about it." He backed up another step and turned toward his own room.

She remained there, leaning against her door, tempting him with her sultry smile. "That's the trouble with you, Duncan McLeod. You think too much."

* * *

Emily's voice quivered in the quiet room, her last note plaintive, dying softly in the end. Applause rocked the saloon. The floor boards trembled as booted feet stomped in appreciation and whistles split the air. Oscar clapped and watched her search the room for him. She smiled softly when she spotted him and moved toward the steps.

"How are you?" she whispered and kissed his cheek.

Tingles raced up his arm as she gripped it, her soft doe-eyes staring into his. "Can I take you to supper?" he asked.

"Of course. Let me get my wrap." She sailed away, gracefully fending off over-enthusiastic admirers.

"Sadie's Cafe is good," she said as they stepped outside and he settled the wrap across her shoulders.

"Sadie's it is, then."

"How is Sam?"

Oscar chuckled. "I would imagine at this moment she is torturing Duncan with a burnt supper and some wild story of how it got that way. Through no fault of hers, of course."

Emily laughed. "You don't think Duncan foolish enough to believe every story she spins, do you?"

"No, I would imagine Duncan is quick to spot one of her tales."

"They're lovely together. Don't you agree?"

Oscar nodded. "Yes, I do."

Emily glanced sidelong at him. "No regrets there?"

Surprised, Oscar stopped. "How did you know?"

"You wear your heart in your eyes, Oscar. And besides, why else would you have followed her here?"

For an instant, he thought to deny he'd been in love with Sam. But he wanted no secrets between him and Emily, no denials or misunderstandings. Not tonight. "You're right. I came because I loved her. My reasons had nothing to do with photography."

"But you found you loved her more than you thought, didn't you?"

Emily started forward again, her arms crossed over her chest to hold her wrap closed.

"I found out I'd confused love with . . . whatever it is Sam and I have."

"She's like the sister you should have had." Emily beamed at him. "The sister stolen away by gypsies as an infant and returned on Christmas Eve, the soul to which you've always felt a connection."

"And I thought Sam spun wild stories."

Emily laughed, the sound cheerful like tinkling bells. "She's right. It's fun to sometimes let one's imagination out to run. Don't you think?"

"I don't know. Sam always did most of that—all of it, in fact. So much so that I became more adept at warding off her wanderings than inventing them myself."

"What does that cloud remind you of? That one, the one crossing the moon right now." She stopped and pointed over their heads.

"It looks like a rabbit riding a donkey."

Emily clapped her hands. "That's exactly right. See? You can do this. Now, what about that one, the one lying in the west."

Oscar looked at the lumpy cloud forming on the horizon. "It looks like Olin Brown's wife . . . lying on a knobby log with . . . an arm dangling off each side."

They exploded into laughter, leaning against each other for support. Her arm went around his waist and Oscar sobered. He reached into his pocket and withdrew the tiny, wooden case. Emily's laugh faded and she stood staring up at him.

"I know I'm not much and I can't offer you wealth or a big house or—"

"I'm not interested in wealth. Or a big house."

"And I know this is sudden—"

"Not as sudden as I'd wished."

Stunned, Oscar paused.

She smiled up at him, unruffled and calm.

"Would you marry me, Emily?" He opened the box to reveal a slim, golden band and a ring with a tiny, blue stone.

"Do you always ask two women to marry you in the same month?"

"No, not always."

"Do you promise never again to say to me that you're not much?"

"Yes," he breathed.

"Then I accept your proposal, Oscar Timmets. I'd be honored to become your wife."

He slipped an arm around her waist and drew her close. She was so slim, so delicate in his arms, spawning a wave of protectiveness fierce and overpowering. He kissed her, his blood thrumming in his ears as he adjusted to the feel of her mouth against his. Desire, unnamed and mysterious, slammed into him and he tightened his embrace.

"I love you," he whispered, his voice coming out choked and strained.

"I love you, too," she returned, her face against his chest, her breaths as erratic and shallow as his.

He took the ring from the box and slipped in onto her finger, then put the box with the gold band back into his pocket. Silver moonlight caught the stone, flashing a fiery blue in the dim light, branding her his.

CHAPTER FIFTEEN

Festoons of summer wildflowers bobbed their heads in the wavering lamplight. The aromas of apple pie, chocolate cake, and roasting pork combined and swirled with the soft night smells of damp earth and trampled grass. Grasshoppers sang, eagerly enjoying the last few days of summer. July would soon be August and autumn snows would quickly sweep down from the craggy heights and silence the grasshoppers' songs.

But not tonight.

Sam waited, her shawl drawn around her shoulders, watching the street for Duncan. Could he have changed his mind? Or was he perhaps called to duty? Impatient, she paced to the other side of the flower-hung bower, affording her a slightly different view of the main street.

"He said he was coming." Mike Finnegan's voice spoke in his soft Irish accent near her elbow.

"Hello, Mike," she said with a smile and was graced with a crinkle-eyed grin.

"Miss Wilder," he returned with a nod.

Mike was one of her favorites stationed at Fort Herchmer. A jovial soul with a rapier wit, he easily got along with the miners, businessmen, and tourists, treating each with equal doses of his brand of humor.

The gold fields had begun early to attract sightseers and groups of men and women who came simply to see what all the fuss was about in the Yukon. Ill-prepared and accustomed to getting their way, the well-to-do could be demanding and rigid in their expectations of the Mounted Police in an environment already fraught with responsibility and duty. But Mike seemed to navigate those treacherous waters with ease and aplomb.

"I was just hoping he hadn't changed his mind about letting Lizzy and Sarah come."

Mike chuckled. "Sure and he's a fool over his daughters. Never seen a more nervous father as that one."

"I guess he hasn't had the years to watch them grow up and get used to the idea."

"Might be a better thing, not having all those years to worry in advance," Mike said.

Sam glanced over at Mike and smiled. He'd brushed his uniform and combed his riotous mop of red hair. Drops of water still glistened in his waves, a futile effort to make the unruly strands behave. As soon as the music started, he'd be out on the dance floor, cavorting with grandmothers and little children without a thought to his appearance.

Three figures approached from the darkness and the gas street lamps caught the shiny brass of Duncan's buttons. An unexpected lump formed in her throat and she blinked away a quick tear at the sight of him striding along, resplendent in his serge, pushing Sarah's chair, Lizzy walking at his side.

They seemed happier with each passing day, less reserved, less angry. Lizzy even smiled on occasion; not a beaming smile, but a smile nonetheless. And yet, as they learned to laugh, Duncan seemed to sink into some darkness he chose not to share with Sam. Sometimes she wondered if she imagined it, noticing the difference only when she caught him in contemplation. Then, a melancholy would seem to claim him, if only for a short time.

"Good evening," he said, his eyes saying more than his words. "Good evening, Mike."

Mike tipped his Stetson and turned to go, throwing the girls an exaggerated wink that set them to giggling.

"Good evening, Miss Wilder," the girls chorused, casting eager glances at the bright lights and laden tables.

"Well, go on then. And don't get into any trouble," Duncan called as Lizzy grasped the chair handles and hurried Sarah toward the gathering crowd, eager for a little independence.

Sam turned to look after them. "They seem much happier than just weeks ago." She turned back and found Duncan studying her with a pensive expression. "What's wrong?"

"I was just wondering if you know how much I love you."

Sam was taken back by his honesty. She ached to smooth his cheek, to pull him back to her room and tell him with her body what words seemed inadequate to express.

"Yes, I believe I do." But words would have to do . . . for now.

"No, lass. I don't think it's possible for you to know."
He took off his Stetson and removed a small velvet bag
from the inside hat band. He opened the tiny drawstring
and spilled a ring out into his hand. "It's not much. I
had a lad good with his hands to make it out of gold
for you. It'll be my promise to you until I can replace
it with a wedding band." He took her hand and slipped
the dainty piece onto her finger, then curled her fingers
into the palm of his big hand. "I'd make you my wife
tonight if there weren't other things to consider."

She was about to ask him what other things when the
band began to tune up their instruments. He kissed her
fingers and pulled her along behind him to merge with
the crowd at the tables of food.

Duncan left her in a chair that faced the dance floor—
boards laid over the muddy ground—and went to get
them each a plate. Her seat directly under a lantern,
she held out her hand to look at the ring. It was delicate,
two bands of gold flowing together in a gentle rope.
Unending. No beginning. The symbol of true love. Hot
tears stung her eyes and clogged her throat. When Duncan returned with two plates, he looked at her face,
lifted one corner of his mouth in a smile, and bent to
gently kiss her. The caress was only a brush of lips,
almost suitable for the public place where it had been
given. Still, they raised a few eyebrows from the white-
headed matrons who clustered next to the dance floor
to find fault with the young.

"It's beautiful," she managed to squeak out as he sat
down on a hastily built bench, crossed his ankles to
balance his plate, and placed his hat beside him.

He looked up, one dark wave dangling over his forehead. "I shouldn't have asked you to keep our engagement a secret. After I thought about it, I wondered if

you thought I was ashamed of what we said . . . what we did. I'm not, Sam. I was never unsure of you, just of me."

She longed to shove his plate out of the way and plop herself in his lap. Maybe she wouldn't even move the plate. She glanced up at the disapproval committee, some looking their way, and toyed with the idea seriously for a few seconds. Instead, she tweaked the lock of hair that tantalized her and leaned closer. "You'd better say thanks tonight in your prayers for the censure committee over there because they're the only thing keeping me from embarrassing us both right now."

Duncan quirked an eyebrow and slanted a quick glance in the direction of the now-swiveling heads. "If my daughters weren't here, I'd take you up on the offer."

Soft music floated on the night air as the abundant food was consumed and couples began to drift out onto the dance floor. Lizzy and Sarah returned to their father's side, ending any more titillating banter between Duncan and Sam. But once they finished eating and Duncan graciously returned their plates to their hostesses, he motioned Lizzy, Sarah, and Sam to the side. He grasped Sam's hand firmly in his and looked at his daughters' wide eyes.

"I want you both to know that I've asked Sam to become my wife and she's agreed."

Sarah squealed and threw her arms first around Duncan and then Sam. Lizzy smiled and wished them good luck, but was reserved in her exuberance, leaving Sam to wonder.

"When are you getting married? Can we be in the wedding? Somebody told me they're wonderful with lots of flowers and ribbons." Sarah clasped her hands together. "Are we going to have a baby sister soon?"

Duncan stiffened beside her and Sam choked down a laugh. Poor Duncan, dealing with adolescent daughters, frustrated sexual urges, and hundreds of thousands of dollars in gold dust all at one time! Well, she thought as she squeezed his hand for reassurance, she could help with one of those problems . . . if he'd let her.

"We'll decide that later," he said weakly. "Right now, I've asked Sam to dance." He glanced down and Sam nodded.

He led her to the dance floor and twirled her under his arm before bringing her close to him, one hand on the small of her back, another holding her hand. He waltzed her smoothly around the makeshift dance floor.

"You're a very good dancer. Where did you learn to waltz like this?"

His warm breath tickled her ear as he leaned in close. "Long, cold winters. No women to dance with. We taught each other."

Sam laughed. "Does the rest of Canada know their beloved Mounties dance with each other?"

He spun her around until the hem of her dress looped out in a wide swirl. "Let any of them that make fun try spending seven snowy months with little to do. We'd have danced with our horses if we could have gotten them inside the mess hall."

A hand tapped Duncan on the shoulder and they stopped in the middle of the floor. Orin Brown's oldest son, Todd, stood with his hat nervously twirling in his hands.

"Inspector McLeod, I'd like to ask Lizzy to dance, but she said I had to ask you first."

Duncan glanced over the young man's head to where

Lizzy stood with arms wrapped around herself, nearly dancing with anticipation.

He quirked his head in her direction and smiled. "Go ahead and ask her."

Todd started away at a trot.

"Todd?"

He stopped and turned as a couple whirled by.

"I want to see daylight between the two of you. Understand?"

"Yes, sir, Inspector."

"Now that wasn't so painful, was it?" Sam looked up into his face and smiled.

"Hurt like hell." He whirled her back into the circle of dancers. "But I figure worse is yet to come—twice."

The next dance was another waltz, but this time a poignant, haunting tune. Duncan leaned closer, the side of his head pressed to hers, an awareness quivering between them. The ring, the playful banter, the soft night all had served to make her want him with an intensity that was painful. Now I know why people prefer short engagements, she thought, as his beard stubble against her hair set every nerve ending in her body on alert.

Duncan stopped and turned. Mike Finnegan stood with a hand on his shoulder. "Can I cut in?" he asked.

Duncan frowned and seemed about to say no, when Mike grinned impishly and raised his eyebrows. "Just trying to save your innocence, old man."

Smiling sheepishly, Duncan moved away and Mike stepped up to take Sam in his arms.

"You've caught yourself a fine man." He spun her away from him so fast that she shrieked, thinking she'd go flying off into the night. Then, he pulled her back into his arms with a fancy flourish.

"Did you learn this dancing with Duncan?"

"Ah, no, lass. I learned this from a wanton woman in Edmonton," he teased.

"And yes, I know Duncan is a fine man."

"The Lord never made a finer one. He's the man I'd want to my back in a scrap. Are the two of you planning a wedding soon?"

"Yes, but we don't know when. Duncan wants to give Lizzy and Sarah some time to adjust to having him all to themselves."

"It's a tragic tale of those two. And a hard thing for him to be taking all the load of raising them." He grinned down at her. "But they need a good laugh or two above all. Something tells me you're the lass to provide that."

Sam looked over where Lizzy and Todd were carefully pacing off the dance, enough room between them for another person, each gazing down at their own feet. Duncan stood in the edge of the crowd, arms crossed over his chest, frowning while Sarah wriggled with excitement at his side.

"What this family needs is a good reason to laugh."

By eleven, only couples remained and the band was gathering their instruments to leave. Families with children had left long ago to tuck them into bed. Lizzy and Sarah had successfully wheedled Duncan into allowing them to stay until the last shred of fun ended. Throwing a shawl across her shoulders, Duncan pointed Sarah in the direction of the wide main street. Down at the other end of town, the night's fun was just beginning. A piano tinkled out an off-key tune while a group of voices caterwauled an unrecognizable song.

"When can we do this again?" Lizzy asked, her smile wide and genuine.

Duncan stopped, started to respond, then paused and said a silent prayer of gratitude. Lizzy had smiled.

"I don't know," he finally said, struggling to hide the emotion. "Maybe soon. How was your dance with Todd?"

Even in the dim light, he could see that Lizzy blushed a bright scarlet. "He's a nice boy." Duncan's heart twisted. How quickly time passed. And he'd missed so much. First steps. First smiles. Christmases. Snowy days. Soon, very soon, Lizzy and Sarah would have lives and families of their own and he'd become unnecessary.

They reached the hotel and both girls moved off to their room, barely able to stay awake long enough to get into bed.

"Do you need some help?" Sam asked and both shook their heads without turning around.

Their door closed with a resounding click. Duncan took Sam's key out of her hand and unlocked her door. She frowned slightly and searched his face. "Is something wrong?"

"No, I just know if I don't put you in this room myself, I'll end up taking you to mine." He pushed the door open. "Good night, Sam."

"Something is wrong. What's happened?"

Bits of his conversation this afternoon with Superintendent Steele rose to haunt him, promising to rob him of sleep. He looked down into Sam's face. Anger nipped at the desire growing within him. How was it a man was saddled with these protective feelings for the woman he loved and yet denied the power to protect her from all that would bring her pain?

"Nothing's wrong. Just suffering an attack of regret."

She touched his cheek, searing a path down his sensitive skin with her cool fingertips. "I have the same regrets, but you were right. We should wait." She grinned. "It'll make the reward sweeter. Especially now that we know what we're waiting for."

Duncan tamped out the contents of his pipe into the fireplace. The hour was far past midnight, leaning toward morning, and still sleep would not come. A thousand regrets circled his brain like discontented ghosts, lost and alone. He propped his pipe on the mantel and wandered to the window. Why, suddenly, did the nights seem endless? He knew the answer. Darkness separated him from the people he loved most.

Raking a hand through his hair, he stared out at the sleeping town. For months now, he'd been responsible for more gold than most men would ever see, ever dream existed. Since his daughters' arrival, he'd had to turn that responsibility over to Inspector Dutton, a young, seemingly competent officer, recently transferred from Fort Walsh. And yet, there was something about the young man that weighed on Duncan's mind. Some little twitch of intuition begging to be noticed. But Duncan hadn't been able to put a name or reason to the niggling thought. Now, after his conversation with Superintendent Steele, his apprehension grew.

He glanced at the wall that separated his room from Sam's and wished with every fiber of his being that his plans for the evening had come to pass. He'd arranged for a visiting minister to give them their vows. He'd made arrangements for Finnegan to stay in his room and watch over the girls. And he'd planned to whisk Sam off to an isolated campsite and make love to his wife underneath twinkling starlight. But duty had moved in and marriage had to wait.

He wished he could talk to Adam McPhail, probably peacefully asleep in his wife's arms in Edmonton. McPhail had fought overwhelming odds to win his wife, Lauren. Now they lived a peaceful life with their son, whom Duncan helped deliver. And although he'd been at Adam's side most of the struggle, Duncan remembered that Adam talked little of his thoughts during those trying times, seeking solace only in the company of his friends.

Duncan turned away from the window and strode toward the door. He'd just look in on her, he told himself. Just for a minute he'd stand over her and remember that tonight she would have been his.

His key fit her door perfectly and he eased it shut behind him. The floor boards whispered softly as he padded across them to stop at the side of her bed and gaze down on her, peacefully asleep on her side, facing away from him.

She wore a cotton gown whose lacy neckline caressed the edge of her jaw. Breaths, soft and even, stirred the hair spread out on her pillow as he watched, a lump firmly jammed in his throat.

Suddenly, she rolled to her back, her eyes wide, as awake as he. "What's the matter?" she asked, frowning.

"I . . . just wanted to see you," he said lamely.

She studied his face a moment before rising from the bed to stand before him. "I know you, Duncan, and something's wrong."

"I can't wait, Sam."

Sam slid a hand down his cheek, sympathy in her eyes.

"Life is uncertain," he began, then swallowed. "My work is dangerous and I never know when—"

She silenced him with a kiss, then drew away and touched his forearm, sliding those delicate fingers down to his wrist. Her fingers tussled briefly with his before entwining with them and tugging him toward the bed.

The warnings poised on the end of his tongue vanished. And all his good intentions followed. She stopped by the bedside, undid the buttons on the front of her nightgown and let the garment drift to the floor. Ripe and full, she stood before him, offering what he wanted most.

She plucked open the buttons on his uniform pants and threw him a teasing glance as she bent over to shove them to the floor. Then, with confident hands, she touched him. He sucked in his breath, his stomach contracting involuntarily. Laughing softly, her hair whispering against his skin, she explored him in places no one had touched before. Sprinkling kisses across his chest, she kneaded him gently. "You're so soft there."

His traitorous body responded to give her more access and his hips arched to press against her palm. A soft groan escaped and he closed his eyes, but not before he saw her impish grin.

She encircled him with her hand, the soft skin of her palm gliding down the length to brush against his abdomen, then away in a motion that made his knees jerk. She chuckled and nipped at his nipple, followed by a flick of her warm tongue.

He was spellbound, every thought focused on the motion of her hand, prisoner to her teasing.

Her left hand occupied, she stepped to his side and ran her other hand down his spine, paused in the small of his back, then over the swell of his buttocks, the cold metal of his ring dragging down the ridges of his spine. Involuntarily, he jerked forward again, seeking her hand. She released him with a throaty chuckle, moved behind him, and wrapped her arms around him, pressing her body tight against his back. She kissed the ridges of his muscles and nibbled at the edge of his shoulder blades.

He turned and captured her in his arms, pressing his hardness against her belly, claiming control. Her breast was soft as his hands closed around her, kneading as she'd done him. Her lips were soft and eager, costing him that last brief moment of sanity. His tongue swept her mouth, seeking hers, probing her as he wanted to do in other ways. Drawing her bottom lip into his teeth, he nipped the tender skin and she jerked in his arms. A hand roamed lower, over the slight swell of her stomach to nestle in that telltale place that said she wanted him as much as he wanted her. She opened to him, pressing her face against his chest and whispering his name as he tormented her with slight movements of his fingers.

"Take me to bed," she said in a choked voice. "I want . . . more than this."

He deposited her on the bed, a thousand warnings ringing in his mind, and she looked up at him, her eyes dark with passion, her hair fanned out around her. For a fleeting second, Duncan entertained those second thoughts clamoring for his attention. This would be no gentle mating, no romantic dalliance. She was no girlish virgin eager for knowledge. She was a woman, his woman, her body his release and the receptacle of his life.

"I love you, Duncan," she said as if reading his hesitation.

He joined her on the bed, hovering over her a moment, then slid inside her. Soft flesh gripped him and she aligned her body perfectly with his as if they'd practiced this routine over a lifetime.

She clasped him to her with her arms and legs, kissing him, nipping at his shoulders and lips, wild beneath him. She was so tiny, amazingly taking all of him, savoring and encouraging the savage pace he was setting. Then, she reached behind her and gripped the rungs of the headboard, reading his body and his needs. He covered her hands with his and plunged to a shuddering climax.

He collapsed onto her, his head on her shoulder, heart pounding, arms trembling. She dallied with his ear and coiled a strand of his hair around one finger, innocent, as if she hadn't just seduced him senseless.

He rolled off her to relieve her of his weight, but she followed, curling against his side like a kitten, where she continued to torment him with flickering touches. He looked out from under his arm and laughed at her fat-cat smile. "You needn't be grinning at me like that, lass. This old man's got nothing left to give you."

"You weren't so old a few minutes ago," she said with slyly slitted eyes.

"One day I'll have a heart attack in your arms and then you'll be sorry," he said, turning onto his side and hauling her against him with an arm around her waist.

She wiggled against him, the movement appearing innocent, but Duncan knew better. He looked down into her clear blue eyes, and wondered at this waif of a woman with a face like a wood nymph and the appetites of a Saturday night doxie. He kissed her nose and she grinned. But as long as those appetites were reserved only for him, he'd not question the odd combination and consider himself granted a second chance at happiness.

Slowly, reality returned, problems and what-ifs. He slid a glance down her slim body, to her stomach, now taut and smooth, and again wondered if he'd planted a child there, a child that might grow and be born with his father in jail.

Duncan put an arm over his eyes and damned his lack of control where Sam was concerned. Gold was missing. Counts and recounts indicated the amount dwindling for no good reason. Assuming the difference attributable to human error, they'd counted again and still the figures did not match. Now, there would be an investigation, an unnerving event for everybody concerned. When the Fort Herchmer detachment was assigned, no one supposed they would be responsible for nor handle so much gold dust. No one could have foreseen the amount of responsibility that would be placed on each man, and Duncan in particular, since he'd been in charge of the group of men guarding the gold. No one could have foreseen such copious amounts would disappear without a trace.

CHAPTER SIXTEEN

All the thunder Thor had to offer couldn't have jarred the ground under Sam's feet the way Oscar's words just had.

"You're going to do what?" She spun around on her stool behind the counter and stared at him as he seated a new bowler hat on his head.

"I'm going to Lake Bennett to bring back Emily. We're to be married on Sunday."

Hurt, sharp and piercing, shot through her. He was her best friend and she'd had no inkling. "When did this come about? How?"

Oscar looked at the floor. "I've handled this badly." He looked up and into her face. "I didn't know how to tell you. You've been so distracted lately and not knowing how you felt about Emily . . . I'm sorry, Sam. I wanted to tell you. I needed to, but . . ." He shrugged and the pain dug deeper.

He'd needed her and she hadn't been there ... at least not mentally or emotionally. Dear, bespectacled Oscar had become a man.

"I'm very happy for you," she said, her throat tight. "Are you really?"

"Oh, Oscar, of course I am." She clambered off the stool and threw herself into his arms. "I'm so glad you found someone. And Emily's lovely."

He held her away for a moment, his eyes, large behind his glasses, searching her face. "You'll always be special to me, Sam, special in a way no one else ever will be. Not even Emily."

She sobbed despite her best efforts. "And you'll always be my best friend. After all, you know the real me."

"I think the real Sam's pretty special." His voice slipped and Sam backed away before they both collapsed into a pool of tears.

She swiped at her tears with the heel of her hand. "So, tell me how this came about."

Oscar shrugged. "How do two people ever find each other? We just discovered we had a lot in common and ... things went from there."

"Will you come back here?"

"Of course. I have the shop. We're going to live here. I'll make a place for you, too," he added a little too quickly.

Sam stared at him, reality dawning. There'd be no place for her in Oscar's new life. She'd given up her dancing the day after Duncan proposed, the incongruity of the two things weighing on her conscience. Now, she worked as a waitress to the hordes of thirsty, hungry men who frequented Charlie's. Oscar would need her no longer. The gray mood she'd been fighting off now crept over her.

Oscar pulled a pocketwatch from his vest. "I have to be going. The steamer leaves in half an hour."

"Good luck," she said as he hurried toward the door—and his future. The bell tinkled as he shut the door, its light sound mocking her.

She reached under the counter and dragged out the small collection of items she'd kept there. Better to make the break while Oscar was gone. She searched the shop for anything she'd left behind and was glad there was little to take. That way it wouldn't be obvious to Oscar when he came back that she was distancing herself from him. If he knew, he'd try to make some amends, try to include her. But Sam knew this was the way it should be.

As she picked up the box and started for the door, the bell tinkled again and Wilton Adcox walked in, accompanied by his brother, Tom. Seeing them was a shock. She'd all but forgotten her original mission.

"Got some more information for you."

"Mr. Adcox, I—"

"There's another shipment going out tonight." He rocked back on his heels and grinned. "And you're gonna be real interested to see who's taking this one."

A chill ran over Sam. "What do you mean?"

"I reckon you better meet me on the road south tonight 'bout ten or so if you wanna find out."

Moisture so fresh it hurt her nose swirled around Sam, creating the same ethereal fog that had cloaked the river her first night spying. Crouched in the same cedar thicket, Sam waited and listened.

Adcox and his brother wore small, knowing smiles that grated on her nerves and put a knot in her stomach. What did they know?

As before, the distant slap of oars broke the fog-swathed silence and a boat slid onto shore. A tall figure emerged from another thicket closer to shore.

"How was your trip downriver?" a voice asked and Sam's blood ran cold. Duncan. She glanced at Wilton and Tom and they nodded with satisfied smiles.

"Not too bad," a second voice answered. "You got it?"

"It's back there."

She exhaled and her head spun. Grabbing a slim sapling, careful not to shake the leaves, she steadied herself to keep from toppling over.

"How long do you think we can keep this up?" the boatman's voice asked.

"Not much longer, I fear. Somebody's tipped off Steele. Is the lad in Lake Bennett going to handle this like last time?"

"Yep. No questions . . . for the proper price."

"Let's get it loaded and you on your way."

The sounds of bags dragging across the pebbly ground replaced conversation until the last one was loaded.

"See you in two weeks," the boatman said, water sloshing against the sides of his boat as he stepped into it.

"Keep safe," Duncan said and his steps faded into the silence of the woods.

Sam and her conspirators waited for what seemed like hours before emerging from their hiding place. Heart pounding, Sam walked the short distance to the thicket where Duncan had hidden. A clear set of foot-prints marred the churned leaf litter.

She leaned against a tree, the strength oozing from her. How could he do such a thing? How could he possibly be stealing gold from the government he'd sworn to protect? There had to be some other explanation.

And with another dose of reality, she realized the foolishness of her mission to expose the Mounted Police. Why on earth had she ever thought these hard-working men who gave up softer lives and the comforts of family would violate the vows they took so seriously? Why had she assumed that because the money was in their hands, so would be deceit?

"You got enough now for your story?"

She glanced at Adcox and the satisfied smirk on his face. He and Tom were up to no good and she'd been gullible enough to go along with it. "No, I don't believe this is what it looks like."

Adcox's smiled faded. "You ain't gonna write this here story and send it to your paper?"

Sam drew in a deep breath. "No, I'm not."

"Just 'cause he's your man, you're gonna let this chance to do right pass?"

"He's not my man. Inspector McLeod and I are merely acquaintances."

"That ain't the rumor circulating."

"Well, I don't care what's circulating. I'm not writing this story. I don't believe the Mounted Police would steal this gold they've been charged to guard."

Adcox lowered a threatening glance. "Mounties is just men in red suits, same as the rest of us. They ain't above greed or stealing. They just got more to lose if they're caught. If you ain't gonna use this information, I'll find somebody who will."

"Nobody who knows the Mounted Police will believe you."

Adcox smiled slowly. "Why not? You did."

A line of ants marched across the tablecloth, their tiny legs hurrying to navigate the bumps and valleys of their red and white checked landscape. Sam lay on her stomach, putting blades of grass in their path, smiling as they overcame every obstacle with dogged determination, nothing deterring them from their crumb of pie crust.

With a growing awareness of Duncan's leg pressed against hers, she tried to keep her mind on the congenial conversation oscillating between Lizzy and Sarah. But all she could think about was Duncan's voice coming to her from the river mist. She glanced up. He sat propped back on his elbows, his eyes closed against the sun that bathed his face.

Duncan couldn't be involved in anything illegal. It just wasn't in him to defy his oath. His honor and reputation meant everything to him. He'd do nothing to jeopardize that. And yet, a small voice chided, he'd made bold love to her again and again with no further discussion about marriage. And last time, he'd given of himself completely, loved her sweetly and sadly, then left her without answers to questions she didn't know how to ask.

She studied him, there in the morning sun, ankles crossed, his tunic hanging open. And wanted him with a desire that slammed at her insides. She took a deep breath and wondered if she'd truly become a loose woman. She shifted her attention to Lizzy and Sarah.

Lizzy's happiness the night of the dance was short-lived—she quickly receded into that black world of hers. Sarah seemed torn between capitulating to her father and remaining loyal to her sister. Poor Duncan swung in the balance. He'd provided them with books and carefully drawn out lessons to occupy the hours when he was on duty. The conversations she'd been privy to had consisted of calm, careful instructions in worldly matters and dutifully defined rules. All in all, their conversations were dull at best and unendurable at worst.

"Let's have a wheelchair race," Sam suddenly proclaimed and scrambled up from torturing the ants.

Duncan looked up at her as if she'd lost her mind. Lizzy and Sarah gaped at her openly.

"Charlie has another chair in the storeroom. He said somebody paid a bar bill with it once. There's a nice, smooth hill near the dock. If we turn over, we'll fall into soft grass."

"Could I have a word with you?" Duncan said in a tight voice, standing and yanking down his tunic in a way that said she was in real trouble.

"Have you lost your mind?" he sputtered when they were alone behind a straggly stand of aspens. "Racing wheelchairs?"

"You've given them everything but laughter, Duncan. They need to laugh. Don't you remember how happy Lizzy was the night of the dance?"

"And I suppose you know all about raising children?" He stalked away, his hands clenched at his sides, and Sam wondered if he was angry at her suggestion or angry because she'd thought of it first.

"No, but I know an awful lot about being one and more than most folks about being one for *too* long. In fact, I dare say I know more about *that* than most people.

You might call me an expert on the subject. Which also makes me an expert on people who act like they're old when they're not."

"Maturity, or the lack of it, has nothing to do with this," he said, turning to face her.

"It has everything to do with it. They're children, Duncan, but they've never had a childhood. They've never lain on their stomachs and played with ants or watched leaves float on the river or—"

"I'm trying to educate them, trying to give back to them the world Rob McDonald burned in his court-yard."

Sam stepped closer, drawn by the anger snapping in his eyes. "Then give them the whole world. Teach them to appreciate the silly and absurd along with the serious and necessary."

He looked completely at a loss for a moment and she wondered if he'd ever had a whimsical thought in *his* whole life.

"Sarah's accident isn't something to be treated lightly," he argued, falling back on the thing about his daughters that pained him the most. He blamed himself for her disfigurement and would listen to no discussion of the topic, no suggestion to improve Sarah's world beyond her wheelchair or crutches.

"I wouldn't dream of treating it lightly. But, what's done is done and they need to realize life goes on."

"We don't talk about Sarah's leg."

"You should."

He glared at her.

"You can't just ignore the fact that she can't walk and part of one leg is missing."

He winced at her honesty and stalked off in another direction. "We can treat it with the respect she's due. All of us," he finished with a pointed look.

"Stop stalking around like a bad stage actor and come over here," she said.

"Why?"

"Because I have something to show you." She withdrew a small, carved wooden figure from her pocket. "An old man tipped me with this last night and I got an idea."

Duncan took the finely detailed horse and turned the figurine over in his hands. "I'm almost afraid to ask, but what kind of idea?"

"Let's get him to make Sarah a wooden leg."

"A wooden leg? Like a pirate?"

"Well, sort of. A man took his off in Charlie's several weeks ago and used it for a poker ante. Then last night, when Mr. Epps brought this in, well it just came to me."

"Well, send *it* back where *it* came from. No daughter of mine's going to hobble around like . . . like . . ."

"Can't think of a pirate? What? With all those books you've assigned them to read, you can't think of the name of one, single pirate?"

"You're being ridiculous." He handed her the horse. "And I'm being ridiculous for even listening to this nonsense."

He stalked back toward the picnic and Sam slid the horse into her pocket. Well, it had been worth a try.

"Papa, are we going to race wheelchairs?" Sarah had turned her chair around and looked up at him with barely contained enthusiasm in her eyes.

Duncan stopped dead in his tracks. Sam halted and watched his shoulders bunch and tighten beneath his coat. Sarah looked up at him, smiling, her eyes glistening with expectation. Even Lizzy awaited his answer with more than her usual interest. Duncan threw Sam a quick glance that made the bottom of her stomach bunch in anticipation.

"Well . . ."

"Oh please, Papa. It'll be fun."

"I'll go get it. Lizzy can come with me," Sam offered.

Duncan glanced around at them all and heaved a sign of resignation. "Go, but don't take forever."

When Sam and Lizzy returned, they stopped beneath the spreading branches of a hemlock tree. In the meadow just ahead, Duncan sat on the ground at Sarah's side, pulling wildflowers and handing them to her. Sam paused, watching father and daughter, their heads bent low over the bobbing flowers.

"You love our Papa, don't you?"

It was more a question of affirmation than inquiry. Sam turned to look into the eyes of a young woman instead of the child her father thought her. "Yes, I do. Very much."

Lizzy turned back to study her father. "My mother left him for another man when we were babies. Did you know that?"

"Yes, he told me."

"She said he'd never amount to anything and that he was the most infuriatingly content man she'd ever known."

"Infuriatingly content. Yes, that would describe your father."

"Mama wanted nice things for herself . . . and for us. So she took us and went to live with a baron." She paused, smiling when Duncan smiled at Sarah. "And left Papa all alone.

"He beat us . . . and Mama, Rob did," she continued without a trace of emotion in her voice. "I think Papa suspects that. He asked me, but I lied and said no. I don't want him to know." She turned her young-old eyes on Sam again. "He feels guilty that he didn't come after us. Rob always thought he would and he kept a loaded gun in the parlor just in case. If Papa had set one foot on McDonald land, Rob would have killed him and we wouldn't have him now."

Sam's knees knocked together as she looked at Duncan's dark head bent over his daughter and imagined him lying by the side of some dark road, a bullet through his head.

"Sarah and I think you should marry Papa right away."

"You do?"

"Yes, and have a baby. Sarah and I would like a little sister."

Sam put a hand to her stomach then slid it quickly away. How odd that Lizzy would echo the very thing she'd wondered about. Did she carry a child? Had she conceived on that dizzyingly passionate night?

Demons had haunted him of late. Sam knew all the signs, but he'd made no effort to discuss his worries with her, withdrawing within himself every time she asked. And he'd not come to her again, hadn't teased or touched or whispered inappropriate promises. Was he having second thoughts about her or was he in some other trouble?

They raced the chairs down the slight swell of the meadow until the sun cast a cloak of dusk across the land. The once-solemn girls laughed and whooped and tumbled in the soft, fragrant grass. They even talked Duncan into racing Sam down the hill and laughed until they bent double, accusing him of looking terrified all the way down. He'd climbed out of his chair, allowing the girls to catch his arms when it appeared he'd stumbled. And as they did so, he'd given Sam a sly wink.

They pushed the chairs back to town, ignoring the curious glances they got for the grass stains on their clothes. Over supper at the Gold Nugget Cafe, Lizzy and Sarah chattered animatedly and Duncan threw Sam glances that made food a secondary priority.

"They had a wonderful time," Sam said, nodding toward where Lizzy pushed Sarah's chair along the uneven sidewalk headed back toward the hotel. She and Duncan followed, her hand tucked inside his arm.

"Yes, they did. And I owe you an apology."

"I know better ways to repay me than words."

"Hummph," was his noncommittal reply.

"Lizzy says she and Sarah think we should get married right away and give them a baby sister."

"I hope things work out in that order." He turned toward her, the question in his eyes.

"I hope so, too," was all she could honestly say. "Let's get married, Duncan. Right away. The girls want it. You and I want it."

A shadow passed over Duncan's face.

"What's wrong?"

"Nothing," he said with a shake of his head. "I just don't think we should . . . not right now. Maybe toward fall."

Were the old fears resurfacing? She tilted her head, prepared to launch into an interrogation, when Duncan turned the full intensity of his blue eyes on her. "Don't ask me any more questions, Sam, because I can't tell you anything else."

"This has something to do with your work, doesn't it?"

He continued down the sidewalk without comment, retucking her hand firmly under his arm. She burned to know, burned to ask him about his involvement in what looked like outright thievery, but his stiff silence said he'd broach no questions. He'd tell her in his own good time. She had to, at least, have faith in that.

A soft knock on the door called Duncan's attention away from the book he was reading by the light of the fireplace.

"Come in," he said, bracing himself for a whirlwind visit from Sam that would torture his loins and exasperate his mind. Instead, Oscar poked his head around the door.

"Am I disturbing you?"

"No, not at all." Duncan closed the book and set his pipe in a waiting bowl.

Oscar closed the door and moved across the room with uneasy steps.

"Have a seat." Duncan shoved a chair at him with a sock-clad foot.

Oscar perched on the seat like a nervous sparrow and knitted his fingers together. "I've—" His voice slipped and he cleared his throat. "I've come to ask some advice," he said, his face tortured with the effort.

Duncan frowned, rose, and retrieved a small flask of whiskey from the table by his bed. He poured a small amount into two cups and held one out to Oscar. "Would you like some?"

"Yes, please," Oscar said, then tipped the cup back and swallowed the contents.

Amused, Duncan returned to his chair with his. This must be some conversation they were about to have.

"What would you like to ask me?" Duncan pursued when Oscar looked a little dazed, probably from the liquor. Hell, even hard drinkers sipped this brew.

"As I'm sure you know, Emily and I are to wed on Sunday."

Duncan nodded.

"And you have known her for some years."

"Yes."

"I . . . well, I'm . . ." Oscar stopped and swallowed convulsively, his exaggerated Adam's apple bobbing. "I'd like you to be my best man."

Duncan let out his breath in a silent whoosh. "I'd be honored to stand up with you, Oscar." He thought the lad had come for wedding night advice and then chuckled at the ridiculousness of that assumption. Why on earth would anyone ask *his* advice on such a matter? His first wife had abandoned him and he was now forced to keep the woman he adored dangling.

"The wedding's at ten. In the morning, of course."

"Of course."

"In the meadow, just south of town. Barring any rain. In which case we'll have it at Charlie's saloon."

Duncan raised his eyebrows. These arrangements smacked of Sam's doing.

"Sam thought it would be a good place in case of rain. Inside, you see and . . . vacant."

Duncan nodded, a sense of impending disaster growing. There was more to come in this conversation than rain arrangements. He shook the flask still in his hand and was grateful that the contents sloshed.

"Ah . . . there's something else." Oscar fidgeted and the chair complained with a loud squeak.

"Out with it, Oscar. You won't shock me. I promise."

"Well, you see, Emily is a lady, as I'm sure you know," he hurried to add with a frown. "But of course you wouldn't know, would you? You'd have to assume and I'm sure that's the assumption you'd make, as most honorable men would. Ah . . . well, she is and I'm . . . I'm not an experienced man, not as you'd imagine or . . . as you *might* have thought at one time, months ago, in Lake Bennett and at the . . . pass with . . . Sam."

"I don't think you slept with Sam, Oscar, if that eases your mind."

"Oh, no. I didn't mean to cast doubts on Sam . . . I mean, I know that . . . I mean, that's why I came to you . . . here . . . because she suggested that I . . . come and talk to you." The last few words rushed out and poor Oscar looked like he'd just spit out a lynx. Claws and all.

Duncan shifted in his chair, using the motion to gather his now-scattered thoughts. Just how much had Sam confided to Oscar? And what had she said to make the poor lad think he was an expert? A small, self-indulgent smile crept across his face despite his best efforts. So, she thought the results warranted passing on the technique, did she?

"You want to know about the wedding night and what a woman expects?"

"Oh yes, please," Oscar said in one breath, his voice desperate and relieved at not having to ask the question himself.

Duncan shook his head. "Can't say I've ever done this before."

"If it makes you extremely uncomfortable, Inspector, we'll just forget this conversation ever happened. I mean . . . Sam, she said that . . . I needed to know . . . things so—. Oh dear, this is so difficult to say. She thought I should know some things so Emily wouldn't be disappointed." He stood as if to leave and Duncan caught his arm.

"Sit down, Oscar."

Oscar sat.

Duncan put the flask on the floor. All the liquor in Dawson City wouldn't make this any easier. He looked into Oscar's face, his eyes expectant and intelligent. The lad loved Emily and wanted to make her happy. How could he deny helping with that? Even if he'd make intricate plans to throttle Sam when he saw her for putting him in this position.

"First of all, Emily is a kind, compassionate woman who loves you, Oscar. Whatever happens, she'll still love you."

His eyes widened. "What does that mean?"

Oh dear, he hadn't meant it to come out just like that.

"What I meant to say was that whatever happens between the two of you on your wedding night will be the right thing and she'd never be disappointed in you. You'll know what to do when the time comes."

"I will? I'll just know?"

Duncan smiled. "Mother Nature is a wonderful thing."

Oscar frowned, obviously mulling over some thought. "Well . . . Sam said that sometimes there are . . . timing problems, I . . . well, she told me that you and she had . . . you know. I'm not one to judge, Inspector. Sam assures me that she loves you deeply and that, well . . . things happened."

He leaned forward, threaded his fingers together, and seemed to gather up some of his scattered thoughts. "But she seemed to be particularly concerned that I know about this one thing."

CHAPTER
SEVENTEEN

Duncan dropped his forehead into his hand and stared at the floor. Leave it to Sam to tell their most intimate secret if she thought it would help someone she loved. And she did love Oscar. Duncan raised his head. Oscar looked horrified.

"I've hit on something sensitive, haven't I? I'm very sorry, Inspector. I'll—" Oscar rose to go, but Duncan tugged him back down by his arm.

"First of all, please call me Duncan. Seems almost necessary at this point, don't you think?"

"Duncan it is," Oscar said, bobbing his head.

"I take it you know the basics? Differences between a man and a woman? How babies are made? That sort of thing?"

"Oh, yes. I'm not so completely ignorant. I know the general procedure. It's the 'fine points', as Sam called them, that I'd like instruction on."

" 'Fine points'."

"Yes, I believe those were the words she used."

Duncan rose and walked to the window. He needed to be on his feet for this one. Crossing his arms over his chest, he studied Oscar's expectant reflection in the glass. Had he really been this eager and innocent once? Had he quivered with anticipation on the eve of his wedding night? He truly couldn't remember. Perhaps time or pain had blocked out the memory. But he had quivered in anticipation of loving Sam. That he remembered well.

"Sometimes when a man hasn't made love to a woman before, he . . . gets a little ahead of himself, in his eagerness to please her."

Oscar adjusted his glasses and looked perplexed. "I'm sorry, I don't follow you."

"No, that would have been too easy," Duncan muttered to himself and turned around to face Oscar. "When a man and woman are . . . in the throes of passion, she would like him to . . . to . . ." How on earth did one say this to a virgin? "She likes it very much if he . . . finishes at the same time she does. Not before."

Oscar frowned, furrowing his brow. "Finishes?"

Duncan glared at him. "I'm sorry Oscar, I just can't be any more specific than that."

Oscar's eyes brightened at the same time his ears started to glow deep red. "Oh, yes. Finishes. And she doesn't want him to finish first?"

"No." Duncan shook his head. Tomorrow he'd never convince himself he'd had this conversation.

"And how does a man go about delaying this . . . finishing?"

"Think about something else for a while. Anything except what you're doing."

"What sorts of things do you think about, Inspector?" Oscar fidgeted to the edge of the chair, his full attention on the discussion, his stutter gone.

"Well . . . I don't know." Duncan floundered for an answer. "Cold water. Very, very cold water."

"Ah, I understand," Oscar said with a huge smile and a nod. "Cold water."

"Works every time."

"Yes, I can see how it would. Do you have any other advice? That you'd care to share, of course."

Well, hell. Why trot out all this blood to scorch his ears for a mere second or two of humiliation? Duncan thought. Why not go for a half hour at least. The poor lad needed instruction and dear, sweet Emily, whose debt he was deeply in, would be the beneficiary. And one day, well, his blood might drain back into his feet.

"Women like to be touched. Caressed. Before."

"Before? Oh, yes. Before." Oscar nodded. "Where?"

"Where?"

"Where do they like to be caressed?"

Duncan could almost imagine Oscar scribbling these tidbits on a pad of paper, so intent was he now on gleaning information.

"Well, all women are different. You'll have to ask Emily."

"I should ask her, then?"

"Yes." Duncan walked back to his chair, sat down, and propped his elbows on his knees. They could dance around this all night or he could come straight to the point.

"When you take her to bed for the first time, lad, there's more to it than getting the deed done. There's the pleasuring of the woman you love. And seeing to her pleasure is as important as seeing to yours. Do you understand?"

Oscar swallowed and waited for more.

"This joining between a man and a woman is a miraculous thing, nothing to be taken lightly. To have two bodies fit together so perfectly and bring each other such pleasure in that joining is surely a gift from God. Take your time with her. Bring her along slowly, touching with your hands and your mouth until she's ready to have you."

Silence filled the room, broken only by the popping fire.

"Well," Oscar said after a pause. He stood and tugged down his vest. "Thank you, Duncan. I apologize for embarrassing you. As has always been true of my relationship with Sam, I have again allowed her to talk me into something my instincts told me I should avoid."

"She loves you, Oscar. She just wants you to be happy." Duncan wished he could ease Oscar's embarrassment.

"I know that this is her way of looking after me yet again, assuring I do not make a complete fool of myself in Emily's arms. However misguided her intentions, they are usually rooted in compassion."

He walked to the door, then paused with his hand on the doorknob. "Do you love Sam, Inspector McLeod?"

The formality of the question caught Duncan off guard. He threaded his fingers together. "Yes, I do. Very much."

"Are you careful with her when the two of you are together?"

Just how the conversation had shifted to put him on the defensive, Duncan couldn't recall. "I'd never hurt her."

"If she were to conceive a child, I'd expect you to do the honorable thing." Oscar turned around.

Duncan looked down at his hands, then back up at Oscar with a newly born respect. "I'd never put Sam in jeopardy, Oscar. I love her."

"I love her, too, perhaps more than you. Did you know that I asked her to marry me?"

Duncan shook his head.

"I did and of course she said no, smart girl. We'd have killed each other inside of a week, I'm sure. I saw then that marriage was not the relationship Sam and I were destined to have. Brother and sister separated in another life, perhaps."

He looked down at his shoes. "I have a deep respect for you, Duncan. You're an honest and honorable man and I believe that you do love her. The point of my ramblings is that I am placing Sam's well being in your hands." He looked back up, his boyish face gone, replaced by the hard gaze of a man. "Guard her well because if you hurt her, all the detachments of Mounted Police in Canada won't keep me from hunting you down."

"Do you, Oscar, take Emily to be your lawful wedded wife?"

He looks so . . . mature, Sam thought as she held the trembling nosegay of flowers, the morning sun warm on her back. Oscar, in his dark suit, his hair neatly combed, beamed down at Emily. So unlike the gangly young man who'd followed her across the Chilkoot Pass only a few months ago.

"And do you, Emily, take Oscar for your husband?"

The priest Oscar had brought back from Lake Bennett smiled at the couple over his protruding stomach. Well, at least somebody would eat all those infernal cookies she'd baked in Charlie's cantankerous oven last night, Sam thought, wishing she could scratch her ankle where a stray blade of grass tickled her skin.

"Do you bring a ring for your bride?" the priest asked and Duncan handed Oscar the slim gold band.

"This ring was made from a single nugget of gold, planted deep in the earth by God for a reason we are not meant to understand and yet we accept," the priest said. "And so is this mysterious union of man and woman. With this ring, do you pledge your love for her?"

"With this ring, I thee wed," Oscar said softly and slipped the gift onto Emily's hand.

Sam glanced over the couple's heads to Duncan, resplendent in his uniform, staring at Oscar and obviously avoiding her glance. They'd argued several more times in the last week about their wedding. She pushed and Duncan resisted until finally he stopped talking about the subject altogether, leaving Sam to speculate as to his reasons.

He didn't look at her as the priest gave Oscar permission to kiss his bride and avoided her pointed glance as the couple turned to smile at the small party of guests gathered in the meadow.

"You look wonderful," she whispered to Oscar's cheek as she rose on tiptoe to kiss him.

He wrapped his trembling arms around Sam and hauled her close. "I'll miss you. I'll miss us."

"No, you won't. You'll have Emily now. Besides, I won't be far away."

"Do you love him?" he asked, pulling back.

"Duncan?" She glanced over to where Duncan had Emily encased in a bear hug. "Yes, God help me, I do."

"He loves you and he's a good man." Oscar frowned down at her. "Don't break his heart, Sam, or I'll give you that thrashing you so richly deserve."

"I won't break his heart."

"No flighty notions?"

She shook her head. "My days of flighty notions are gone."

"Indeed? Should I look behind your back to see if your fingers are crossed?"

She glanced back at Duncan, now walking toward his daughters, on his face the tender look she'd learned to adore. "I'm a different woman, Oscar, from the one who climbed Chilkoot Pass."

"Yes, you are. Somewhere in this you've grown a woman's heart."

Oscar left her standing there in the morning sun, her wilted bouquet dangling from her fingers, while he loaded his bride into a borrowed buckboard. How Sam's heart ached for this happiness to be hers. To be the bride waving at her guests as she drove away to begin a new life in her husband's arms.

But Duncan was showing no signs of relenting, leaving her puzzled. She'd tried reason and then seduction, to no avail. He wouldn't let her into his mind or back into his bed.

A slight stir at the edge of the crowd drew her attention away from her self-pity. Superintendent Steele and Mike Finnegan worked their way through the crowd, nodding and greeting the guests. They stopped at Duncan's side and the three men exchanged words. Duncan's face darkened and he shook his head. Mike glanced at her, the pain in his expression palatable even across the distance. Something was terribly wrong.

She started toward Duncan, but he whirled and walked off toward the road behind the other two men. Sam began to run.

"Wait. Duncan!" she called, drawing the attention of several guests.

"I have to go back to the fort," he said when she stopped at his side. "Something's come up."

She looked up into his eyes. "What is it? It's something terrible, isn't it?"

"Promise me you'll take care of my girls." His grip on her fingers tightened and his expression darkened.

"Duncan, what is it?"

"Promise me."

"You know I will. Tell me what's wrong." She pivoted. "Tell me, Mike."

Finnegan glanced at Duncan and then at Steele before carefully examining his boots.

Duncan took her arm and led her a short distance away. "There've been some problems with the gold that's stored at the fort."

"What kinds of problems?"

Duncan looked down, his face unreadable, closed. "I can't tell you, Sam. Police business."

Wilton Adcox drifted through her mind. But, weeks had passed since their last trip to the river. With her refusal to write the article, Wilton had dropped out of sight and she'd heard no more from him. Surely he and his lazy brother wouldn't take their discontent further.

"I'm going back to talk it over with Steele." He slid his hand down her arm to encircle her wrist. "It'll be all right. See that the girls get home safely."

"Is that *all* you meant when you said take care of your

girls?'' There was more he wasn't telling her. She could feel it in his touch.

"Yes." He glanced over her head, then back to her face. "See that they get into bed on time." He lifted her hand and, keeping his eyes on hers, kissed the ends of her fingers. "I love you, Sam. Never doubt that." Then, he let her fingers slide away and brushed past her to rejoin the other men.

"When's Papa going to come back?" Sarah asked as she hopped toward the bed on one foot, then sat down on the edge.

"He'll be back soon. And he said to make sure you got to bed on time." Sam lifted the covers. "Now in with you."

Sarah scrambled underneath the quilts. Her damaged leg was barely noticeable at times as she'd learned to compensate well in her movements. At fourteen, she behaved like a much younger child, thanks to her childhood of denial and abuse. Now, warm in the light of her father's love, she had bloomed into the child she'd never been.

"When are we getting my wooden leg?" she asked.

Sam sat down on the edge of the bed. "Shh. You're not supposed to tell that. That's between you and me and Mr. Epps."

"And me," Lizzy said, snug in her bed across the room.

Sam turned and found Lizzy smiling at her over the edge of the quilt. "And I'll keep it a secret, too."

"Is Papa in trouble?" Lizzy asked.

"Oh, no. I'm sure not. He'll probably be here when you wake up in the morning. But if he's not, you're not to worry. Superintendent Steele might have sent him on an assignment.''

Sam tucked the covers around Sarah, who smiled up at her. "When are you and Papa going to get married?"

"Sarah, that's none of your business," Lizzy admonished. "And if they've decided, I'm sure they'll tell us."

"I just wanted to know," Sarah answered with a pout as she flopped over onto her side and snuggled down into her pillow.

"We haven't decided, but you'll be the second to know," Sam said, rising and turning down the lamp on the table.

With the extinguishing of the lamp, moonlight gained possession of the floor again, boxing rectangles of silver onto the smooth boards. Sam moved to Lizzy's bed and sat down on the edge.

"Something's wrong, isn't it?" Lizzy whispered.

Sam looked down at the shadows playing across the quilt. "I think so, but he won't tell me."

Lizzy studied her face. "If he's done something wrong, you won't leave him, will you?"

"No, of course not. I love your father and he wouldn't do anything wrong. I'm sure whatever it is, it's a misunderstanding."

Despite the small fire on the hearth and the cozy quilts on the bed, Sam's hotel room loomed huge and empty. Cross-legged in the middle of the bed, her face buried in her hands, she sobbed out her misery. She'd cry tonight, she promised herself, just for a little while, and then she'd dry her eyes and cry no more. Somewhere in Dawson City, Oscar and Emily lay content in each other's arms, loneliness very far away from their cocoon of happiness.

Yes, she was jealous, Sam admitted to herself as she blew her nose into a handkerchief. Pea-green and ashamed. Oscar deserved happiness. But so did she, reasoned her inner voice. And that happiness seemed so very distant at the moment.

A soft rap at the door brought her off the bed and scrambling across the floor. Wiping away the last of her tears, she yanked open the door, expecting and hoping for Duncan.

"Miss Wilder?" Superintendent Sam Steele stood in the hallway outside her door. "I realize it is late and this is an awkward situation, but could I come in for a moment?"

"Of course." Sam held the door open and stepped to the side.

Sam Steele had made quite a name for himself over the last few years. He'd been appointed Commanding Officer of the North West Mounted Police in the Yukon in July and was already known for making up laws as necessity required. He was a wise and good man. And to have him here at her door at such a late hour spoke to the seriousness of the situation.

"May I have a seat?" he asked, taking off his Stetson and motioning to the chairs by the fireplace.

Sam nodded and Steele eased his long frame onto the edge of a chair seat. "Inspector McLeod is being detained in Fort Herchmer and he asked me to come and let you know. I believe that his daughters are here in the hotel with you?"

"Yes, they are. What do you mean, detained?"

Steele twirled his hat and looked down at his boots. "He's been arrested on suspicion of theft."

"Duncan never stole anything in his life." The words burst from her on a breath of frustration and guilt. Somehow, her nocturnal spying with Wilton Adcox figured into this. As surely as the sun would rise tomorrow.

"Inspector McLeod does indeed have an exemplary record, but with the mounting evidence . . ."

"What evidence?"

"I'm not at liberty to discuss specifics," Steele answered, his voice curt but his eyes compassionate. "I know this is a shock to you. Inspector McLeod told me the two of you planned to be married."

Planned. Past tense.

"Yes, we plan to marry soon."

"Perhaps you should consider delaying the ceremony." He spoke softly, calmly, knowing nothing of the churning fury in Sam's stomach.

Sam swallowed and reined in her anger and fear, funneling that regained energy into clearing her mind. "Do you think this will be that serious?"

He stared at her, his eyes sorrowful. "I truly wish I could tell you more, Miss Wilder. Perhaps in a few days, I can divulge more information, but for now I must beg your tolerance."

He stood, walked to the door, and seated his Stetson on his head. "You are welcome to visit Inspector McLeod tomorrow, if you wish," he said, turning. "The jail is in my office."

"I wish to see Inspector McLeod."

The young constable looked up from his modest stack of papers and swallowed. "Yes, ma'am," he said with a nod, shoving back his chair. He lifted a ring of keys out of the desk drawer and opened the heavy wooden door directly behind him. Beyond, jail cells formed from stern, iron bars filled a small room.

Sam brushed past him as he murmured, "Just knock when you're ready to leave."

Duncan sat on a slim cot, elbows on his knees, his head in his hands. Clothed in ordinary brown pants and a white shirt, he looked lost and small, now formally divested of his scarlet suit of armor.

"Are you all right?" she asked, flattening herself against the unrelenting bars.

He raised his head and smiled, then stood and met her at the bars. "I'm fine."

Sam reached through the bars and hooked an arm around his waist to bring him closer. "What's happened? Please tell me."

He cupped the back of her head and brought her face close enough to touch her lips. His eyes slid closed and his breath rushed across her cheeks. "I wondered if you'd come."

"You doubted I would?"

"Sometime in the wee hours this morning—yes."

"Was this what you wouldn't tell me?"

He released her and stepped away, an unconscious effort to prepare her for what he was about to say, she sensed.

"We've been shipping gold downriver outside official channels. There's nearly two hundred thousand dollars' worth in that tiny storehouse at any given time; Steele feared that the temptation would become too great and we'd be robbed, endangering the lives of the men. So, under the cover of night, we've been shipping it out a little at a time."

The nighttime meetings she'd observed. "How?"

"Officers from Lake Bennett, disguised as miners,

bring a boat here, load up the gold, and see that it's moved downriver like ordinary cargo. A month ago, an entire load disappeared. Two men were injured and the gold vanished." He looked down at the floor. "I was the one who loaded it. Somehow information came to Steele that I arranged the disappearance. Then, several hundred dollars in gold was found in my barracks, hidden beneath the floor under my bunk."

"But why would he believe such a thing about you?"

"The accusation was packaged well, made to look like I needed the money to support Lizzy and Sarah . . . and you." He threw her a meaningful glance. "Supposedly, I was overcome by temptation, a sin of which I've already been guilty several times, as I remember."

"I'll wire my uncle. He'll send a lawyer and—"

"No, Sam." He moved back to the bars. "I want you to stay out of this. I need you to look after my girls." He caught her hands and entwined her fingers with his. "Promise me you won't get mixed up in this. Promise." He squeezed her hand.

Sam looked up into his face and wondered if she was imagining the slight droop of his shoulders or the defeat that dimmed the intense blue of his eyes. He was a proud man, now stripped of that pride, his reputation and honor besmirched. He'd lost the only two things that had kept him going these last long, lonely years.

"All right, I promise. But he has no proof other than this person's word."

"He has proof. Two men from Lake Bennett have come forth to say they cooperated and a third has confessed to piloting the boat over Whitehorse Falls. That's enough to convict me."

"Do you know these men?"

He shook his head. "No, I never saw them before."

"How long before the trial?"

Duncan shrugged and kneaded her fingers. "Three weeks, most probably. A judge will have to come up from Edmonton." He yanked her close, pulling her against the cold, metal bars. "If this should not go favorably, go home to San Francisco and take Lizzy and Sarah with you. I've no one else to ask, Sam."

"I have a little money put by," he told her. "I've told Mike where it is. Take that with you. I've nothing else to leave you for their support. I know I'm asking a great favor." He stopped, his throat working. "I'm glad now I didn't marry you, else you'd be bound to a prisoner."

Sam ran a hand through his dark curls, her fingertips reveling in the warmth of his skin, his candor rending her heart. "Don't you know the marriage took place long ago? The wedding's only a piece of paper and a few words. We won't leave you, Duncan. This'll work out. You'll see."

He kissed her again, his lips gently brushing hers. "Just make sure you've got no part in the working out of it."

CHAPTER EIGHTEEN

The mules scrambled up the sharp incline, their broad hooves sending small stones rattling down behind them.

"You're going to get me killed yet," Oscar complained, grabbing the saddlehorn to haul himself forward. "And if you don't, Emily will when she finds out what you've talked me into this time."

"Wilton Adcox has refiled on the claim he lost months ago. Don't you think that's a little suspicious? And he and Tom ran up a huge bill at Orin Brown's and paid it all off in gold dust."

Oscar shrugged. "They could have made a strike on their claim. Men do it every day. Orin's used to taking in gold dust."

"Whose side are you on, anyway?"

"I'm just playing the devil's advocate, Sam. Even if we find out something, it'll have to be foolproof to convince a judge in the face of the evidence somebody's been able to put together.''

"And Wilton was awful anxious for me to know that the Mounties were shipping gold downriver."

"You should have been suspicious then."

Sam shrugged. "You're right. I should have been, but I was just so anxious to write the perfect story."

Oscar grunted and more rocks clattered away. She glanced over her shoulder to make sure Oscar and his mule hadn't plunged over the precipice they were skirting.

"Well, if you're going to do a stupid thing, do it for Duncan and not for a byline."

Sam pulled her mule into the shade of a spreading hemlock and waited for Oscar. Sides heaving, his mule followed and stopped, head hanging. She turned in the saddle to face Oscar's scowl. "It has nothing to do with articles or bylines. Adcox framed Duncan and I'm going to prove it."

Oscar shook his head and cursed softly under his breath. "Does Duncan know you're coming here?"

"Of course not."

Oscar folded his hands over the saddlehorn and shifted forward with a groan. "And how do you expect to prove it when the Mounted Police have been working on this for weeks?"

Sam smiled, secure in the genius of her plan. "They're not women."

The Adcox claim was unremarkable, a crude, muddy shanty leaning precariously against the sheer, stony mountainside. A stream of murky water poured past the front door. Sam stepped over a pair of snowshoes, a pan, and an assortment of shovels and picks abandoned in the yard. She rapped sharply on the door and heard scrapes and thumps from inside.

Tom Adcox peered out the cracked door, his eyes bloodshot and hooded. "Whadda you want?"

"Is your brother in?" Sam asked as sweetly as she could.

"Wilton. Nah, he's out back at the stream."

"Fine. I'll just scoot around there then." She lifted her skirts and hurried around the corner of the house.

"Have you truly lost your mind?" Oscar hissed. "They could kill us both and nobody would ever find the bodies."

"Shh—and watch," she cautioned, striding across the rutted and trampled ground that led down to the stream.

Wilton crouched at the water's edge, patiently sloshing a shallow pan, occasionally gouging at the contents with a stubby finger.

"Mr. Adcox. How nice to see you."

Wilton jumped, dropped his pan, and staggered to his feet, his hand pawing at the holster on his hip. Undaunted, Sam pursued him in his stumbling retreat, her skirts held delicately out of the mud. Oscar's heart pounded and he swore he could already smell the gunpowder.

Wilton eyed her and then Oscar. "You'd scare the wits out of a man, wouldn't you?"

"Oh, did I startle you? I'm very sorry. I was so anxious to find you."

"Why?" He threw a glance over their shoulders as if he expected a detachment to come galloping over the hill.

"During our dealings before, you struck me as an astute businessman."

"What's that mean, 'astute'?"

"Good."

"Oh. Well, go on."

"I have a proposition for you."

His nerves apparently settling, Wilton scanned her from head to foot in a manner that bristled with threat, then assessed Oscar with a slitted glance. Oscar swallowed and shifted his attention to the small derringer hidden in his coat sleeve.

"What kind of proposition?"

Sam boldly returned his gaze, sweeping his length with a slow, assessing study.

"Say, don't you dance in Charlie's, too?"

"I did. I'm retired now."

"You a writer *and* a dancer?"

"Yes, Mr. Adcox. I'm a multitalented woman."

Wilton frowned and looked at Oscar. "What's 'multitalented' mean?"

"It means that a person does several things well."

He returned his gaze to Sam, accompanied by a lazy smile. "I'll just bet you do, little lady. What's your offer?"

Sam swallowed and subtly rearranged her face into one of delicate anguish. "I find myself in a compromised position."

"Compromised?"

"By Inspector McLeod."

She was truly out of her mind. Oscar shifted his feet and wondered how far a derringer could shoot.

Adcox's face fell. "That bastard," he said with venom.

"My sentiments exactly. And as Inspector McLeod is destined for a life in prison, I need a husband."

Oscar wanted to roll his eyes and fling up his arms in dismay. How dense could Adcox be not to see through this one?

"You and the Inspector . . ."

"Yes, you see I was overcome with . . . compassion for him one evening after he told me of his wife's tragic . . . and mysterious death. I wasn't thinking properly and he was . . . well, he was . . . forceful."

"He forced you?" Adcox leaned forward, intent, his pan and gold dust forgotten on the ground.

"Yes." Sam sniffed and swiped at her nose with the back of her hand. "It was horrible."

Oscar moved over a step, away from Sam, just in case the old adage about being hit by lightning for lying *was* true. Perhaps he should just shoot Adcox anyway before he accidentally reproduced.

"Well, how come you thought of me?"

"Well, you were kind enough to point out the fact that Duncan, I mean Inspector McLeod, might be embezzling money and even though I was just too blind to see it, you did. And since he will be of small use to this tiny life I carry," she placed a hand on her abdomen. "I must find a man willing to give me his name . . . for the sake of the child."

Not even Ruby, the mule, now grazing peacefully under an aspen tree, would be gullible enough to fall for this line, Oscar thought.

"Now why would I want to take on a wife and somebody else's young'un?" Adcox said, narrowing his eyes.

Oscar glanced back where the mules were hitched. They could cover the ground in seconds, if necessary. His derringer held two bullets, one for each brother. There'd be no second chances.

"Because I have five thousand dollars to give you in exchange."

Adcox's eyes glittered with greed. In another minute

he'd be licking his lips. No, Adcox wasn't nearly as bright as Ruby the mule.

"How do I know you ain't lying about all this? Maybe you want to know where McLeod hid the rest of the money."

"I assure you," Sam said smoothly over her shoulder as she pivoted and started for her mule, "that I have no interest in Inspector McLeod's ill-gotten gains." She reached into her saddlebag and lifted out a plump, cloth bag. Weighing it in one hand, she walked back toward them. "I anticipated your reluctance, so I brought good faith money." She stopped in front of him, picked up one of his mud-encrusted hands, and fitted the bag into his palm. "Five hundred dollars in gold dust."

Adcox stumbled forward a step, staring down at the bag. Oscar wondered if his own face registered the same amazement. Where had Sam gotten that much gold dust?

"Honey, you got yourself a husband."

Duncan smashed his fist against the log wall and winced with the pain. "Why'd you help her do something so stupid . . . and dangerous?"

Mike leaned his chair against the wall and repositioned his feet to balance it there on two legs. "Sure and she's the best liar in Dawson City," he answered in his soft Irish brogue. "And, seemed to me and Steele, your last resort, lad. Nobody's come forward to dispute the witnesses' statements. Both of 'em still swear you hired 'em to steal the gold. 'Tis a matter of your word against theirs and they've got two more than you on their side. And then there's the matter of the gold under your bunk."

"I told you I don't know how that got there."

Mike slid his knife out of the leather pouch at his side and began to shave softly curling slivers of wood off a stick. "I know what you told me, lad. I believe you, but will the judge?"

"Doesn't my fifteen years mean anything?"

Mike shook his head. "Not when there's more than a hundred thousand dollars at stake. The judge'll figure a saint could be tempted by that."

Duncan braced his hands on the wall and stared at the floor. "What about Adcox's place? Have you looked there? Maybe he hid the gold nearby."

Mike flipped a shaving between the cell bars. "McPhail and I went up. He concocted a tale that Steele had ordered a physical for all miners because of the typhoid epidemic. They bought the story. He slipped them both something in a tonic and while they were out cold, we searched the place. Nothing. Not a hint. Up in those rocks, bags of gold could be scattered in a dozen places. He could spend it a little at a time for years and no one would be the wiser."

Duncan watched the blond shaving slowly uncurl, unraveling like his life. The judge would be here in less than a week and they'd found no evidence to support Duncan's contention he was innocent. Dozens of people had been questioned by the members of the detachment to no avail. "What, exactly, is she going to do?"

"Just ask a few questions in Charlie's. Give them a dance or two to loosen them up. Nothing more. I promise. Steele and I figured she couldn't get into too much trouble doing that. In fact, he thought it a noble gesture when she came to him with the idea. After all, Charlie's is the perfect place for a man's tongue to get loose enough for him to talk."

Duncan shook his head and laughed. "She's duped the two of you, too."

Mike grinned and ran a finger down the smooth point of wood. "Don't worry so much, old man. There's not been a lassie born that could pull the wool over Michael Finnegan's eyes."

"I want a really big one, Wilton." Sam hung on Wilton's arm as they gazed in the window of Langdon's Jewelers. "I want that one right over there." She pointed to a huge diamond set in soft, warm gold.

"Jesu, Sam. That one's near two hundred dollars."

Two white-haired women walked by, sweeping aside their skirts and muttering something about a tramp. Sam threw them a venomous glance. Word had circulated around town that she'd abandoned Duncan in favor of Wilton Adcox and his money after his rumored gold strike. But she cared little for public opinion. She'd play the strumpet if it meant freeing Duncan. Truth was in the eye of the beholder, she'd learned early. Her reputation could be easily mended with a little glue and plaster in the right places. Duncan's was another matter.

Soon, she knew the rumors would work themselves to Duncan. She could only pray that his faith in her was unshakable and that he'd somehow know this was a ruse for his benefit. She couldn't tell him, for once he knew, he'd move heaven and earth to stop her.

"Please?" She turned cow-eyes on Wilton and saw him melt into a fawning, sickening puddle at her feet. "It'll make all these old biddies pea-green with jealousy."

Wilton glanced down the street at the righteously swishing skirts and smiled. "As big and tacky as you want, darlin'."

The ring was indeed tacky and gaudy and a dozen other synonyms for excessive opulence. Why anyone would want such an eyesore, she thought, testing the weight that seemed to drag at her hand. Next to her breast, sewn into a tiny bag inside her chemise, lay Duncan's ring, beautiful in its simplicity.

"How much?" Wilton asked the jeweler and reached into his pocket. He withdrew a small bag, spidery writing crawling across the far side, unreadable.

Would he be so bold and foolish, she thought, as to keep the gold dust in the same bag he stole it in? Damn, she swore when she couldn't get a good look.

The jeweler carefully weighed out the proper amount of dust, then drew the bag closed and handed it back, apparently noticing nothing amiss.

"Why don't you and me take that ring someplace and give it a trial run?" Wilton suggested with a prickly sniff to her right ear when they stepped outside the shop.

"I can't. I have to go to work," Sam shot back. She hadn't figured on him being quite so eager so soon, although she'd been sure he'd want to sample the wares, especially since he knew she was no virgin.

"Work? Ain't no woman of mine gonna work." He flung a smelly arm around her shoulders and yanked her closer.

"Well, Wilton, I'm still a single woman and I've still got to eat."

"Here." He withdrew the bag again and dangled it in front of her. "Now you ain't gotta work." The bag twisted on the string he held it by, rotating closer . . .

closer . . . then swinging back. Still, she couldn't read the writing.

"I'll accept the ring, but I won't take any money from you . . . until we're married, that is."

Wilton frowned. "You ain't funning me after all with this marriage business, are you?" He slitted his eyes, the dullness replaced by a dangerous sparkle. "Don't nobody mess with Wilton Adcox and get by with it."

Sam breathed in to steady her nerves. "Of course not, Wilton. A deal is a deal and we made one. Right? I never go back on a deal."

He studied her closely and she remembered once seeing a black-eyed snake assess a mouse in Charlie's storeroom with the same expression in its eyes . . . just before it ate it.

"Come and watch me dance." She gripped his forearm. "You've never seen me dance, have you?"

The dangerous glimmer was again replaced—by lust. "Once. Made my dick get hard."

"Well . . . maybe you should come and see me again." She faltered, bravery fleeing in the face of his blatant language. Perhaps she'd underestimated Wilton's potential to do her harm. Perhaps she should have listened to Oscar. Perhaps she shouldn't have lied to the entire detachment of Fort Herchmer. "I've changed my routine."

Her voice had lost its ring of confidence. Even she could recognize the fear in her words.

"All right," he agreed, his eyes hooded in anticipation. She knew he was already envisioning her naked beneath him.

* * *

"Didn't your mama ever yank up your skirts and spank your bare behind?" Gertie asked, tugging up the neckline of the red satin dress. "Well, she shoulda, cause you're the stubbornest woman I did ever see," she finished without waiting for Sam's answer. "I thought you was done with dancing like this when you found out the real thing was better."

Sam felt a flush of embarrassment climb up her neck at Gertie's blunt words. "I couldn't think of anything else to do." Sam yanked the neckline back down until the smooth round of her flesh showed above the rows of ruffles.

Gertie planted her fists on her hips and scowled. "Well, anything'd been a damn sight better than this idea."

"I can take care of myself. And besides, if he gets drunk enough, he might tell me where he hid the gold."

"Sure, and I'm the Pope's daughter," Gertie mumbled.

The piano player struck a chord and the crowd quieted down. "That's my cue. Wish me luck." Sam smiled and ducked through the curtains.

She performed her dance with more enthusiasm than she felt, knowing that Wilton was sitting in the front row, his gaze fixed on her cleavage. She'd instructed Bert to ply him with whiskey and hoped that by the end of the evening he'd be drunk enough to confess and too drunk to want sex. When the music ended, she knew she was wrong.

"We're going upstairs," he stated, then leaped on the stage and grabbed her wrist. A murmur went through the room, but no one offered help. Word of their engagement had circulated around town quickly.

Wild Sam Wilder had made her bed and now she had to lie in it.

Literally.

Wilton yanked her toward the stairs, taking them two at a time. Sam stumbled and fell, then regained her footing, her mind frantically searching for a way to escape this fate and still get what she wanted.

"This room right here's ready." Gertie appeared in the hall as they rounded the corner, holding open a room door. "Got it all ready for you. I figured you two couldn't wait for the wedding."

Had Gertie lost her mind? The last vestiges of sanity fled and Sam clawed and scratched at Wilton's iron grasp. But as he dragged her in the door, Gertie leaned close.

"When you get inside, go behind the screen and pretend to take off your clothes. Then go along with what happens," Gertie whispered as she pried one of Sam's hands off the door facing and shoved her into the darkened room.

Puzzled, Sam stumbled into the room and tottered for balance as Wilton released her and staggered over to the bed. Candles burned by the bedside and the drapes had been drawn tightly to shut out light from the street lamps. There was barely enough light to make out Wilton's silhouette as he sat down on the bed with a groan. Rubbing her bruised wrists, Sam edged toward the screen, trusting blindly in Gertie's whispered words. "I'm going to take off my clothes."

"No. I want to sheee you undress," Wilton slurred, the liquor finally catching up with him.

Sam swallowed. "Well . . . I have to . . . wriggle around some to get off my corset and it would . . . ruin the effect."

She heard a button bounce off the floor as he pulled off his shirt. Then, he grunted and fumbled with his pants. "I don't care what you do. Just get naked before I bust."

Sam ducked behind the screen and ran smack into a naked woman.

"Sable?" In the dim light she could barely make out the exotic face of one of Gertie's most requested girls.

"Yep," she whispered and the fragrant smoke of a cheroot drifted around them both, its end glowing red in the dark. "Just stay back here. Don't come out 'lessen he says something, then come stand by the bed and answer him. I'll take care of the rest."

"You're not going to . . . but won't he know it's not me?"

"Honey, when they're this horny, they don't care who or what you are." Sable sashayed away, trailing the smoke from the cheroot in her fingers.

"You a smoker?" Sam heard Wilton ask as the bed springs groaned. "You smoke them nasty cigars? Damn."

"Hmmm," Sable replied.

More groans and squeaks from the protesting bed.

"Gawd almighty," Wilton said, sucking in his breath as the squeaking settled into a regular motion. "Good Gawd blessed almighty."

Sam backed up against the wall, trying to shut out the noises of lust.

"Dammit, watch them ashes. You burned me with that thing."

"Shut up," Sable said in a throaty growl, keeping up the rhythm that grew faster and faster until the head of the bed slammed against the wall.

Wilton climaxed with a deep groan and Sam stuck

her fingers in her ears to shut out the sound that stirred her stomach into a froth. She waited, then took out one finger. No noise at first. Then, the squeaking began anew.

"I wouldn't a never thought you was a woman who'd come back for seconds," he said, his words slurring more and more as Sable attacked him again. "Ow! Damn, woman, put out that cigar."

A hand closed around Sam's arm and pulled her from behind the screen and out into the darkened hallway. "Get outta here. Once he passes out, me and Sable'll dump him outside in the alley. Tomorrow morning he'll have a new respect for you," Gertie said, hurrying her toward the steps.

Quickly, Sam changed back into her street clothes and ducked out the back door. She started for the hotel, then paused halfway down the sidewalk. If Wilton was unconscious, she could search his pockets. She might not get another chance.

She picked her way back to Charlie's and ducked inside a convenient doorway. Minutes dragged by and she leaned her head against the smooth door frame. An evening chill crept under her clothes and numbed her feet. She jerked awake, then stepped back into the shadows as Charlie's back door scraped open.

Gertie poked her head out, looked right and left, and then Sable stepped out, a bright pink silk robe wrapped around her. She nodded to Gertie and together they rolled a body out into the alley. Wilton groaned softly, then lay still. The door closed and Sam waited for a few minutes before squatting beside him. He was lying on one side, an arm stretched out in front of him. Sam slipped her hand in his pocket. Nothing. She checked

his pants pocket, front and back, cringing as she probed
his clothes and still found nothing.

With a hand on his hip and one on his shoulder, she
rolled him to his back, arms and legs sprawled out in all
directions, and continued to search through his clothes.
Her fingers closed around the small bag of gold dust.
She wrestled it out of his pocket and hurried to a small
patch of light reflected from a street lamp. The scrawled
writing that had held so much potential said, RED PEACH
SNUFF.

Her heart sank. Hot tears stung her eyes. She'd been
so sure, so confident that the proof to free Duncan lay
just within her reach, so sure that she could do what
the entire Fort Herchmer detachment could not.

Wilton moved, groaned, and rolled over onto his side.
"Sam?"

Sam backed into the shadows.

"When I get my hands on you, you little bitch! You
did this to me." He clamped both hands on his head
and moaned, then shoved himself to his hands and
knees.

Sam glanced down the alley. She was trapped! The
back of the livery stable formed a box end to the narrow
corridor—Wilton was between her and the street
beyond. She reached behind her for support and her
fingers closed around a shovel, probably left there when
Charlie shoveled mud away after the flood. Maybe she
could ease past Wilton while he was still getting his
bearings. She started forward. His hand shot out and
clamped around her ankle.

"I could smell that rose perfume of yours," he said,
raising his head and glaring at her with furious eyes.

She stumbled backwards and raised the shovel. Her
courage faltered. She raised the shovel higher, calculat-

ing the force of blow necessary to render him unconscious. With a certifying glance over her shoulder, she
rotated the shovel until the back faced Wilton.

A hand caught her wrist.

"If you bash him that hard, lass, we'll be picking up
pieces of him," Mike whispered in her ear.

He stepped around her, but as he did, Wilton, still
addled, lunged toward her. Mike rapped him sharply
on the back of the head with a small, black club.

Wilton collapsed at her feet. She knelt and felt his
pulse, which beat steadily beneath her touch. Sam
glanced at the weapon in Mike's hand, a weapon obviously meant for concealment in a man's clothes.

"I wasn't always a Mountie." He said nothing else
and slipped the club into an interior pocket of his tunic.

"What are you doing here?" she asked.

"Gertie sent for me." He flashed her a grin. "She
said she knew you wouldn't have the good sense to leave
well enough alone."

Mike rolled Wilton onto his back, bent down, and
hoisted him over his shoulder. Something sparkled in
the faint light as it fell onto the soggy ground. Sam bent
and pulled a round, shiny disc from the mud, a length
of wire attached. She scrubbed the object against her
skirt, then hurried to the end of the alleyway and into
a circle of light cast by a street lamp. The letters
N.W.M.P. were stamped into the steel tag.

A broad grin spread across Mike's face. "That's the
tags we use to tie up the bags of gold dust." He lifted
it out of her hand and trailed his fingers down the
dangling wire. "If the arrogant bastard hadn't kept this
as a souvenir, we'd never have proved he had the gold."

CHAPTER NINETEEN

"Papa, be still." Lizzy's slim fingers slid underneath the tight neck of Duncan's tunic and fumbled with the gold emblems that graced his collar.

"It's too tight." He ran a finger inside his satin-backed neckband.

Lizzy fisted her hands on her hips and sighed. "It's no different than it was yesterday or the day before. You're just nervous."

He stared at his reflection in the mirror. A strand or two of gray flecked his dark hair and tiny lines fanned out from the corners of his eyes. What was he thinking, marrying a woman ten years his junior? When she was thirty-five, he'd be forty-five. And when she was forty-five, he'd be fifty-five. And when she was fifty-five, he'd be—

"Stop worrying, Papa," Sarah said with a sweet kiss to his cheek. "She's not too young for you."

He smiled down on the bright face. "Now, how did you know what I was thinking?"

"Because that's all you've talked about for two weeks," Lizzy grumped from across the room as she folded his clothes and placed them in his valise. "I'm surprised you haven't talked yourself out of this wedding."

He returned to the face in the mirror and adjusted his emblems one more time. "I may be wrinkled, but I'm not stupid."

Lizzy snapped shut the valise. "You're all packed."

Duncan turned to face his daughters and yanked his tunic into place. "All right. What's the final verdict?"

They smiled broadly, no trace left of the sullen, lost children who'd swept into his life. "You look so handsome, Papa." Sarah limped to his side and encased him in a hug.

"How's the wooden leg, Blackbeard?" he asked, pushing her back a little.

She beamed, her blue eyes sparkling. "It's wonderful and after Sam put some lambskin on it, it doesn't hurt anymore when I walk."

One of many miracles he owed the woman he was about to make his wife. And one in a multitude of things she'd lied about. Sitting in the Fort Herchmer jail, he'd realized Sam Wilder was never going to give up her lying ways. If a little lie eased the way, either for herself or someone she loved, she'd spin a story worthy of the situation. But she'd never lied about her love for him or his girls. That truth shone in her eyes every time she looked at him.

"Now, Aunt Emily's going to bring us out to the cabin day after tomorrow." Lizzy handed him the valise with an affirming nod. "And we'll bring the last of the furniture with us."

Duncan nodded, concentrating on keeping thoughts of Sam under control.

"Are you sure you don't need more furniture there than just the bed?"

Her question bounced off him, then came back and smacked him mid-chest. "What did you say?"

"I said are you sure you don't need more furniture out there than just the bed? We have a whole wagonload, you know."

Her stormy eyes lightened and one corner of her mouth twitched. Lizzy McLeod was making a joke. And a risqué one at that. Floored, Duncan could only stare at the woman-child before him. When had Lizzy become an adult? And where had she learned such irreverence?

From Sam, of course.

"Well . . . we have a chair and a table. . . ." Words fled. Embarrassment crawled up his neck as his innocent daughter's eyes danced at his discomfort.

"Oh, Papa. Don't worry. I was only teasing," she soothed and plucked at a piece of lint on his tunic. "I'm old enough to know what goes on when people get married."

She worried the braid on his sleeve and straightened his cross belts. Finally, she lifted her eyes to his. "You deserve this happiness, Papa. Always remember that."

Duncan nodded, a lump in his throat choking off words.

"And I hope someday I'll find a love as special as yours and Sam's."

* * *

Sarah stumped down the aisle of the little chapel on the leg old man Epps had carved for her, grinning in a manner unbefitting a proper best man. As she took her place beside Duncan, she looked up at him and patted her pocket where Sam's ring resided. The wedding guests tittered and Sarah flashed them a smile of triumph. She'd begged to be the best man, even over Lizzy's frantic arguments that such things just weren't done. In the end, Duncan ended the argument. He and Sam had already made such a spectacle of themselves, what did it matter?

Oscar came down next, obviously ill at ease in this reversal of roles. But he winked as he passed and Duncan wondered how much badgering Sam had had to do to get Oscar to agree to be her maid of honor.

The priest shook his head and looked to the heavens with a silent plea. The congregation rose to their feet and turned. Duncan licked his lips and breathed deeply, his heart hammering. In all the years of storms, Indians, and whiskey traders, he wondered if he'd ever been more terrified than he was at this moment.

Then she appeared and his heartbeat calmed. She was stunning and delicious in a flowing light blue gown that had probably been Emily's contribution. In the softening afternoon light pouring in the windows, she looked almost unearthly, like an angel dropped to earth.

She started toward him, a soft smile on her face, looking only at him as she maneuvered the narrow aisle. Then, she was by his side, wisps of hair teasing her neck . . . teasing him. She turned to smile at him and Duncan knew he would always remember these few brief seconds when their eyes met and their souls mated. A shiver ran down his spine. How amazing that God had made so perfect a creature and given her to him.

They said their vows while a cold wind rattled the windows. Autumn was upon the Yukon and soon snow would blanket the scarred and gouged earth. But here, inside the snug, warm church, they promised their lives and their hearts to each other.

Sarah dug the ring out of her pocket with a grin and gave it to Duncan. He took Sam's fingers into his hand, curling the cold tips against his palm.

"With this ring . . ." He paused, lost in her eyes, lost in the emotion of what he was about to say. Mike Finnegan cleared his throat with a soft *harrumph*.

"With this ring, I thee wed." He slipped the band onto her hand.

The priest declared them man and wife and said a prayer for their union. When all heads were bowed and the chapel was peacefully silent, Sam turned to him, her eyes glistening with tears. "I love you," she mouthed.

The prayer ended. Voices chattered as he kissed her with a polite brush of his lips, wanting more when her eyes flashed a promise of so much more to come. Then, she turned to demurely thank a well-wisher. Before he knew it, he was sweeping her into his arms and depositing her into a waiting wagon. Waving their good-byes, they left their family and friends behind and headed for the new cabin they would eventually share with Lizzy and Sarah. But for tonight, it was theirs alone.

Duncan squatted by the fireplace and rearranged the logs with a poker. He traced a finger over the rock hearth and remembered the sweat and hours of work it had taken to lay each gray stone. Like the events of a man's life, he mused. One stone at a time. Hammered and chipped until it fit where it belonged. Then another and another until a hearth was built, strong and sure. A place for cooking and warming and stockings at Christmas.

He heard the door to their bedroom creak open behind him. He rose and slowly turned, savoring the anticipation. Sam had something planned. She hinted all the way from the church until he wasn't sure he could wait like a good bridegroom. She stood in the doorway wearing some long, filmy thing that showed her curvy silhouette underneath, yet revealed no details. Her hair was still twisted up on her head, soft tendrils drifting down to tease her ears. She was devastating.

Sam moved toward him, trailing a yard or two of the blue stuff behind her. Tiny bare toes peeked out from underneath the blue cloud and firm breasts steepled the fabric that lapped across her chest, showing an immodest amount of cleavage. Duncan swallowed as a rush of desire and eagerness stabbed through him unlike any he'd experienced since he was a young man.

Firelight becomes her, Duncan thought as she stopped at his side, the yellow flames warming the rich glow of her hair. He reached for her, but she backed away with an impish smile on her face. Without preamble, she let the filmy blue garment slide down her arms to the floor and stood before him naked and glorious.

"When I am old," she said, backing toward the window, "I want to remember that I walked naked through this house on my wedding night."

Duncan moved toward her, drawn by the same force that seemed to have robbed him of all cohesive thought. She stopped in the curtainless window, moonlight softening her hair, brazen in her seduction.

He stopped stock still as she sauntered toward him

and touched the same collar he'd fiddled with that morning. "And you, husband, are way overdressed."

She flicked open the buttons of his tunic and slid her hands inside to skim it off his shoulders and arms. Then, she discarded the carefully groomed serge garment with a fling.

"You know, you Mounties wear too many clothes." She snapped his suspenders off his shoulders and worried open the buttons of his shirt, which joined his jacket in an undistinguished heap in the corner.

Duncan forced his hands to stay at his sides and let her have full control. He closed his eyes and thought of the coldest part of the Yukon River as her fingers found and undid the buttons down the front of his pants. Her throaty chuckle as she brushed cruel knuckles over him was nearly his undoing.

"Whitehorse rapids on a January day," he murmured.

"What?" Her hands stilled . . . far too close to areas throbbing for her attention.

He caught her wrist in a firm grip. "I'll finish."

He sat in a chair and sucked in his breath as his bare back touched the cold wood of the chair seat. Sam giggled and loosened her hair so it fell to her shoulders. Quickly, he discarded his boots and socks and stood. Before he could move, she skimmed his underwear down his legs and backed away, waiting for him to kick them off.

Feral would be the word she'd use to describe her husband, Sam thought, sobering as the firelight gilded his skin a golden hue. Feral and dangerous. A thrill ran through her at the imagined peril. In their times together before, she'd spent little time looking at his body, intent only on passion and the fleeting nature of their stolen moments.

Finely shaped muscles defined him. A smooth chest bore a thick mat of dark hair that traveled down his abdomen. Strong arms waited to hold first her, then their children. Large, gentle hands, capable of delivering both justice and pleasure, reached out for her.

She stepped away, staying just beyond his grasp, struggling to remember the seduction she had planned, resisting the temptation to give in too soon.

"Sam?" He frowned and stopped.

She moved to the newly finished table and ran a hand over the smooth wood. His eyes widened.

"It'll be our private joke," she said with a grin, trailing a hand down the table top.

He looked at the table, then back to her. "You're not serious."

"I'm very serious." She climbed onto the table and sat on the end, her feet dangling, and held out her arms.

His eyes darkened, despite the smile on his lips, and he stepped into her embrace. Warm skin chafed against hers. Chest hair prickled her sensitive breasts and his arousal nudged against her stomach. A gentle nip to her earlobe resulted in a trail of kisses against her temple and a soft groan in her ear. "Life with you will never be dull, will it, wife?"

Wife. So wonderful a word when it rolled off his tongue. Sam shivered a little with delight.

"Are you cold?" he asked, drawing back to look at her face.

She shook her head. "No. Not as long as I'm in your arms."

He kissed her, probing deep in her mouth, hinting at other activities yet to come. Always, from the first time, his kisses had left her weak-kneed and hungry for more.

Tonight she wouldn't go to bed hungry.

He slid into her, adjusting her hips until the planes of their bodies met. A soft grunt of pleasure ruffled her hair as he stopped and held her tight against him. His head against her temple, he seemed satisfied to simply stand there claiming her body with his, wordless.

Sam locked her ankles behind him and he began to move within her, touching places he hadn't touched before, searing her with a fire that radiated from their point of joining. His mouth firmly on hers, he rocked, driving her toward completion more quickly than she'd ever imagined, stealing away her breath and all her carefully laid plans.

Abruptly he stopped and lifted her, their bodies joined, and headed toward the bedroom.

"What are you doing?"

"I'll not explain to my son that he was conceived on the supper table." Duncan tumbled them both onto the bed and kissed each of her eyes.

"Stick-in-the-mud."

"Temptress."

"Do you have plans to explain to our children where each of them was conceived?"

He arched within her, exploring deeper each time, his face shadowed by the faint lamplight. "No, but I'd never eat another peaceful meal at that table."

A comeback rose into her thoughts and then melted away like spring snow as he shifted positions. "I wanted to wait longer. I had more . . . ideas." Sam struggled to put words together as her body sang with satisfaction. "I wanted to make tonight special."

He slowed and looked into her eyes. "Any night with

you will be a memory." He raked his fingers through her hair. "Most of them good, I hope." He smiled and nibbled at the edge of her collarbone.

Slow and steady, he lifted her on the tide of passion, holding back, ignoring her pleas that he hurry. She clawed the bedclothes, held prisoner by his body and the wanton needs of her own. At his mercy, she could only look up into his blue eyes and meekly beg for more.

He poured his life into her with a bruising kiss and her own body greedily took what he would give. Sated, he rolled to his back and pulled her with him until she lay spread-eagle on his chest, her hair fanning over them both. Beneath her cheek, his heart fluttered like a wild bird.

"God, Sam," he whispered into her hair, skimming it off his face.

She raised her head and smiled at him through the curtain of auburn strands. "Do you think I'm pregnant?"

He chuckled and wrapped his arms around her. "Should I take that as flattery?"

She levered herself up until she straddled his waist. "No, really. Think, Duncan. A baby."

He captured a lock of her hair and teased a nipple to attention. "A chance to do things over, do them right."

"Lizzy and Sarah—"

"Want a little sister. I know. I've heard that for weeks, now."

Sam leaned forward and kissed him, lingering until he reached for her and then she pulled back, her eyes sparkling with mischief. "You interrupted my seduction, you know."

"And if I hadn't, I'd have been sporting splinters for

a week. In uncomfortable places, I might add." He lunged forward and nipped at her mouth, his teeth skimming her lower lip. "My inventive little wife who'll be the death of me. What if we had broken the table? How would we have explained that?"

Sam stretched out beside him, snuggled into the bend of his arm, her head on his shoulder. "Well, we could say—"

Before she could react, he'd rolled over and stuffed her beneath him. "No more lies."

"No more lies," she repeated as his eyes darkened again in passion. She put her arms around his neck and tugged his head closer.

"We'll save that imagination for more productive uses."

"Um-hum," she mumbled around his kiss, her fingers crossed behind his head.

THE HEALING

North West Mounted Policeman Mike Finnegan left behind a dark and troubled past to serve justice when he enlisted in the Mounties. Now, stationed in the Yukon Territory, he finds himself embroiled in a murder case that will resurrect those painful memories and cost him his heart.

Pregnant, broke, and desperate, ex-prostitute Jenny Hanson wants only to find a quiet, peaceful place to have her unborn child. But that dream is endangered by the fact that she has recently killed the cruel lover who brought her to Dawson City. A woman well-versed in turning adversity into advantage, Jenny hopes to hide her sins amid the hustle and bustle of the Gold Rush. What she doesn't count on is falling in love with the man sent to bring her to justice.

COMING IN APRIL 2002 FROM
ZEBRA BALLAD ROMANCES

__WITH HIS RING: The Brides of Bath
by Cheryl Bolen   0-8217-7248-1 $5.99US/$7.99CAN

Glee Pembroke had always been secretly in love with her brother's best friend, Gregory Blakenship. So when she learned that he must marry by his twenty-fifth birthday or lose his inheritance, she boldly proposed a marriage of convenience, while planning to win his love.

__THE NEXT BEST BRIDE: Once Upon a Wedding
by Kelly McClymer   0-8217-7252-X $5.99US/$7.99CAN

To Helena Fenster, the only thing worse than her twin sister marrying the man she loves, is having to tell him that his fiancée has jilted him. Rand Mallon's reaction is quite surprising—he's prepared to marry Helena in her sister's place. Yet how can she marry the man she adores when it's obvious that, for him at least, one woman is as good as another?

__NIGHT AFTER NIGHT: The Happily Ever After Co.
by Kate Donovan   0-8217-7273-2 $5.99US/$7.99CAN

Maggie Gleason never wants to marry. So when she hires a matchmaker, it's to find a teaching job, not a husband. Scenic Shasta Falls, California turns out to be the perfect match for an independent woman determined to start a whole new life. The boarding house where she lives even has a magnificent library . . . if she can get past the mysterious recluse in the room next door.

__LOVER'S KNOT: Dublin Dreams
by Cindy Harris   0-8217-7072-1 $5.99US/$7.99CAN

Dolly Baltimore, Millicent Hyde and Rose Sinclair had conquered their past heartaches to discover that love was more than possible—it was irresistible. Lady Claire Killgarren isn't so sure, but with help from her newly happy friends, and a very special man, she's about to find that she'll give anything to be caught in a lover's knot . . . for all time.

Call toll free **1-888-345-BOOK** to order by phone or use this coupon to order by mail. *ALL BOOKS AVAILABLE APRIL 01, 2002*

Name _____

Address _____

City _____ State _____ Zip _____

Please send me the books I have checked above.

I am enclosing $ _____
Plus postage and handling* $ _____
Sales tax (in NY and TN) $ _____
Total amount enclosed $ _____

*Add $2.50 for the first book and $.50 for each additional book. Send check or money order (no cash or CODs) to: **Kensington Publishing Corp., Dept. C.O., 850 Third Avenue, New York, NY 10022**

Prices and numbers subject to change without notice. Valid only in the U.S. All orders subject to availability. **NO ADVANCE ORDERS.**

Visit our website at **www.kensingtonbooks.com.**

DO YOU HAVE THE
HOHL COLLECTION?